BINDING BLOOD

Bonds of Blood: Book III

DANIEL DE LORNE

For my husband Glen,
who waited a long time for the first book,
and even longer to get his name here,
but if not for him, I wouldn't have got this far.

PROLOGUE

He rose from darkness into an expanse of gray. A shapeless, endless landscape rolled around him and enclosed him above and below. The only difference was him, an unsteady point in this unfamiliar place. He looked behind him—*felt* back with his awareness—without needing to turn. Nothing followed him, but something had sent him there, something he'd wanted to escape.

Something still out there.

He drifted, not knowing where to go or if the *something* prowled before him or behind. It didn't matter which way he went. A drab vastness extended in all direction towards a horizon that never came nearer. Yet inside himself grew an uneasiness brought from wherever he'd been before. It clawed out of the deep, still hidden in shadow, but its approach became harder to ignore. He hastened.

How had he got there? How could he leave? He traveled, checking back often to see if whatever was after him—yes, something *was* after him. Something had chased him there.

Breath had gouged his throat, his insides cut with little hooks—

Hooks?

No… Teeth.

Biting into him. Taking chunks out of him. Except not chunks.

Blood.

The teeth had taken his blood. Drained him of it. Exiled him there. Wherever he was. He couldn't return.

Not yet. Not yet.

It wasn't safe to go back.

Not yet. Not yet.

But those teeth that had stolen the life from him would follow. And he had nowhere to hide in all this gray. Nothing to defend himself with. Nothing but his hands—

He raised them and waggled his fingers. Yes, *his* hands. He could use them to fight. But as he looked, they shattered and reformed into glowing shards of purple crystal. It vanished and his hands reappeared. He looked down at his body, his bare chest, and ran his hands over it. Solid, yes, but neither hot nor cold. And then his body disappeared, replaced by purple crystal. The fear intruded more. He swiveled. It was getting nearer. Whatever *it* was. Whatever had hurt him.

Whatever was coming to hurt him again.

He spun, and the gray rotated around his axis as he shifted between flesh and light, blinking between one and the other, spinning faster and faster. He wouldn't return. But where was he? And what was he becoming?

He flashed. He spun. He beckoned.

And the horizon changed.

A figure melted out of coalescing clouds. He stumbled back but kept his eyes forward and locked on the figure as it neared him. He couldn't run but trying was instinctive.

However quickly he covered ground, the figure—a woman—drew closer. Raven hair waving in a breeze that wasn't there, a benevolent smile and sparkling eyes, her body close despite his retreat. She reached out a hand ready to touch him. He wheeled, fell, and cowered.

"Don't be afraid," she whispered. "I'm here to help you. We've been looking for you." Her hand stroked his cheek, and the suddenness of it hoisted him to his feet. He jumped back and bunched his fists.

She vanished and reappeared behind him, catching him. "I'm not trying to hurt you." Her soothing voice smothered her lies. Everything there was designed to harm him. He should have been safe—safe from the thing that sent him there—but he'd landed in another trap.

He jolted out of her arms and positioned himself where he could see her.

"I've searched for you for so long." She offered him her hand. "You shouldn't be here, but this is not the end."

He flinched. What did she mean? And how could she help him? She was a part of this. He didn't know how but he *knew* it deep inside him where the thing lurked. Because of her, he was there. Anger stirred inside him and unleashed a torrent of shouted words. His mouth moved, he yelled, but she didn't hear him. She couldn't decipher whatever he said, and concern chiseled into her pale brow. Around him the light flared, a violet haze sparking as he raged with the transformation.

Slim hands raised. "Calm yourself, please. I'll guide you back."

Back? No. *Back* was where he'd be torn apart. He'd be... He'd be killed!

Her hand came nearer, and he tensed. He'd destroy her if he had to; just to get away from her. Just to be safe.

To be whole.

She froze, and her eyes drifted over his shoulder and into the distance. "Get behind me." She rose up, growing bigger, and guarded him with her body.

He followed her wide gaze, and his heart plummeted. The thing he'd been fleeing stalked out of the gloom. The woman had grown three times her original size, and he peered around her.

A demon strode out of the oppressive clouds. Wings the color of tar, horns gleaming like polished obsidian, impatiently thrashing a pointed tail, eyes glowing crimson.

The demon didn't come alone. Men and women swept across the plane to surround them. The space between his gasping breath and this army of death shimmered.

"Well done, Sinara." The demon's voice rumbled with the destructive glee of an earthquake. "Thank you for finding it."

She snarled, an inhuman sound that sent him stumbling away from the protection of her back. Menace swept from the warriors with a stickiness that cloyed at the back of his throat. Trapped. He wrapped his arms around himself, but still his body shook with enough force that he feared he'd burst into a shower of splinters.

"If I were you, I'd make this easy. Give it to me now and I'll let you leave unharmed." The demon leaned forward and glowered with a toothy grimace. "Then again, I'm not you, and I'd prefer to see you beaten and burned."

"I'll die before I let you control it," she growled.

"Let's hope so. Proceed."

The army opened their arms and light burst forth. He braced, preparing to be blown apart by their magic—yes, magic, he knew of magic—but the attack rebounded. The hail of red power streaming towards him struck a shield that covered him and the woman. She checked points on it, tension held at the corners of her eyes. She protected them, but her muscles clenched the longer the assault lasted.

"I have to get you out of here," she grunted. "You're needed elsewhere."

She grabbed his wrist, but her words had the touch of prophecy and he rebelled in her grasp. He wasn't going to be used again. He'd already suffered for it once and that's what…

That's what had brought him there. That's what had brought him close to—

A chill crept up his feet and legs, into his belly and his torso, freezing his heart.

I'm dead. I'm dead. I'm dead.

"No, don't think that. You're alive," she said in a hurried whisper. "You just got lost." Desperate eyes stared into him as if her saying it could make it so. But the cold had almost engulfed him, and the fear was draining. Whatever they thought they could do to him, they wouldn't get the chance.

"We'll find you." Heat bloomed through her hand into his wrist, and her warmth kept him alive.

He screamed silently and thrashed. The heat intensified. The siege roared around them and the sound of stone cracking lifted his eyes as a jagged line spidered across the shield. His body seared with the blaze of her magic, and as an explosion shuddered around him, her power propelled him down to where the vampire waited to finish what he'd started.

Oberon's consciousness slammed against his skull. Air punched into his lungs and heaved his torso off the ground. The violent jolt whipped awake the agony coiled in his body.

But he was alive.

He held the breath, a pause in mid-air before his strength dissipated, and he collapsed back on the singed carpet.

Alive. And in pain.

A shoulder ruined by fangs, a violated asshole, a crunching ache in every bone and muscle, and a migraine drilling through both eyes: all converged to gnaw on his feeble energy.

Was *he* still there?

Panic sparked through his weakened body. His lead-lined eyes struggled to open, then battled to focus. Lights from the street cast shadows through the window across the sofa, the broken candles, and the crumbling living room wall; signs of his efforts to fend off Olivier, but no sign the vampire remained. The search exhausted him, and he slipped back into darkness.

We'll find you.

His eyes sprang open. Who'd said that? As real and as recent as if they'd been in this shithole of a room. Air scoured his lungs. Something was after him, and he couldn't stay.

He released what should have been a simple jet of power. Sweat drenched his body, but he managed to bring his phone within reach. How could there be so little in him? He rested before he punched at the screen, letting his body steal a few precious seconds of his waning life force to recover for a further attempt at saving himself. Talons scraped through his body, while the prickles of the carpet fibers dug into his flesh with each shallow gasp, reminding him of how weak he'd been when facing that fuck Olivier.

He'd tried to help the vampire and been half-killed for

his trouble. He focused on that invasion, and fury at being brought so low galloped through his body. He hitched his soul to it until he bucked with its violence. He should have been able to stop that bastard from—

He wrenched his mind away from the memory, not wanting to relive it, inside or out, not while this naked and exposed, this close to death. Survival came first.

Through drooping eyelids, he keyed in the number for emergency services. Thank Christ it was so short. The tinny voice of the operator came up the line. He pleaded for an ambulance, gave his address, told her he'd lost a lot of blood. Speaking snatched the last of his strength, and the phone slipped onto the carpet. He didn't know what was said after that, whether they were coming, what would happen next.

He fought against the dimming of his mind, but he was too feeble, too far gone. A desperate rattle of alarm at finding the vampire waiting for him sustained his consciousness for a second, but then that too evaporated and he floated into nothingness.

"Can you hear me?"

Words broke through the fog. Latex-coated fingers pressed at his wrist, then his neck.

"Please..." he whispered.

Please don't let me die.

His awareness rose and fell as his body lurched off the floor, as he was covered, as the door banged, as the trolley rattled, and the ambulance lurched.

"Hold on," a woman said. "Don't be afraid."

Don't be afraid...

Why did that seem so familiar? Like he'd just heard it. The more he focused on those words, the more his connection to the planet evaporated, the more gray swirled around him.

And something told him he had to stay away from the gray.

He hunted for something that would keep him tied to Earth, and then, scrabbling with desperation at losing time, at losing life, he found it.

He sank all of himself into where the vampire's teeth had torn his skin and marked him.

And it pulsed with life.

Everything else—thoughts, words, the grayest of mists and the glittering of obsidian—all vanished below the blazing vengeance and shame and disgust.

Because the vampire wouldn't get away with what he'd done.

I
THE HEART OF A VAMPIRE

Present Day

I

Olivier's world shook with his roars, and the stone walls repaid him threefold. Locked in this circular dungeon in a darkness as black as his soul and strung up with his arms outstretched and his ankles shackled, he tested the limits of his power. His desiccated skin rubbed against the manacles, grating against the join between one piece of metal and another. He slammed his arms forward, pulling the chains taut. He was stronger than any man or woman alive, stronger than any beast. How could mere chains hold him, for fuck's sake?

But they weren't mere chains. And Aurelia had him right where she wanted.

He snarled, and the echo rebounded. An animal prowled in his voice, fettered like one for whatever purpose his sister had in mind.

She'd said he was needed and that Thierry's time for vengeance would come. But what she said hadn't concerned him then. He'd been too wounded by Thierry's eagerness to destroy him—and from the weighted silence that yawned within him.

He hung suspended in this lightless cell truly alone, cold trickling down his body and through the inactive mental bond between him and his twin. Aurelia hadn't obliterated it completely, but he had no way of reviving it. Drained of blood to feed Thierry's bitch-whore, his brother's emotions should be coursing through him like syphilis. The thinner the blood, the thinner the veil: that's how it worked.

He scrabbled through himself, digging in the dirt of his inner being to find some root to nurture.

But Thierry was gone, and the blackness within was worse than the inky blackness without.

He rattled the chains again, hoping Aurelia's power would fail, even for a second. Then he'd snap these chains and be gone from there and back to—

Back to where? Wherever Thierry had been, he'd been home.

Until his brother's betrayal.

No. Home had never been home, just a mess of hurt: the grip of Henri's fist on the back of his neck as he'd pinned him down; Aurelia's smug satisfaction, pleased her brother was getting what he deserved. Ghosts crowded him and probed with their pokey fingers. They broke through the skin and gouged the infected wounds around his heart. He shifted and caved against their examination; his breath shaky as he forced it out along with their assault.

Fuck you all.

He bared his fangs, then clamped his jaw shut. What he needed was blood. Any blood. His stomach tightened the more he thought about it, thought about it the more it tightened. He fought to calm the clawing thirst. He slammed the back of his head against the stone behind him, but it wasn't hard enough to dull the pain. The stone remained inviolate. That way offered no escape.

He'd have to hang awhile, imprisoned with his thoughts, his hunger, and the ghosts in their crowded cell.

Henri with his malice.

Aurelia with her resentment.

Thierry with his disgust.

And their mother…?

Ashes and dust. Too many people writhed inside his head like worms in muck. Besides, how could he hold a grudge when he could barely recall her face?

He let her go.

The darkness crushed him, and he fought again, testing the limits of his sister's prison. He cursed, and a sound broke out verging on a pathetic cry before he cut it short. But it squatted in his throat, pressure building until it joined with the weeping in his heart. He strained against his bonds, snorting with the effort like some demented minotaur, scrabbling against the stone to find any leverage. He'd tear his hands off if he had to, to get out and get away. And once he was free, he'd decimate his remaining family members.

Aurelia. Thierry.

Dead.

And then?

Then he'd truly be free.

II

Olivier's screams mixed with a disturbance on the astral plane that cut Aurelia's spine. Her heart steeled against them, and she blocked her hearing a second before the connection she shared with her mother, Sinara, wrenched inside her and forced her to her knees. She braced against the floor. Palms pressing into cool stone, dress tangled about her legs, inner realm tilting… She delved to check the conduit to her mother's power.

More timid than ever, she stretched her shaken awareness to the reassuring source that twinned with her own…

There!

Her desperate sigh righted the world. Sinara's power still flowed, still enhanced her own, but… What the hell had happened? The connection wouldn't reveal any details, only that Sinara may be in danger. She hurried down the hall to her room and rushed to settle on the bed.

"Aurelia, stop!" Hame burst in with Carn following hard up behind him.

"Sinara needs me." She lay back and searched the rock ceiling for something to focus on. She needed stillness then she'd be out and with Sinara and there'd be an explanation for—

"You won't find her." Green eyes brimming with knowledge implored her to stop. Hame's hand slipped into hers. "She's gone."

Her molars ground together. He lied. The connection remained. "You're wrong." The words came out jagged.

"Xadrak attacked her and she's vanished."

Her breath vibrated. Couldn't he see he was delaying her from doing what must be done? Xadrak wouldn't attack Sinara. He'd never been so bold before, so why now?

"I still have her power, now leave so I can find out what's really going on." She sharpened her eyes on a crack in the rock.

"You want to know what happened? Fine." He nudged her over, forcing her to make reluctant room.

Carn's blue slate eyes met hers, and his disapproval—of her, of what Hame was doing—knocked her.

"You're not going out there," Carn said.

"I'm not going anywhere, but she will see what I saw."

Hame lay down and shut his eyes. His mind nudged at the edge of hers, growing more urgent, more forceful. Carn sank into a chair by the wall, his elbows pitching on his knees, his chin resting in his hands, his eyes watching Hame, watching them.

She tried to swallow, but what little saliva she had tasted of chalk. What would Hame show her? She settled next to him, his fingers linked theirs together, his grip strong and resolute, but it paled to the insistence of his mind. She must see, as much as she didn't want to. Her eyes closed and she opened to him.

Here is what happened.

Hame's memory drowned her, bringing Xadrak and an

army of his followers—twenty, thirty, forty!—before her. They surrounded Sinara in her demon form as she protected a…a…a…person? Human-shaped but bathed in violet light, its features indistinguishable, a soul on the astral that Sinara shielded with her body and life. But more than human, it was—

The key!

She shivered with the possibilities. After all this time, it had been found. An end, previously abstract, solidified in their future.

She wanted to dart forward and interrogate the vision, but an opaque shield hid the key as Xadrak's forces attacked. Were they insane? Were they trying to kill the key after all?

Aurelia covered her mouth with her hand while magic rained down and Xadrak roared—that's what she'd felt earlier. His frustrations. His fury. He added his strength to the assault and cracked Sinara's defenses. An explosion erupted where she and the key had sheltered, and Aurelia closed her eyes against the blast.

When the light faded, Sinara was gone.

The key too.

The vision ended.

Fresh air hurried to refill her lungs.

If you knew this was going to happen, why didn't you warn her? she asked Hame.

It's not a vision. I was sucked into observing it as it happened.

Where is she?

More importantly, where's the key? Hame said.

She shoved him out of her mind and opened her eyes. Hame squeezed her hand, but she pulled away and climbed off the far side of the bed to pace.

"You see? Sinara's of no use to us now," Hame said. "Not until she returns to a form that's recognizable."

Carn swore. Then swore again.

Of course.

He'd not received Sinara's power. After two hundred years of Xadrak's enhancement, he was again ordinary. He still had his strengths. But he—like much of Aurelia's coven—would remain weaker against Xadrak's army.

Xadrak's *large* army.

There had been at least forty. Had Xadrak held any back, even to retrieve such a prize out of Sinara's clutches? His arrogance may have allowed it. She curled the end of her braid.

"At least we know the key exists," Hame said. "We can find it."

"And how are we meant to do that?" She glared at Hame.

"Easy, Aurelia," Carn said.

"It's fine." Hame waved away her outburst. "She's right. We're back to being just as lost now that Sinara is gone."

His words inflamed the wound in her heart. "She's not gone!" Her voice cracked. She'd managed for centuries without her mother's aid but now so much more was at stake. They balanced on the edge of a chasm that a child's breath could knock them into. She tugged at her hair with a force that whipped her mind out of its fugue.

Find the key. Bring forth Xadrak. Open the portal. Send him back to Crion.

That was the plan.

So simple.

So direct.

Without Sinara, it had never seemed so impossible.

"But we'll get through this." Hame's warmth encircled her mind, offering a comfort she allowed herself to seek respite in. For a moment. Until her heart repaired. Until the worry over Sinara's whereabouts—of losing her mother yet again—dulled.

"Should we be worried about Thierry and Peter?" Carn asked.

"Your son is safe," she murmured. Xadrak's future earthly vessel was under guard with his family in Tuscany. "But Thierry—"

Her fingers twitched to reach for her braid.

"Maybe it's time to put him under house arrest," Hame said.

"But whose house? We can't have him here with Olivier." The thought of locking Thierry away, so soon after he'd rediscovered Etienne—Alex—soured her stomach. Her brother should have some freedom, some joy, but weighing that against their need to keep him safe…

Perhaps Thierry could have it both ways.

"We saw about forty acolytes during the attack," she said. "Do you think Xadrak has more than that?"

Carn scratched his throat. "Maybe," he said in a way that was more yes than no.

Her twenty-nine against their forty—or more. She didn't have enough. And only a handful of them were linked with Sinara's strength.

"We need to thin the herd."

"We need to *cull* the herd, but how do we do that?" Hame asked.

The idea that had whispered inside her head had been small but certain. A cold decision. If she wouldn't lock Thierry up, then he must pay for his freedom.

"We'll team Thierry with a squad of witches. Use him as bait."

"That's risky, Aurelia," Hame said. "Verging on stupid. If they capture him, they'll have half the portal."

"Even if they did, they still can't use him without the

key and Olivier. This way we can keep an eye on Thierry, he's not locked up, and we can even the numbers."

"What if Xadrak's entire force comes after him?"

"It's a chance I'll take, and they're unlikely to resist sending a few after him." She paced again, wishing the room were bigger. "We capture one or two, interrogate them, get the information we need to find more."

"What if they've gone for Thierry already?" he asked.

She stopped. Did Hame really consider her such an amateur? She had only recently reconciled with him; would his doubt of her abilities be one of the things she'd have to repair? "His presence is masked."

"I want to help," Carn said.

Hame's head whipped round, and a fierce light shone in his eyes. "No, you're not strong enough."

Carn winced. "No one builds a better shield than me. I can protect Thierry and hide our forces so Xadrak's army won't know they're there." He turned to her. "I need to do something."

"I would have thought you'd want to watch Peter."

Carn gave a small shake of his head, and this giant of a man, who towered above her and Hame, shrank. He massaged his palm with the thumb of his other hand, marking a small circle built with a force that bulged the muscles in his arm. "I know what must be done, but I don't trust myself not to try to stop it. Let me help take down acolytes."

Hame brushed Carn's fringe from his forehead. "Are you sure? I don't need you to be a hero."

Carn smiled like the first warm day after a long, dark winter and basked in Hame's sunshine. "No chance of that. But I've sat on the wrong side of this fight for too long to take a break. I'll be safe. I'll come back to you."

"And I'll be watching you every step of the way."

"I suppose it's too much, considering what I'm about to do, to ask you not to go onto the astral plane."

Hame shrugged, his eyes twinkling. "An oracle's gotta do what an oracle's gotta do."

"We need him, Carn," Aurelia said. "He might find the key."

"We live in hope." Hame chuckled with more bitterness than mirth.

She rubbed her arms to distract from a chill she couldn't melt. "We should get moving. Xadrak's forces would have scrambled. I need to talk to the others, and we can pull together the teams to take his army down to manageable levels. Carn, watch over Thierry and Alex. I'll follow with a squad."

"Will you tell Thierry what's going on?" Carn asked.

She bit her bottom lip. Always she'd hinted at Olivier's importance, at his future as a sacrifice, while obscuring Thierry's. It had seemed kinder. It had given him hope. But now...

"I don't know. He might be more pliable if he's kept ignorant, but there's a greater chance of things going wrong if he's not aware. Either way, hold off making contact with him unless it's necessary."

Meanwhile she'd check on Peter and let his guards know what had happened. The last thing they needed was to wake up and find Xadrak standing in front of them.

III

Aurelia emerged out of the ether on the gravel driveway leading to the villa. The house in the village of Monsagrati was of the usual type, a two-story terracotta-colored building with arches, shutters on the windows and a few blue glazed pot plants positioned out the front to offset the yellow. It was more than adequate as a place to hide Carn's son, Peter, and his family.

Before she knocked, Zoe opened the door and greeted her with a big white-toothed smile. "You're just in time. We're about to play charades."

Aurelia rolled her eyes.

Games at a time like this?

Aurelia entered, and Zoe looped their arms together as they walked down the hall. Her friend's easy companionship muscled its way inside her heart, nudging aside some of her concerns about Sinara. Being with Zoe made it easier to escape.

The newfound friends were in the living room, wine glasses—some empty, some half-filled—littered the coffee table. A collection of chocolate wrappers and plates with smears of leftover cream and raspberry coulis were dotted about.

On one couch sat Peter with his wife, Jane, her slightly protruding eyes giving her an endearing quality, a church-mouse kind of woman. Diana, petite yet chubby and sand-wiched between her parents, fixed Aurelia with an intense stare that prickled her skin before she'd seen it. The little girl tracked her across the room.

On the other sofa lounged Zach, who was closest to Peter, and the two had smiles beaming. Auburn-haired Mira perched in an armchair. Somewhere in the house must have been another few of her witches, because someone had to be controlling the family's mind.

Peter jumped up and offered his hand, stumbling from clumsiness or wine. He gave his name and introduced his family. There was little doubt who Peter's father was. Their coloring was different, Peter's hair russet to Carn's wheat, but both were tall, broad of face and appeared warm and welcoming—when Carn was in the mood to be so.

She forced a smile. Seeing Carn's son's family together, even in this fantasy, she wished it had turned out different, that Carn could be here, and that she could have enjoyed herself as well.

Snap out of it.

Whatever was being done to keep the fantasy going, she needed to help. She smiled easier this time.

"I'm sorry I'm late, I hope I haven't kept you waiting."

A momentary flicker across Peter's and Jane's eyes, and their faces becoming slightly neutral, before the narrative was reformed in their heads and Aurelia's presence slipped in as easy as if she'd always been part of the group. But even though they were controlled, it was easier to talk without them listening.

She froze the family and stoppered their ears. "How

have they been?" Peering into Peter's eyes, she hoped for some sign that Xadrak lurked within. But his eyes were the same stormy blue as Carn's.

"Fine," Zach said. "They respond well to mind control, and there haven't been any slips or struggles. They've actually been fun to hang out with."

"Don't get attached." The words flew out.

"We're not getting attached, Aurelia," Mira said behind her. "We're doing our job. All Zach is saying is it's much easier than we thought."

"And no sign of Xadrak? No acolytes?"

"They can't find us. We're locked up tight."

"Then how did I get up to the door without being stopped?"

"Because we knew it was you," Zoe said, a tough tone in her voice. "We knew you were here the second your feet touched the ground, and if it were anyone but you, we would have been gone in an instant."

She'd overstepped, calling her soldiers' abilities into question. She should have known better. She'd trained them after all. She swallowed hard, her skin prickling at knowing she was wrong. The old Aurelia would have ignored it, but these were trying times and she didn't have the luxury of burning her bridges—just acolytes.

"I'm sorry for questioning you." The words came easy. "You've all done really well."

Zach looked at Zoe then back to her. "Are you feeling alright? You're sounding a little...off."

She sighed. She may as well tell them. "Sinara is gone."

"What do you mean 'gone'?" Zoe took Aurelia's hand. "We've still got her power."

"I know. I do too, but Hame saw something. She fought

Xadrak and his acolytes and they attacked her. She didn't make it out of the fight."

"But she's spirit. She can't be dead. We'd know. Wouldn't we?"

"I'm sure we would but it worries me. Not everyone's been given her power—Carn for one—but that's not the worst of it."

"There's worse?" Zoe asked.

"Sinara found the key and was protecting it but that's gone too, and we can't find it."

"You're shitting me," Zach said.

"Afraid not."

"And Xadrak definitely doesn't have it?" Zach looked at Peter.

"We're sure." While her witches fidgeted, their nerves making them clench fists or rub their mouths with their hands, she screwed herself in place to be pilloried with their questions. She squeezed her wrist as the only outlet for her fear.

"And he can't get through without some outside help, right? I mean, Xadrak would have emerged when we took Peter otherwise."

"Carn says there's a spell involved, that the acolytes need to be physically close to Peter, but we don't know if Carn was told the truth."

"Great. So, we could be sitting here and Xadrak could emerge at any second." Zach paced the room. "Christ, what about Diana? What about Jane? They're going to get caught up in all this. We need to get Peter away from them."

"Calm down." She fought to quell the panic rising up her throat. "He gains little from exposing himself now. He'd lose the surprise—"

"Waking up to find Xadrak in here would be a big fucking surprise if you ask me," Zach snapped.

Mira and Zoe hadn't said much, but she'd be surprised if they didn't share Zach's concern. She did. Regardless, they had to remain focused.

"The family is to stay together. Zach and Zoe, you keep watching over them, but, Mira, I'd like you to help track acolytes."

She explained the plan with Thierry and Alex. Mira agreed that it was risky but had merit. Meanwhile, Zach and Zoe looked increasingly uncertain about Peter.

"We don't mind staying, Aurelia," Zoe said, "but we want to be sure it's the right thing to do. Perhaps it would be better, safer, to…"

"Killing Peter is not an option."

"But why not?" Zach couldn't hold back. "We don't have the key. Sinara is gone. And if Xadrak comes through, we're royally fucked. Surely, we can get Xadrak here another way, a safer way."

"This is the first time we've ever seen the key and now everyone's looking for it. If we lose Peter, then we've got no hope of bringing Xadrak across and chucking him through the portal."

"But without Sinara to help us——"

"We can do this without her." She didn't sound as reassuring and confident as she would have liked, but she hurried on. "We have Peter, we have the two halves of the portal—all we need is the key. We're in a position of strength."

Silence settled, and the frozen figures of Peter, Jane, and Diana gave off a vibe like some house of waxwork horrors. Why then, if they should be assured of their advantage, did it feel like they were on the losing side?

"You're gambling with a lot of lives, Aurelia," Mira said.

"We've been doing it for centuries," she said. "And this is the first time we've ever come close to finishing it."

Zach slumped back onto the couch. "I don't like it."

"Neither do I, but we will get through this. We will be victorious. And Sinara will come again."

He snorted. "I wish I had your confidence."

"Keep vigilant. Xadrak can't get through without a ritual being performed. We'll find the key before then and then we'll have our victory."

He sighed and his head hit the back of the seat. "If we end up dead, I'll never forgive you."

"I promise to make it up to you in the next life."

Despite his reservations, he trusted her, they all did, and their loyalty warmed her—but it also scalded her. She was putting their lives in danger, but she had the experience, the hunches, and that would have to be enough. That and the power.

She unfroze the scene and let the facade of friendship fall back into place. Taking Peter's offered hand, she shook it and introduced herself.

And wondered how soon it would be before Xadrak stood before her.

IV

THE STENCH OF ORANGES FILTERED THROUGH THE GAP AT the bottom of the door and twisted Olivier's gut. Before the degradation of his imprisonment, he would wrinkle his nose, flare his nostrils, and twitch against Aurelia's putrid scent. With his body wailing for blood, he ground his back teeth together to stop from retching.

After the smell came the click of the lock. Light crept into the dungeon and his pupils dilated. He readied himself to confront his captor, peering into the shadow of her face before the room illuminated and she was revealed: black hair pulled and tied behind her ears, her green eyes as toxic as algae, and a severity to her features that belied the youthful skin and girlish figure. The years had not been kind to his little sister.

She glided into the room, footsteps lost beneath the fall of her navy-blue dress, her hands clasped low and a little too rigid in front of her. The muscles at the top of her breasts tensed. The whole sorry mess brought only a little warmth to his heart. It would burst aflame again when he stood over her bloodless corpse. He bared his fangs at the anticipation of that moment, and they ran wet with his eagerness to delve into her remains.

"What do you want?" she asked, flat and worn.

He closed his mouth, unwilling to speak to her, to acknowledge her existence beyond what he had already shown. Hunger shredded his stomach, its claws tearing into him, his abdomen spasming. He wanted to be still, to be stone, but he wavered on the verge of shaking.

"I didn't summon you," he growled.

"No, but your childish screaming got on my nerves."

"Wait 'til you're in my position, *sister*, and we'll see who can keep hold of their screams."

She raised an eyebrow, then deliberately focused on his manacled wrists pinioned to the wall above his head. "I don't think I have to worry, *brother*."

She turned, probably satisfied that her magic held. She'd let a flicker of panic slip, despite the bravado. She was not infallible. She was not all powerful.

She could fall.

But he needed blood, and if she'd come down once, maybe she was amenable to his requests.

"Blood," he said to her retreating back.

At least the bitch stopped. Her head turned slightly, enough for him to see the thin smile slash across her mouth. A growl rumbled in the back of his throat.

"Thirsty, are you?"

Black tar bubbled and burst in his veins. He scraped his tongue over his canines. "I never pegged you for much of a torturer, Aurelia, but Henri probably fucked that into you."

She sped towards him and stopped close, a snarl contorting her face that he'd be hard-pressed to match. He chuckled, relishing the impact of that one thrust. The starvation was worth it.

"It would account for you turning into such a

monster." Her voice dripped scorn, but the rest of her was rock. He'd wounded her, but not enough to incapacitate. He needed his strength back, and to get that he needed blood and no amount of flattery would make her ease his bonds. He had to find another one, another idiot more pliable.

He smirked at her. "Can't say it's not had its uses. Though, now that I'm entirely at your will for whatever wicked purpose you have intended for me, I begin to wonder if I'm really the worst one in this room."

She blinked and swallowed; her neck tight. Then she made herself breathe; a slow, shaky inhale. A long, quiet exhale. Stalling.

"Whatever you want me for, I'm not going to be much use to you if I'm dead—you've already shown your hand." A sour streak trickled down his throat. "I want blood."

"You'll live without it."

Thierry holding Alex's mouth to his wounds, taking his life, his blood. And then, once the transformation was complete, tossing him away like an old piece of meat to be chewed on by a stray dog.

Oh brother, you are brother no more.

"Perhaps. Perhaps not. Thierry's whore took a lot of what little I had left. It's already leaching out of my veins and sucking on my remaining strength. Who knows what state I'll be in if you leave me to continue as I am?"

She studied him like someone looking at a piece of modern art and trying to decipher it. Finding no answers, her head straightened, and she hitched up the sleeve on her right arm.

His lip curled. "Not yours."

"It's mine or no one's."

"I'd rather starve."

"So be it."

"Look, you don't want to feed me," he purred, though

this being Aurelia, a woman lacking in any sensuality, the effect was likely wasted. She believed she was his superior and she expected to be treated as such, no matter how little he'd done so over their history. She wanted to be treated as emperor to slave, not general to general. "It'll weaken you —not only physically but in my esteem. No, your blood —*you*—won't do."

She pushed down her sleeve. "Then you get none."

"I can wait you out, Aurelia. Or perhaps I can't. Perhaps I'll be a sack of empty skin by the time you make a decision and give me what I want. Tick—" his head tilted to the left before shifting to the right, "—tock."

"Do you think people are lining up to be your blood donor?"

He chuckled. "You'd better believe it."

She peered up at him from beneath hooded brows, a grizzled schoolmistress one moment, a vile adolescent the next. "Ever the egotist."

"Ever the *bitch*."

Her eyes narrowed to slits. "You're not *that* important that I wouldn't let you starve."

"I'm important enough to give me some loser's blood and you know it. But by all means, take your time. It's not like I'm going anywhere." He pulled himself back to press against the wall and rest his head. He watched the ceiling, but she remained in his periphery. Her hand reached up to play with the ends of her hair.

Gotcha.

"How about that witch you ordered to follow me? His blood wasn't completely ruined by all the citrus. That is, if he's still alive."

"I don't know who you mean." Her thumb stroked her index finger like she was trying to calm a nervous dog.

"How many times over the years have I told you you're

a terrible liar?" he said. "You'd think you'd get better at it but no, you refuse to learn." He sighed for dramatic effect. "The witch you sent to spy on me. The boy who thought he was strong enough to run with wolves."

He'd been a minor annoyance, a failed helper, and an easy thing to vanquish. But his blood, for all its aftertaste of oranges, tasted sweeter than most, and he'd left him just enough to live on with his failure. Perhaps that was the victory.

"While I'm not much of a fan of weakness, I'll drink from him. Assuming he pulled through. If he didn't, maybe he has a brother who's just as pretty?"

"Why bother? I could force-feed you."

"You're wasting time. He could already be dead. I guess it's been a few days."

She blinked three times. Her cheek twitched. She moved when she tried not to. She caught him staring, held his gaze, then left, shutting him into the darkness.

But she'd taken the bait and the hook stuck deep. One weak-willed witch coming right up.

Freedom is on its way.

He could taste it.

V

Monsters chased Oberon in and out of consciousness. Voices coaxed him into wakefulness only to let him fall back down again. He needed time to heal, they said. He could heal himself, he wanted to reply, but they wouldn't have listened. Instead they dropped him back into the waiting jaws of vampires lurking in the murky depths. But each time he plunged down his kicks and screams strengthened, propelling him up and into unfamiliar surroundings. No more terrors, just the beeping of machines, the murmured discussions between nurses and doctors, and the rattle of the trolleys.

His eyelids fired open to stare into fluorescent light. He inhaled sharply, stomach swaying on a sea of nausea, and propped himself up on his elbow. Steadying himself helped ease the punches pummeling his stomach. A tube connected his arm to a pump, and a clip locked onto his index finger measured his pulse. He was alive. That was something.

And he was getting out of there.

"Nurse!" He pressed the call button. If he could shout, he didn't need to stay. "NURSE!"

The world tilted, and he closed his eyes to stabilize himself again, forcing breath in and out as if it were a question of ballast. If he got the oxygen right, the room would stop swaying. Then he could leave.

A woman, probably not much older than him, thin, and blonde with a ponytail, entered the room, her attention immediately fixed on the numbers and waves on the monitor. He closed his eyes again. Breathed.

Keep breathing.

"You're back with us, I see." She wrote the observations down on his chart.

"I want to leave." He coughed and reached for the jug of water on the table with a shaking hand. How could he be so weak? He focused on keeping the water level, but it shook more. He had to show he was strong enough to leave even with sweat plastered on his forehead.

The nurse reached over, poured him a drink and passed it to him as if it was the easiest thing in the world. He grimaced but took the plastic cup. She didn't let go until he gripped it hard enough to buckle the sides. He raised it to his mouth and drank. His throat bulged with the effort of swallowing, but it flushed the fear and panic attempting to climb out of him. He gasped with the effort of drinking and held the cup out for more.

She poured him another. "The doctor has to see you first." She handed him the cup and leaned in close. "And I believe the police are interested to hear what happened to you." She indicated with her head to the two men standing outside at the nurse's station.

The men were dressed in suits, not uniforms, but they carried themselves as if they stood on the side of the law—

what little it would do them in a world where evil played free.

"Are you ready to speak to them?"

"How long have I been out?"

"Three days."

Three days and still weak. If he'd been at his full strength, or even half of it, he'd vanish and not look back. Or cloud their minds. Make them believe he'd already spoken to them, that their report was mistaken, that he wasn't a victim. And definitely not someone they could help.

He closed his eyes and checked his strength. A weak pulse beat beneath his skin, akin to his heartbeat, but more treasured. His power trickled through his arteries. A reassuring presence even if it had let him down when the vampire—

He half-dropped the cup, and the nurse took it.

"Do you want to speak to them? You don't have to. After what you've been through, I'm not sure I'd want to talk about it yet. Can I call someone to come sit with you? Do you have any family? A friend? We couldn't find a next of kin."

He fixed her with a glare. She was trying to be nice. Trying to make the best of a bad situation and all that useless shit. But some situations couldn't be made better.

"Let's get this over with so I can get the fuck out of here."

She blanched but retreated.

He pressed the button to raise the bed, his strength weakening to the point where he'd collapse on his back like a corpse before too long. Supported, he scraped his hand through his hair a few times, then folded his arms across his chest. His thumb rested on his bicep and rubbed the skin where the tattooed Ô was.

With each pass back and forth, he smoothed the sensations of the vampire's attack, feeling the strong hand pressed into the middle of his back, his violations, the puncture wounds on his shoulder, all of them rising and flooding his body with cortisol, and bile bubbling at the back of his throat. His eyes stung with the effort of restraint, and he blinked, looking for something to throw up into. He rubbed his bicep harder, faster, as the two cops entered his room.

"Glad to see you're awake and looking so well, Mr. North." Lines radiated from the corner of the cop's hazel eyes. Despite a slightly bulbous nose and lips that were too thin, he had a reassuring face, if it were possible to be reassured at such a time. He offered his hand but pulled it back when the handshake wasn't returned. "I'm Detective Chadstone and this is Detective Gillies. We're from Major Crime Squad."

Staying at the foot of the bed, Gillies' mouth struggled to form a smile. All it did was make his beady eyes disappear and his fat face rounder. "Can you tell us what happened?"

Oberon tongued the roof of his mouth and looked from one cop to the other. "I'm not pressing charges."

The lines on Chadstone's face deepened. "It was a pretty nasty assault."

Rape. Let's be honest, guys.

Nails dragged beneath the surface of his chest and up his throat, carrying words ready to launch and tell them everything. But they didn't look at him with anything resembling concern. Whether that was because he was just another victim, or because he was a *male* victim…or maybe it was because he was weak. They couldn't help him, even if they were inclined to.

"Yes, I'm sure."

"Is that because it was consensual?" Gillies' mouth resembled an asshole. An unviolated one.

His thumbnail gouged into his bicep.

Chadstone shot Gillies a sideways glance. "What my partner means to say is we get many people not wanting to talk about the things they've been through, but when they do, they find it helps. The paramedics were called to your apartment around three am on Saturday morning. They found you naked on the floor…"

His voice summoned the scene. A young twenty-something male, gay, naked on the floor of his apartment. Blood covering his back and his ass. Wounds in his neck. Lost a lot of blood. Around him a home in disarray, plaster broken on the cracked wall, furniture overturned, perhaps catching the smell of burned carpet, burned something. It would have looked like a hook-up gone wrong. They happened. That's what you get for letting unknown people into your house.

What you deserve.

"I'd like you to leave."

Chadstone looked at Gillies. Gillies rolled his eyes.

"You see, Mr. North." Chadstone adopted a harder tone. "The marks on your shoulder are similar to those we've noticed on other victims around Perth recently. I'm sure you're aware of the unusually high number of murders that have happened. You're the only one who has the marks and lived."

The vampire.

Or his twin brother.

Probably both.

He'd done nothing to stop the rising body count or to cover it up. That hadn't been his brief. And he was paying the price for it. Well, not for much longer.

"So, if you could tell us who you were with—"

"You think I subjected myself to this willingly?"

"Well, Mr. North, there's no sign of forced entry so we have to assume you knew whomever you let into your apartment. What happened afterwards tells us you didn't know this person very well."

The other officer crossed whatever invisible barrier had kept him from coming closer to the bed. With his advance came the waft of stale cigarette smoke. He peered down and tried to use his body where words had failed to intimidate.

"Look, mate, we only want to catch the guy who did this. We don't care what kind of shit you get up to in the privacy of your own home, but this guy has killed a lot of people, and you're lucky to have escaped with your life."

He sneered the last word. It was a familiar sneer, one worn by many when they considered the merits or otherwise of his 'life'.

Chadstone chewed his lip. Under normal circumstances, he'd be the kind of guy anyone could confide in. He probably had kids and coached a football team on the weekend. Let him father someone else.

"You think I'm lucky? You go through what I did and tell me how lucky you are. Until then fuck off."

Gillies' cheeks flushed. "Look, you little faggot—"

"Enough!" Chadstone barked.

Despite his weakness, power swelled beneath his skin and swirled in the center of his chest, a blaze awakened, ready to scorch the earth. He breathed hurriedly, unsure whether he was stoking or suppressing it.

"We'll leave now, Mr. North." He pushed Gillies towards the door before turning back to place his business card on the table. "If you want to talk, give me a call."

Oberon didn't move, didn't even look at the card, just held Chadstone's eyes with a glare. He waited until they left then collapsed—heaving with adrenaline—back into the bed.

That fucking arsehole cop. He wished… He wished…

He could have obliterated him. He could have rained down torment on him that would make his eyes bleed and his soul crack.

Then why didn't I?

"I'm not strong enough."

"You are."

Instinct brought power surging to his hands and into a ball of fire that he launched towards the voice. Sweat drenched his body, and he collapsed back into the bed, his heart racing and his breath panting, but the fight-or-flight response streaming through his system summoned strength to hold a second attack ready. He wouldn't have enough for a third.

The fire didn't strike its target, but instead froze mid-air, surrounded by a force that diminished and extinguished to reveal Aurelia in a blue dress.

"Get the fuck out!"

His room door closed as she approached. His hands shook with the effort of holding on to his second attack and waiting for the moment he could get his revenge on her for feeding him to her brother. She seemed unfazed by the danger she was in and instead reached out a hand as if to lay a benediction rather than a curse.

"Don't touch me, Aurelia."

Her palm rested on his forearm, over the scrawl of tattooed Latin. His prepared attack faded, his energy calmed, though his heart still hadn't recovered from the shock of having someone—her—appear in his room without his knowing.

What if it had been the vampire?

He tried to shake her off, but her hand clamped down.

Through the connection of skin on skin, warmth trickled into him, a heat prickling from head to toe, outside to in. What was she doing to him? But while his mind resisted, his body craved it, craved it more than water on a blistering day. He breathed like it was the first time, his lungs ripening into their full capacity, and his pulse resounding like the beat of a drum calling warriors to arms. His blood hummed, and his power—oh God, his power—restored to its full strength and thrummed along with his heartbeat.

Strong again.

Alive again.

Thanks to Aurelia.

But she'd get no thanks from him.

He cast her hand away, able to do it now, and threw back the covers to escape. He pushed through the worry that his legs would not support his weight, but even falling seemed a small inconvenience to get away from her. He ripped the drip out of the crook of his elbow and left it to leak onto the bed. He silenced the beeping machines. He searched for his clothes before realizing they had probably cut them off him.

Aurelia's faraway eyes swam up to his, then she blinked. "Do you feel better?"

"You lied to me."

She pursed her lips and sank into a chair. "I warned you about the danger involved."

"You said I'd be strong enough to handle it. He just…" He closed his eyes, but the vampire's face materialized, and he opened them again. It didn't help that he saw some of that bastard in Aurelia. Less madness, perhaps, but still a determination that bowed others to her will. He wouldn't bow again though, no matter what she offered. "He raped me. Like it was the easiest thing in the world."

Clearly it was.

"I'm sorry." She said it softly, no doubt meant to be consoling, but her voice was disconnected. She told him what she thought he wanted to hear.

"I couldn't stop him. You held back from giving me full access to my power." He stabbed the air with his finger.

She glowered before wrestling her affront into submission. But he'd seen it. She knew he'd seen it. She smoothed her face anyway. "I gave you everything you were capable of. I learnt my lesson long ago not to deny others their full potential."

"That's reassuring," he sneered, "to know that I'm unable to stop a *vampire* violating me."

"He's no ordinary vampire."

"No, he's your brother. I'd expect him to have all sorts of enhancements. I wanted to—" He didn't want to let the hate win.

"You wanted to kill him," she finished, answering as if his wish were the most normal thing in the world. As if everyone wanted the creature dead.

Perhaps they did.

Shame no one had succeeded.

"I'm sorry I can't offer you his life, but I can give you something else."

"We have nothing to say to each other." He leaned against the wall, cushioning his backside with his hands. "All I want is to get far away from your whole fucking family."

He didn't want to be that person. He had never wanted to be a hater and despise the world. But the vampire had tarnished everything. His chin dropped onto his chest, and he studied the scuffed floor. "What help?"

"I can give you immortal life."

A shiver burst at the base of his spine. His head jerked up. "Why would you give me that?"

"So this short life can be salvaged and filled with more joy than sorrow, more peace than strife."

So I can outlive that monster.

He kept his hands behind his back lest they give him away. "Immortality hasn't made you any less angry, any happier."

"We all have our callings in life. As you know, mine is to fight—and win—this war with the demon Xadrak. It was decided before I was born, and I have accepted it. Your life, however, can be whatever you choose."

Immortality had its perks, and one life was never going to be enough for him. But he'd yet to find a witch willing to give him eternity. And like some prophecy Aurelia appeared asking him to sign on the dotted line with his own blood. There was always a catch, and there were bound to be many.

"I'm sure you demand something of me. Help to fight your battle? Nearly dying obviously wasn't enough so what do you want?"

She took a deep breath and stared at him, examined him.

"I need…" she paused.

It's about him.

He held up both hands and shook his head. "I'm not interested."

"You haven't heard what it is yet."

"I know it has to do with your brother, and if I get anywhere near him, I will kill him." His hand closed into a fist, and he paced as far as the small room would let him. He had to keep moving, the fear urging him to run.

"I wouldn't ask this if I wasn't desperate."

"So, it's true?" He stopped, and his voice turned breathless. "You want me to face that monster again? You'd better fuck off before I lose it."

He already was. Pins tap-danced across his chest, each little strike repeating a routine that was building to a climax and making him twitch with each slap-ball-change. He had to get away from this or he'd be crushed underfoot. But his attempt at escape only took him five steps towards the door then five steps back. He rubbed the Ô until his skin burned with the rest of him.

"What about Thierry? Surely he's keen to help his brother." What that brother got up to he'd been only vaguely aware of. Olivier had been the more visible of the twins. Literally. It had been easier to follow Olivier's path of destruction than Thierry's.

She cleared her throat. "Thierry has even less reason to want to be near Olivier than you. Help me and I'll help you."

Thierry hated Olivier? Maybe that could be useful. Not that he'd ever go near either of them again. And even though she offered something, that didn't mean he'd take it.

"I helped you last time and I ended up here. If I help you again, I'm going to end up dead."

"But you won't."

He stopped his back and forth. "You'll make me immortal *now*?"

She didn't answer.

"I thought so. Gotta dangle that carrot a little longer while I get beaten to a pulp with the stick?" He massaged the back of his neck, trying to undo some of the knots that had formed.

"You have my word."

"Your word isn't worth shit, Aurelia."

"Look at it from my perspective. If you offered me immortality in exchange for completing a task, would you give it to me before or after?"

He jutted himself forward, his fists punching the bed, and snarled in her face. "You can bet I wouldn't be asking you to go anywhere near your rapist."

Her eyes widened and dissolved the neutral demeanor. Her usually pallid color reddened and the air around her sparked like electricity jumping pylons. Power buzzed through him.

Such strength. What he wouldn't—

He swore at himself.

"You have no idea what I've done in my life, Oberon. The sacrifices I've made, the things I was forced to do because it was my duty. You are not the center of the world, and your problems are not special. All of us must make hard decisions and unpleasant choices, but that's life. I am offering you immortality. I am giving you the chance to exact a kind of vengeance on the man who attacked you. I know what it's like to conquer your own rapist."

Shame frothed in the bottom of his stomach. He hated her for holding a mirror up to him. But was self-pity worth losing this opportunity?

He forced the words out of his mouth. "What would I have to do?"

"Keep Olivier alive."

The vampire's lips closed over the holes in his shoulder and drew out the memory of blood stolen. His muscles tensed, his power surged, and he vanished, leaving Aurelia and her impossible request behind.

VI

"Thierry, open up, or I'm letting myself in."

Aurelia and Carn waited on the landing outside Alex's apartment. After three knocks, Thierry still hadn't responded. He probably smelled her before she'd even rapped her knuckles on the recently repaired front door.

"Go away, Aurelia," he growled from behind the thin wood. "You and whoever you've got with you."

She sighed and released a whispered word of power. The handle unlocked beneath her touch.

Filtered light through threadbare curtains cast a funereal pall. An ordinary, small apartment: a couch, a kitchenette, and a room and bathroom down a shortened hallway. Her nose wrinkled from the mustiness, the linger of naked bodies exercising in ecstasy.

"You can't run, Thierry, so you may as well make yourselves visible."

"Who's the witch?" His disembodied voice circled the room.

Carn closed the door. Energy shimmered through her as his shield slid into place.

"His name is Carn. He works with me. We're here for your help."

"No chance. You still owe me for Olivier."

She stood in the middle of the room, but rather than pivot and search for him she remained still and spoke to the hallway. "Help me and you'll get what you want, but I'm not going to talk to an empty apartment for much longer. And you won't like it if I get impatient."

Two tense seconds passed before Thierry cast off his invisibility to reveal himself standing a few feet in front of her. A dark scowl shaped his eyes and brow, a reflection of his twin's, and her heart skipped a beat.

Not Olivier. Not Olivier.

Thierry's hand gripped Alex's, and the gaze of the blond healer-cum-vampire darted between them. Both were naked to the waist, their lithe torsos of perfect muscle, enhanced by the vampiric power that animated their bodies. They wore shorts, no doubt hastily pulled on when she arrived. Thierry had ever been the nudist.

"I knew we should have left days ago. What do you want? We were quite happy without you."

"Mind if I sit?" She sank into the couch's soft cushions. Carn's large and formidable form guarded the edge of her vision.

"Make it quick, or we're out of here," Thierry threatened, but she wouldn't be rushed. It had nothing to do with the difficulty in finding the right words.

"Alex, how are you?" It couldn't be easy, this new existence of his.

"He's fine." Thierry cut across Alex's stalled response. "Get on with it."

Alex's head drifted dreamily towards her and Carn. "Oranges, violets," he whispered and breathed deep, "and blood." His eyelids fired open—shocked? excited?—and fangs protruded to pin his lip against his bottom teeth. Thierry held onto Alex harder. It wasn't for support. She charged her hands. Alex swooned. Blood bloomed on his lip. He needed to feed. Desperately.

That could work to her benefit.

"Very well," she said. "My coven has battled another for centuries, and you and Olivier are the prize."

He frowned at her, the lines deepening that marble skin, his head coming forward a bit like he tried to hear her better. Elder brother disbelieving younger sister. "Excuse me? For years you've told me Olivier is the important one. *He's* the one with some higher purpose. You said I'd get to be with Alex and that would be the end of it." His voice raised, his words clipped and steady.

"It's a little more complicated than that." She used a lighter tone to balance Thierry's building anger, but she couldn't outweigh it. "Neither of you are exactly what you appear to be."

"We're not vampires?"

She leaned back into the couch and locked her hands together over her lap. He'd struggle with whatever she had to say so the only thing to do was lay it all out. As much as was necessary.

"Not *just* vampires. You're two pieces of a portal that opens our world to another."

He coughed a breath. "Since when?" The color of his eyes shifted from their rich brown to that of glowing embers.

"Since always. When the portal opens, we intend to send a demon through it and back into his world."

"Is that so? Funny, I hadn't noticed any locks or door handles on me over the past *six hundred fucking years*." Thierry's eyes opened wider to let the blaze burn bright. He stalked the room, fists ready and searching for something to punch.

Alex backed up and wedged himself into a corner, crossed his arms over his chest and watched Thierry pace.

Aurelia's legs tensed ready to launch. "There's no use getting upset."

"Upset? What else haven't you told me? Or will we need another century to cover it all? Let's start with you telling me who this demon is."

She straightened the line in her dress before smoothing it out. One Band-Aid answer coming right up. "His name is Xadrak, but you knew him as Henri d'Arjou."

He froze. "Father? I thought you killed him. A long time ago."

"Yes," she said, "and no."

He tilted his head back and his whole body sighed. "I'm tired of riddles, Aurelia."

And she was tired of arguing. She roped down the annoyance bloating like indigestion in her stomach. Hadn't the brothers had their freedom and fun while she'd been forced to serve? If he wanted the truth, then he could have it. "Do you remember Mother?"

"What's she got to do with it?" That frown again. She was beginning to hate it.

"Mother and Henri are not from this world. They're both demons from another realm."

His laughter machine-gunned the stale air.

"Why are you laughing?"

"It explains *so* much. So, what about the horns? I'm assuming they had horns, these demons."

She sucked her tongue. His childishness stung her like march flies. "Their bodies were human; their souls demon. They fought a battle in their world, fell through a portal into this one, and got bound up in our mortality. They produced you, me, and Olivier."

"Demon spawn. Figures." His fists squeezed and his knuckles popped. "And it's our job to put it right, is it? How do *you* know all this?"

She forced herself to go on. "From Mother. After she left us, she returned filled with magic and taught it to me. When you and Olivier were turned, I killed Henri, but doing so released the demon into the astral. He lacked a physical form, but he was still dangerous."

Thierry opened his mouth to speak, but she held up her hand to silence him. Perhaps locking him up would have been the better choice. Definitely less aggravating.

"For centuries she and I have been working together to keep Xadrak—Henri—from committing any serious harm. Meanwhile we've been looking for the key. Without it, we can't send Xadrak back to where he came from, and if he remains, he'll seek to rule."

Thierry crossed the room and stood next to Alex. "Good luck with that, Aurelia, but I'm not getting involved. Find another way. Use Olivier. Tear him apart. But I'm staying here with Alex."

"It doesn't work like that." She rose. "But when this is finished, you will still be here, and Olivier will be gone. That much I can guarantee."

"How can I trust you? How can I trust Olivier? He'll double-cross you. He'll swap places with me and *I'll* get sent to some hell dimension."

His accusations burned. Olivier was the one she warred with, not Thierry. They were meant to be beyond this hate and mistrust. But if she'd done it differently, she might have already lost him.

"I promised you you'd be rid of him and you will. *He* will go, not you. And you *will* remain with Alex."

His eyes narrowed. "Why spill your secrets now?"

"The key has been sighted, and we're trying to locate it."

"Before the demon gets it?"

She nodded stiffly.

He rolled his eyes and raised one hand as if holding up her arguments for examination. "But why the warning? Why not come to me when you've found it?"

She wanted to reach for her braid; instead she interlaced her fingers and held them in front of her stomach. How to explain this without setting off any fight?

"Because we have to even the odds. Xadrak's forces are larger than mine, and we need to wipe a few of them out."

His hand fell against his arm, the slap of skin on skin as loud as a gunshot. He blinked to process her words and each rapid-fire open and close built the arguments for his refusal. She was going to lose him.

"Thierry, it's not—"

"You want us to fight?! Go up against an *army* of witches—an army who wants us captured or dead?"

Alex's breath shuddered out in a long, shaky stream. Thierry clasped his hand again but didn't see the pleading in Alex's eyes. He wouldn't last much longer, and then Thierry would battle against her to get his lover fed. She had to pull this trigger.

"You'll be doing us a service." She took a cautious step towards them.

"You're turning us into a fucking target! I will not allow Alex to be used as bait."

"That's fine because *you're* the one who's going to be the bait." She raised her voice, and Alex screwed his eyes shut. "Alex can sit it out, but whether you like it or not, you are going to help us bring down Xadrak's acolytes."

"Why bother telling me if I don't have a choice?"

"I thought I owed you the courtesy, but now I'm having regrets. You've been under *my* protection since you were turned and despite what's happened to you, it's not even a fraction of how bad it could have been." She reared up to his snarling face. "My coven is ready to attack and kill any who come near you, but we need to draw out as many as possible. And if you know what's going on, then you're less likely to fuck it up."

"Forget it, Aurelia, I am not—"

"It's either this or I lock you up like Olivier. Maybe *with* Olivier."

"You wouldn't dare," he snarled, fire filling his eyes.

"Just try me."

"If you think—" He shoved his finger in her face.

"Please, Thierry," Alex whispered, pulling on his arm, and dragging Thierry's anger away from her. "I need to feed. If it brings someone close that I can kill and it does some good, then let's try." His Adam's apple bobbed up and down with a hard swallow. "I'm sure she won't let anything happen to either of us."

Relief trickled through her chest and splashed her heart, but her body remained battle primed.

Thank the heavens for Alex.

Thierry's face smoothed into an impassive mask. How he must have warred with his nature. Wanting to protect himself and Alex while his lover was the sainted voice of reason. Etienne had been the same.

He rolled his tongue around inside his mouth like he juggled marbles. "How many will protect us?"

"Ten of my strongest."

"This won't work. You know it won't."

"It'll work well enough. Besides, if Xadrak gets control of you, he won't care whether you come back to Alex. He'll use you, discard you, and that'll be that."

Alex slipped an arm around Thierry's waist. He rested his head on his shoulder, his face pallid even in the shadows. But no worse than Thierry, who looked like he'd lost the battle, the war, and his life.

"The coven has this place surrounded, and Carn is in charge of shielding you. Trust him. He'll keep you safe."

"When do we start?"

She faced the two vampires. Without all the history, without knowing what they were, they were just two young men who wanted to love each other in peace. Despite her promises, despite her wishes, and despite all her best efforts, she had no guarantee they'd survive and get their happy ending.

"Now. I don't think Alex can go much longer without blood."

He winced before his face brightened with an ironic grin. "Please, don't say that word." He hugged Thierry tighter.

She smiled. This could work better than she'd hoped.

VII

THE CHARCOAL ENDS OF BURNED CARPET SPIKED THE BARE soles of Oberon's feet. His ruined apartment was as he'd left it—the overturned furniture, the cracked wall he'd attempted to push Olivier through. He could put it right with a little magic, but he didn't trust himself to not bring the whole complex down. The fractures in the exposed concrete showed how much force he'd used to defend himself and even that hadn't been enough. Another of the cop's business cards sat on the coffee table. Failure surrounded him. Coming home—no, no longer home—had been a mistake.

He wouldn't stay long. Aurelia's request hounded him. She couldn't expect him to go anywhere near Olivier, let alone willingly feed him his blood. He reached over his shoulder, and his fingers slipped beneath the hospital gown and over the gauze patch. He picked it off and touched the puncture wounds. The flesh had healed except for two raised bumps. If he went near Olivier again, he'd get more of the same, though next time they might be in his neck. Never again. He'd never let the vampire near him again.

He marched into his bedroom, ripping the gown from his body. He'd shower later—elsewhere. He pulled on underwear, a black tank-top, blue torn jeans, socks, and shoes, then vanished from the apartment. Less than five minutes and the walls had already compressed his lungs to the point of suffocation.

He emerged in the entrance to an alley, hitting the ground with a fast stride, the feeling of being watched chasing him out of the ether. His breath panted in and out of his mouth. He couldn't stand still and was too nervous to look behind him in case anyone was there. In case *he* was there. But, no; if Aurelia wanted his help, then she must have Olivier somewhere. Imprisoned, she'd said. He should feel safe.

He dashed down the street, found the right door, and ducked inside.

The odor of antiseptic stripped his nostrils. The tattoo parlor smelled cleaner than the hospital.

Julie squealed. "Obe! Haven't seen you in ages." She came out from behind the counter and pulled him into a hug. She squeezed him until his vertebrae popped then shoved him back to arm's length and appraised him as well as she could with one eye half-covered with a purple fringe rigid with wax. She clucked her pierced tongue. "You look like shit."

He gave a half-hearted laugh, which raised her studded eyebrow. Even to him it sounded pathetic.

"Sit." She pointed at one of the black broken-vinyl chairs before walking to the back of the shop.

He perched while the tattooist's needle buzzed from behind a curtain. Julie returned with a bottle of water in her ink-decorated hand and thrust it at him.

"Drink this."

His mouth dried at the sight of it; he hadn't realized

he'd been thirsty. The adrenaline had finally burned out. As the cool water wet his throat, it melted some of the tension that had been keeping him upright, and he uncoiled into the chair. His head hit the wall with a hard thwack, and he jerked forward, spilling the water and coughing as it went down the wrong way. He rubbed the back of his head, before opening his eyes and looking sheepishly up at Julie who studied him like he was…

No, Julie wouldn't think anything bad about him. She didn't seem the type, not without cause.

He sighed and leaned back again—with caution.

"So, what's it going to be?" she asked.

There wouldn't be any prompting or sympathy if he didn't ask for it. And he wasn't about to do that. Sympathy would get him nothing. Only one thing could make this right, and until he got the chance, he was going to burn away as much of the pain as he could.

"A brand."

She pursed her lips. "You sure?"

He glared at her. "I got the rest of this done, didn't I?" He waved his hand in front of his chest.

She laughed, and he crushed the bottle. He wasn't like some clients who walked out with full body work done, sleeves, genitals, skulls, even the parts where the hardcore hesitated. Julie herself had more ink on her than most of the guys in the city. The four pieces he'd had done were nothing compared to them, but still he took pride in his art, a defini-tion of his identity that needed no more embellishment.

Until now.

"I want a brand on my shoulder, will you do it or not?"

"Hey," she barked. "Don't get stroppy with me, Obe. It's my job to make sure you're sure so you don't chicken out halfway through."

"Did I flinch before?"

"No, but a brand is different. It won't come off."

"Do I look like I want it to come off?"

"You look angry and angry people have regrets."

He looked her in the eye. "No regrets."

"K." She shrugged and walked back around the counter. "What do you want it to be?"

He stood opposite her, took the offered pen and drew on the pad. It had to be simple. The branding process couldn't handle the intricate work of a tattoo, and the length of the procedure might be another problem. How long could he withstand the iron burning through multiple layers of skin? How different would it be to just another tattoo? Anticipation stirred in his belly and whipped up a cold air.

When he was done, he turned it to face her.

"It's long. You sure you want something this detailed? It's not going to turn out pretty like the rest of you."

"It's not meant to be."

She looked from the pad to him and her eyes lingered on the tattoos she could see. Delicate, graceful work yet he was going to get this scar?

"Where do you want it?"

He pulled his shirt over his head, turning as he did so. He pointed over his right shoulder, ran his fingers over the raised bumps. "Here. I want the *i* to go in between the dots."

She came around, grabbed his arms, bent him to her height so she could get a better look. "What the hell? Who did this to you?"

"It doesn't matter. Will you do the brand or not?"

The whirr of a needle in the background stopped. "For fuck's sake, Jules," Bill shouted from the back. "This is a business. If he wants the fucking brand, he can fucking have it."

A guy—the customer—laughed and then hissed as the needle punctured him.

Oberon slipped his shirt back on. Julie wasn't smiling. Hard concern, like a lioness watching her cubs play too close to crocodile-infested waters, stalked her eyes. *Thank you* vibrated on the end of his tongue, but he kept it contained. Gratitude would come later.

"Fine," she said stiffly. "Come back tomorrow and I'll do it then."

Panic seized his neck and dug its fingers through to the muscle. "No!" He pounded the counter with his fist. "Now. It has to be now."

Julie flinched. "I think you'd benefit from a little time to think about it, Obe."

"I have thought about it."

"I'm sorry but—"

His hand latched onto her wrist, and his fingers pressed against her pulse. He swallowed his apprehension and released a simple persuasion spell. "You'll do it today," he whispered. "And I don't want any more arguments."

She fought for a second, a testament to how much she was against the idea. His heart twisted, but he needed it done today. He wasn't going to be in town tomorrow.

"Then let's begin."

OBERON LAY FACE DOWN ON THE WHITE CLOTH WITH HIS left arm alongside his body to keep his shoulder flat. His right arm bent at the elbow, and his forehead rested on the back of his hand. His skin tightened under the air conditioning pumping down from above. Julie had gone off to finish the stencil while the cauterizer warmed up on the stand next to him. Meanwhile, Bill continued to work behind the curtain on the guy who didn't make much noise. Once he swore but little else indicated he suffered under Bill's needle. It whirred and whizzed, started and stopped, continued humming away, lulling him into a place where his mind stopped, and he drifted into blessed nothingness.

He didn't know how long it lasted before Julie's sigh-laden return wrenched him back. "This what you wanted?"

He lifted his head to look at the tracing paper with the design on it dangling above his head. "Perfect."

It vanished with a flutter, and his skin prickled as Julie swabbed his shoulder with alcoholic wipes. She repeated the cleaning a couple of times, each time harder than the one before. If only everything could be so easily cleaned. She copied the design onto his skin.

He'd never wanted a brand before, which wasn't to say he hadn't been attracted to them. The ink had seemed a better fit at the time, the black seeming to emerge out of him, an uncovering rather than an application. A brand seemed much more violating.

But he'd been forced to wear the vampire's mark and only an equal show of force could neutralize it.

The cauterizer looked like a chunky pen with a piece of metal on the end that glowed when hot. It would draw third-degree burns onto him and wipe out the pain receptors. He'd rebuild himself as the letters formed words. His stomach fluttered and his legs fidgeted as he waited for his flesh to sizzle beneath the self-inflicted trauma.

"I'm going to say this one last time—are you sure?"

"Yes." His voice came out flat and low. His muscles clenched waiting for a blow to come out of nowhere. He breathed deeply, a little too fast, but he needed it to keep himself still. He needed to control his power in case he lashed out or tried to protect himself.

He wanted this. He needed it. He needed it to hurt.

She cleared her throat and her rubber-gloved hand pressed his shoulder. She didn't stretch the skin, didn't want it to pucker. She picked up the cauterizer, and he braced himself as an aura of heat neared him then pressed into his flesh.

The fire cut through the surface of his skin, down through two layers of skin to kiss the third. The tang of burning flesh scraped the back of his throat. He was glad he hadn't eaten. As Julie continued, the thought of food drifted away but it wasn't annihilated with the agony he'd expected. The pain snuffed out as soon as it flared and as she traced each letter, its mildness spread throughout his body. His skin stung, different to that of a needle, but just as bearable.

"Are you okay?"

What could he say? He'd wanted it to hurt. He'd wanted it to reach through and ignite a pyre that burned everything Olivier had done to him. But instead it drifted through an already barren and blackened land. His tongue tasted ash.

"Keep going."

She continued the procedure. Her hand braced his shoulder, the wounded skin burned, but it quickly faded, and despondency blanketed him. It weighed down on him, slowly, consistently, and dreadful in its immovability. It would crush him and continue on once he'd been ground out of existence.

She spoke—he thought she spoke—and probably wanted him to stop, wanted to take a break, but he must have given her muted encouragement to keep going. It all happened beyond him while leaving his soul to weep for something more, something to spark the pain, to obliterate what that monster had done to him. He couldn't feel and so he'd sought to scar himself in a greater fashion. As if that could have made it right.

Look how easily I broke you.

Olivier's voice slithered into his head and wrapped around his heart, his poison dissolving through the muscle. Julie continued, humming to herself. He forced his eyes open, unable to close them in case the vampire's face loomed. He didn't want to relive what he'd been through, didn't want to experience it, even if it meant feeling something other than this nothingness.

"I'm finished," she said, but he barely heard her.

A fog enveloped his mind.

She asked if he was okay, gave him some water, showed him the brand—all dark red and angry—in the reflection of the mirror, then took a photo of it on her phone so he could see it as it really was.

Jamaïs encore.

It was meant to be a promise to himself and a warning to the vampire. Never again would he suffer what he'd been through. Never again would he be weakened. But it was naive.

The monster had taken up residence inside his soul, stripped it bare, and no burned skin was ever going to evict him. He'd have to do more. He'd have to go further.

His thumb ran over the tattoo on the inside of his forearm, the first one he'd gotten.

Aut inveniam viam aut faciam.

I'll either find a way or make one.

Perhaps Aurelia's request wasn't so absurd after all.

VIII

Scorpions scuttled through Olivier's veins, their tails stinging him as what little blood remained dripped ever more out of his ancient body. Every lost ounce became another beat counting out the seconds of his diminished existence. Defeated by something as simple as hunger, time now the drain on *his* life force. She would return. He mattered—she'd said so—but what state would he need to be in for her purpose?

It took too much effort to keep his head raised. His skin had turned crêpe paper–thin and crinkled in the dead air of the dungeon. Would he soon blow away? Or would he even fail to take flight, as if flight were only for living things?

He hadn't been alive all this time, not in the way of normal things. In others he'd been more alive than any of them, more alive than any human, any vampire, any mistake of creation. Burying his face in the thick of it, lapping up all the sweat and blood and viscera that bubbled forth to coat his tongue in all its putrid richness.

How he reveled in it.

And how it now tormented him.

Stuck. Pinned to a wall. Exhibited in some forgotten room for some bug collector. A relic. The world had died, and he was forced to die with it.

Hold, said the voice. His voice. Quiet in the darkness. Whispered. But assured. An insider, a companion to help him avoid the pitfalls of his loneliness. It promised freedom.

But the hunger stole so much of his strength.

Perhaps it won't be long. Perhaps it would be better to—

A scent brushed his nose, so faint he might have been mistaken.

It concentrated and dominated.

Lightning lit his dried heart. He raised his head and inhaled deeper, reaching for that smell. He pushed aside all others and grabbed at it, sweeping it towards him so he could breathe it in, hold it, and sink in his fangs. Heady, heavy, and vile: the fetidness of oranges.

Oh, yes. Oh, yes. Oh, yes.

He clenched his fists and pulled himself up, rolled his shoulders, stretched, and chased those maudlin, traitorous, *weak* thoughts away.

In the remaining calm, he sharpened his senses, sharpened his *need* to the finest point where all his attention focused on where the door would open, and in would walk that skin-covered sack of blood. Saliva filled his mouth. It mattered little that it had only been a handful of days— *days!*—since he'd gorged. His body had suffered too much to mean that time was irrelevant.

Oh, yes. Oh, yes. Oh, yes.

His body hummed as the smell intensified, but he wasn't about to appear eager for his saucer of milk. He was a lion. He waited. He prepared himself. The prey was going to come to him.

He exhaled all the fusty air that had clung to him, its sticky dustiness expelled, along with any errant thought that he could have ever allowed *this* to triumph over him.

He was Olivier *fucking* d'Arjou, and he would never be defeated.

After all, hadn't Aurelia brought him exactly what he'd demanded? Not that there'd ever been any doubt who was really in control. The chains were an illusion; they were her crutch, not his prison. And that other witch… Well, he was going to have plenty of fun with him.

Oh, yes. Oh, yes. Oh, yes.

IX

Like every sacrifice there ever was, Oberon wished the walk to his doom would both end and last forever. Aurelia didn't look back to check he followed as she glided down the circling tunnel and deep into the mountain in which she'd built her home. He'd contacted her the day after leaving the tattoo parlor and she'd come to take him away with nothing more than a smug smile.

Now he was in the heart of her lair where a dungeon contained the beast. The tunnel's outer walls were rough granite, but the floor and the ceiling were smooth and built of stone slabs. Aurelia carried light, a glow that emanated from her and just covered him. Looking behind him, all was darkness.

His shallow breath caught in his throat to stop the screams from getting out.

A fitting place to tether a monster.

All too soon, Aurelia stopped outside a stout wooden door with a metal handle and a lock. There was no sound —from him, from Aurelia, from Olivier. He kept his eyes within the light, afraid of what hid in the shadows, afraid of the possibility that Olivier might have escaped and waited for him.

His shoulder blade itched. Fingers picked at the brand, attempting to open the skin.

Aurelia turned to him. "Are you ready?"

Was he? Everything still hurt. The draining, the rape, the branding, and his near-death. Yet there he was, hoping vengeance would make it all better.

And it would. One immortal life in service of another. Nothing seemed more fitting. Taking away what Olivier valued—his strength, his vitality, his position—and using it in service to the one he'd wronged. Aurelia would never have let him in if she knew his plan, but she'd act as an unwitting accomplice. He'd get her to fulfil her promise before he sent that motherfucker to hell.

"I'm ready." The coldness in his voice sent ice spidering across his skin. He needed the numbing.

The door swung inward to a pitch-dark room. His fists clenched ready to fight Olivier if he'd somehow got free. Too much potential lurked in that blackness. If he was going to come down regularly, he'd have to leave the light on. In the back of his mind, he laughed at the childish sentiment, but fear quickly froze it out.

Nope, can't laugh about this yet.

With a wave of her hand, the light extended and illuminated the cell. Olivier didn't lift his head or search for who entered; he was already watching them. No, watching *him*. His lips parted in an obscene smile and revealed his fangs. His eyes glowed with so much arrogance it was as if the manacles weren't there. Oberon's stomach shriveled.

Walking in blind would have been better.

Olivier's gaze possessed him as surely as when he'd held him down and raped him. Seconds stretched until only the two of them existed. His focus localized on the vampire's beautiful and alluring face made grotesque from their shared past. Yet still he remained entranced. He'd managed to pass through the Devil's door, but this second test of facing what was inside almost had him beat. Could he be in the same room as this fiend?

The last time he was alone with Olivier, he'd nearly died.

Jamais encore.

The link snapped, and the light brightened. He raised his head, spine popping as he straightened. Aurelia entered and he followed.

The vampire kept his stare fixed on him, but it didn't hold the same intensity, like being watched by a security camera as opposed to an armed guard. There, but distant.

Chains bound Olivier to the wall. With arms pulled wide, he had barely enough slack to let his hands fall forward. His feet were the same. His naked back pressed against the stone, allowing him very little leverage. Not that mere metal chains would be enough to keep him bound. Enchantments ran through it all, keeping him in place—enchantments Oberon would add to.

"I see you've brought me some scraps," Olivier said, his voice low, verging on a whisper.

The sound rasped against his skin. "Beggars can't be choosers, leech," he snapped back.

The vampire chuckled. "Speaking of begging, you never did get around to it the last time we met. I'll have to remedy that."

"Enough," Aurelia said.

He stopped but didn't turn his attention to his sister.

"Oberon has agreed to feed you, but if you cause any trouble, I will leave you to starve."

"How kind, dear sister. Even if you witches taste like shit."

"Better that than an empty stomach, am I right?"

"We'll see. Give me your wrist." Olivier's command speared his chest and lodged into his spine.

He looked at Aurelia and caught the slight nod. He would have preferred to do this without an audience, in case he wavered, in case the fear got too much for him and he panicked. But he understood Aurelia had to know he could do this.

He stepped forward, feeling the enticing threat rolling off Olivier. He'd sensed it in Perth when he'd first seen the vampire, the way he attracted people. They knew he was bad. They knew he was dangerous. Irresistible. Knowing it was the magnetism's fault and not his own weakness didn't make it easier. He drew nearer and Olivier's tongue primed his lips.

At that moment that slow, seductive swipe bothered him more than the fangs.

Blood thundered in his ears so hard he suspected Aurelia could hear it. He presumed Olivier could. It must have been music to his finely tuned hearing. He took one step after shaky step until he was closer to the vampire than he'd ever wanted to be again. His foot kicked a stone ledge, one positioned on either side of the bound creature. All had been provided for. He rose a few inches off the ground, but the action had him thinking of guillotines and the final moments of the condemned. When he straightened, he aligned with Olivier perfectly.

"You stink." Gold ringed Olivier's brown eyes.

"You're no bed of roses yourself." Which wasn't exactly true. Olivier didn't smell of anything, not even death. But he would be fucked if he was going to let an insult from this bastard go by.

"Gently, Olivier, and stop when commanded," Aurelia said as Oberon offered his right wrist.

"But the witch likes it rough," he said with a smirk. "I remember."

The last was whispered, and Oberon struggled to keep from incinerating the monster's face. As it was, the air around his hands crackled. Olivier's nose wrinkled before he latched onto the proffered arm and sank his fangs savagely through the flesh.

Iron nails hammered into skin and muscle. A sharp, thick pain tore up his arm like hot mercury sluicing through his veins to pull on his heart. He wanted to heave, barely managing to keep the sick down, but he couldn't stop the panic rising.

He won't let go. He'll never let go.

He clenched his jaw until it hurt. He couldn't believe he was there; couldn't believe he allowed this fiend to feed from him willingly. He would have wept at this further shame, but he hung on and his chest strained against his draining.

Enough. He's taken enough.

He had to stop this before the bloodsucker took too much. Olivier's nose scrunched while he slathered over him. His lips and tongue stroked the underside of his wrist, a sensation barely perceptible above the feel of the fangs inside him.

Out of the corner of his vision, Aurelia inched closer. He didn't want her to stop this. He had to be the one.

"Enough," he squeaked.

Olivier ignored him.

"Enough!"

The corner of Olivier's mouth twitched.

The fucker was laughing at him.

Wrenching his focus away from the aches pulsating

through his body, he turned his fear to anger. Anger at being caught like this. Anger at Olivier thinking he could control him and treat him like shit again. He bubbled and boiled, stoking his power until it seethed through his legs, torso and arms.

The beast continued to gorge.

Fuck you, Olivier.

Blue light erupted in his hands and exploded into Olivier's skull. The vampire threw his head back and howled. Freed, Oberon maintained the flow, stepping down to face the parasite. He opened his other hand and a second bolt flew into Olivier, making his body spasm and jerk. He'd stopped roaring but he still writhed.

"Stop, Oberon," Aurelia commanded, somewhere beside him. Where she was, he couldn't be sure. All that mattered was burning this sick bastard into nothing but ash.

A white light and a boom filled the chamber, and he was thrown back and cut off from his power. He skidded across the floor and slammed into the wall. The light faded back to normal and, groping for the power, he found it returned. But the look on Aurelia's face told him using it would be a mistake.

Behind her, Olivier hung unconscious.

"You're here to feed him, not kill him!"

"Why? Why does he get to live?"

"Because right now Olivier is one of the most important things in the world. More important than you and more important than me. Anything happens to him and we're in deep trouble. Understand?"

"No! I refuse to understand why this…this…this…motherfucking piece of shit gets to drink *my* blood. Tell me what he's being used for or our deal is off." Immortality would have to be sought elsewhere. This was too much. Far too much.

She glowered, towering over him as he stared up at her, showing as much defiance as he could, while inside he quivered with rage. They stayed like that for seconds, and the longer she said nothing, the harder it got to follow through with his threat. But he'd leave. She had one minute to explain or else—

She closed her eyes and expelled a shaky breath. She said something about a portal, the demon, and searching for a key. There was a lot to take in, and her words plucked a string inside him, sending a vibration through his spine. Whatever it meant, it faded when he reached for it, gone beneath the realization he'd not get to kill Olivier himself. His heart plunged, knocking out his stomach as it fell.

"I know you want to kill him. But I can't allow it. It's either this or nothing. Will that be good enough?"

The withered voice of reason told him that this was better, that Olivier would be put to good use and suffer for it, that this was justice of a kind. And until then, until he served Aurelia's purpose, Olivier would be at his mercy.

He hoped they never found the key.

He agreed with a small nod, but he couldn't look her in the eye.

She hovered for a moment, seeming as if to say something, but instead swept past him and out of the dungeon. She didn't wait for him to follow.

Olivier hung from his shackles; his lips stained red. Was he awake? How much had he heard? What Aurelia had said about him being important would swell his already-inflated ego. The bit about his demise however… Best to keep that close to his chest.

Raising his wrist, he traced a sigil in the air over the puncture wounds and they closed without leaving a scar.

After the last time, Olivier would never leave another mark.

He turned his back on the unconscious vampire and marched from the dungeon. The light remained; he wanted Olivier to see his prison. Then he closed the door, the lock sliding into place, and ascended the hallway.

X

HAME'S FULL-THROATED ROAR HIT AURELIA'S EARS AT THE same time as his frustrated thoughts stampeded into her head. Forced away from scrying over Thierry and Alex's attacks on acolytes, she gripped the edge of the table she'd been sitting at and shored up her mental defenses until the sound faded and the intrusion eased. If not for the inner understanding of Hame's thoughts, she'd have worried that he'd seen something awful. Still, his agitation caught in her throat.

She breathed as slowly and as measured as possible, her fingers straightening until they lightly rested on the table. She raised her hands to her head and smoothed her hair back to press down any errant strands. Pushing back from the table, and the black and still surface of the scrying bowl, she walked down the hall to Hame's room and knocked.

The door wrenched open to reveal Hame, bare-chested, sweating and eyes wild. "It's impossible. It's just fucking impossible."

He turned from her and buried a hand in his fiery

locks, unkempt and tangled as usual, pulling them as he stalked the room.

"What did you see?" She stayed in the doorway. His irritation heated the room and warmed the surface of her skin.

"Nothing, that's the problem!" He stopped at the end of the bed, his hands gripping the footboard until his muscles bulged. She wished there was a window they could open.

"I can't do this without going onto the astral."

"Then why aren't you there?"

He hung his head. "Carn's right. It's not safe out there and what if it doesn't do any good?"

She sat on the edge of the bed, noting its warmth. How many hours had she left him alone as he grew more disheartened?

"Let me help you. I can protect you on the astral."

He held her gaze for a while before looking down and picking at his thumbnail. "I know that. But what if—" He made a strangled noise that squeezed her heart.

"What if you're attacked? What if you're killed? What if it destroys Carn?" *What if it destroys me?* "Without wanting to point out the bleeding obvious, you're the oracle. What-ifs aren't meant to be a problem for you."

He smiled, one of those small heartfelt ones that seemed to radiate through the fire of his hair. Smiles that had been too rare of late.

"So, is that a yes? You'll let me help you?"

He straightened and the smile stayed. "Sure."

She patted the bed next to her. "Then let's get on with it."

Hame stretched out next to her and his hand held onto hers, heat passing from his palm into her and up her arm to cradle her heart.

Just the two of them.

Though it wasn't really. Carn and Hame had joined their minds before he'd gone on vampire-watching duty. She buried the small, spiky ball of hurt.

Are you ready? Hame's presence appeared inside her head, the channel between them opening wide. For safety. For expediency. For comfort.

I am. Let me go first, and I'll take you out with me.

Lead on.

She slowed her breathing to the point where it became measured and easy. Her body relaxed until finally she drifted free of it and hovered over her supine form. She saw Hame's dulled physical shell before he poured his consciousness into his astral form and surrounded his body with a soft glow. Only when it burned bright and didn't waver did she reach down and grasp his hand.

He rose out of his body, her power extending to circle him as she layered protective shields around them to guard against evil eyes. His hair cascaded down to his shoulders, bursting with light as pure as lit magnesium and the sight of it elevated her heart. His eyes twinkled, and she rose on the strength of that happiness.

Shielded, determined, they soared. The physical gave way to the ethereal; the ethereal to the lower astral with its flat gray, and finally to the dusty white as far as they could reach. Too encumbered by the ties to their physical bodies, she couldn't take them to the lofty heights of pure spirit, but she could come close enough. Looking around, even though all was white, she breathed a sigh at being free to reach this place once more yet knowing Sinara would not be waiting for her. And that its beauty was harder for her people to reach with Xadrak roaming unchecked.

"Can you work here?"

"Almost," he said. "Give me a moment."

He stepped away from her, the protections stretching to keep him covered. What if it wasn't enough? What if the acolytes—what if Xadrak—found him? She massaged the top of her sternum to quell the panic burbling at the base of her throat. Were there enough spells in the world to keep Hame safe?

As she smothered her worries lest she descend too low, Hame summoned a grove of lush grass surrounded by towering oaks that stretched beyond her vision. He raised his arms and out of a ground made of rich soil grew a dolmen of granite, two standing stones and a capstone. The grove was as real as if it existed on Earth, or if she were standing again in the real thing. The breeze rustled through an ocean of leaves.

Hame had come home.

"Beautiful," she said when she was able to speak again. "If I dug, would I find Loic's bones too?"

Hame laughed. "You will."

They stared at the dolmen, and the air between the stones shimmered with possibilities. Would Hame's visions flow? Would the path forward be clear? Would he be open to all secrets?

And whose death would he witness?

"Are you sure you're up for this?"

"I am." His answer came out as well made as the stones in front of her, and he glimmered in the knowledge of what he was born to do. His doubt was gone. "And you've got work to do as well." He kissed her on the cheek. She was being ever so gently dismissed. A buzz at the back of her head conveyed his excitement and eagerness, but it hit a wall of her own apprehension.

"I'll lay down added protections once I leave, but don't step outside the grove. Please, if not for your sake, then mine and Carn's. Don't leave the grove."

He squeezed her arm. "Whatever you say."

She quickly turned and walked away, or else she'd find herself standing guard for hours. She'd already lost her mother; she wasn't keen on losing her oldest friend. The mission gave her feet the strength needed to walk away. She vanished before she reached the oaks.

She lay shields around the grove and strengthened them threefold. If Xadrak and his acolytes somehow reached this height, their search should be fruitless. But once complete, she hesitated over where to go next. With Hame plunging into the prophecies, and her witches—and her brother—hunting acolytes, her best option would be to find out where Sinara had gone.

But where to begin her search?

She turned her thoughts to take her to where Sinara would be if she still resided on the astral. But no matter what pressure she applied, she could no longer deny that Sinara had gone. She'd have to try something else.

The astral retained echoes of everything that had happened within it and by exerting enough will, she could pick up the essence of something from long ago. It had only been seven days since Sinara's demise, and with such an application of power, the resonance should have rung loud. Aurelia focused and the world shifted around her, she traveled as the astral traveled, bringing the two of them together until she stood in an empty landscape.

Her body vibrated with the residue of power. The world had turned a little grayer as she descended to the edges of her enemy's territory. Thinking the demon's name this low may have brought her undue attention. She tapped into the energy that surrounded her and rebuilt Sinara's last moments. But confronted again with the strength of the acolytes' power, her grip loosened, and she jolted out of the memory with a hard shudder.

"It can't hurt me," she said to herself, hoping the words would calm her hurried heartbeat.

But the longer she stayed out, the quieter the nothingness seemed and the more exposed she became. She had to do this quickly. Steeling herself against the sudden onslaught of the past attack, she plunged back into the memory, freezing it in place to get her bearings.

She stood in front of a shield, Sinara in full demon form in front of her, glaring with teeth bared at whatever stood behind her. Turning, her heart slammed into her throat. Xadrak loomed in all his oily darkness, his eyes beaming with hellfire, while his tail thrashed behind him, his black wings expansive, and that sneer across his face that menaced and mocked.

Just a memory.

Xadrak's acolytes circled Sinara. Cloaked in their own shields, she couldn't make out who they were individually so she could not find them later. And when they dropped out of the astral, she'd be unable to follow them without latching on to the real soul. The bottom of her stomach opened at seeing so many who'd been drawn to Xadrak's power and his wickedness.

But for Sinara to have been bested?

She hated to turn her attention from the horde, but they taught her nothing. She orbited Sinara, the demoness in a defensive stance. One hand held back, her body positioned to shelter the key.

A shard of purple light stood behind the demon, yet for its hard edges, it appeared to cower, drawing nearer to Sinara's presence and protection. Without a doubt this was the key; the final piece they needed to open the portal to Crion. Her heart thrummed with exhilaration at finally seeing what she'd searched so long for; of having confirmation that it existed, that it was ready. She reached out and ran her fingers along an edge of diamond. The whole thing was smaller than her, and Sinara dwarfed it. But its true form was irrelevant. She needed to know where it was now. And perhaps she would discover it—once she'd again witnessed her mother's obliteration.

She retreated about twenty yards, keeping her view of Sinara and the key unobstructed. Xadrak remained within her peripheral vision. She breathed deeply, calming herself and strengthening her psyche to watch what she must see.

When she was ready, she unfroze the memory.

The acolytes released their onslaught, while Xadrak and Sinara traded barbs. The energy flowing around her, from the demoness and from the acolytes, jolted through her body. The shouting and the cursing threatened to distract her, but she kept her eyes locked on the key, hoping for some clue as to its identity. It must be someone, the way it clung to Sinara's body seeking comfort revealed its humanity, or at least a sentience, yet it stubbornly refused to revert to its other shape. Perhaps the memory of this place only recorded truth.

The battle raged around her, and Sinara's face and body strained with the effort of protecting herself and the key. Aurelia would have given anything to help slaughter those who had chosen the evil path and dared to attack her mother. Sinara obstructed her view of them as the shield slid in place and within all too short a time it shattered and exploded outward.

A far too strong grip cut off the air to her lungs. She struggled to break free, stumbling out of the stranglehold before it crushed her windpipe.

She's not dead. She's not dead. She's not dead.

She had known that before, but it was hard to think otherwise, especially when the air cleared.

Sinara and the key were gone.

Acolytes picked over whatever remained of Sinara and the key. In his mania, Xadrak scooped down and plunged his claws through the bodies of two of his followers, hoisting them high into the air and burying his fangs into their necks, destroying them with his fury. He cast their bodies off and stalked towards his acolytes, frozen between running for their lives and remaining behind as loyal minions. One who stood directly in front of the demon, whether struck by fear or duty, was ripped into chunks.

"You have failed!" His voice rolled over the silent acolytes.

One chose to speak, and Aurelia almost cheered at the stupidity of it, knowing another would soon be dead, one less for her coven to hunt and kill. "But my lord, the demoness is dead and—"

Xadrak grabbed him in his claws and tore him apart. His soul ripped to tatters and somewhere on Earth, another acolyte fell dead.

"The key is all I care about. Find where it went. There will be no excuses, or you will *all* feel my displeasure. Go!"

The acolytes vanished immediately. They would have reeled from the hard return to their bodies, but a few bruises were worth escaping with their lives.

Left alone, Xadrak stalked over to the spot where Sinara had stood. He sneered down at it, where nothing remained but an imprint of energy. He lifted his head as he sniffed at the residue, growling as he did so, a sound so animalistic and primal that it vibrated through Aurelia's body. She hissed, and Xadrak turned. His head tilted and his red eyes narrowed.

He couldn't know she was there; this was a remnant of something that had gone before. But the malevolence with which he stared was unmistakably directed at someone. She looked around in case someone else had been there at the time, but it was only her. And when she turned back, Xadrak had gone.

The sight of nothingness sent an icy hand groping along her spine. She released the vision, but the uneasiness remained. She forced herself to think her way out of the fear that had her caught like quicksand. She could trace parts of Sinara's soul, though, after seeing this level of destruction, it could only go to one place, and that was not somewhere she could follow through to the end. Fighting the panic that threatened to destabilize her and throw her out of the astral, she focused on the remnants of the demoness's soul and once finding the faintest thread, latched onto it and traveled as far away from this tainted place as possible.

Even so she couldn't travel far enough or fast enough to escape the smear of Xadrak's evil.

***

THE TRAIL LED AURELIA TO THE GATEWAY TO THE LAND OF the Dead, but while it continued through, she was forced to stop well before it. Two columns supporting a blank pediment stood in the middle of nothing, but through them rolled white clouds pierced with sunshine. Was Sinara still in there? Had she been reborn? She could make out no faces, no vaguely human shapes, just a cloudy sky.

A world at peace.

And one she would have to disturb.

She strode to the gate, careful to keep back a few feet. If she fell, she would never get out the same way.

She gathered her power, transforming it into a pulsing beacon laced with Sinara's name that she released through the gateway. But once it reached the other side, the focused power diffused, bursting in a myriad of directions.

She waited.

One of the threads twitched.

Then yanked.

She braced. Anything could be clawing its way to her yet hope skipped through her body at the possibility that it could be her mother.

The progression of whatever was coming took on a rhythm of one hand going after another, a slight tug at each connection. She strained against the pull on her energy, feeling more and more being taken out of her as this lifeline brought forth—

"Loic?" She gasped as the face of the old oracle and Hame's tutor surfaced.

Her power slipped, and he faded, but she scrambled to recover and strengthen the spell. He returned, his wizened smiling face hovering on the other side, so near she raised her hand to touch it. He hissed and drew back sharply, and she blushed.

"You should be more careful, Aurelia."

While the last time the two had spoken he'd been possessed with Xadrak's madness, he had only friendliness in his voice and a benevolent familiarity. What Hame would have given to see him again.

Her heart ached for her friend. "Why haven't you moved on?"

"Someone needed to guide the souls to where they had to go, and who better than an oracle?"

"Gaming the system?"

He chuckled. "Just trying to bring a little happiness into the world. Of course, they don't have to take my advice." His face darkened. "Xadrak never did."

No surprises there. Xadrak's earthly incarnations had always been overripe with arrogance. But she already knew enough about *that* demon.

"And Mother?"

"She has *always* taken my advice." He gave her a wink. "But not always followed it."

"So, you've seen her? Recently?"

He nodded, the levity gone and his face fading a little. "She has returned to Earth, and you need to bring her forth."

Claws sank into either side of her belly and stretched the skin. Talons sent a network of dared-not-hoped-for-possibilities sparking beneath the surface.

It's time?

She leaned a little closer to the gateway, pumping more power down the link to Loic. "Tell me where she is."

"In the womb of an acolyte."

His words shredded her hopes and scattered them on sulfurous air. "So, they have her?"

He nodded. "But they don't know it yet. You need to go to her, rescue her, and speed up the pregnancy."

"I've never done anything like that. Is it even possible?"

Loic smiled, a tight grin no doubt meant to be reassuring but it struck her as smug. While he'd been a spirit for more than half a millennium, it appeared not all his humanity had sloughed off. Oracles had ever loved being the holder of secrets; no matter their appearance of altruism.

"Then you've seen what happens?"

"Bits of it, but there is too much uncertainty. It's always been this way. Power gets thrown around, too many variables. But the portal will open. Whether Sinara or Xadrak or both of them are there, I cannot say."

"So, I have to find Sinara and bring her to term before Xadrak finds her and finds the key?"

Another bob of his head. "And hurry. If the acolytes

discover Sinara is in the womb, they'll seek to keep her there."

"They don't want her dead?"

"Of course not. They want to pitch her back through the portal, and a fetus is much easier to throw than a fully-grown demon."

XI

A loud drumbeat pounded Oberon's temples and stretched the skin with each strike. So far the headache had lasted nearly two days, and he couldn't put it down to a lack of blood. He'd healed himself, replenished his stores, but still the pain bore into his skull. Broken sleep didn't help, what with his thoughts keeping time with the march of the thudding. He couldn't stand to look at the fissures in the stone above his head any longer, and the sound of voices in the corridor—raised voices, arguments, about him, Olivier, Loic?—had kept him secluded. Aurelia had left, and Hame had shut himself away. Searching, he'd said. Oberon was alone, in pain, and verging on becoming sick, if not physically, then at least of his own company.

He swallowed and dissolved a little more of himself to expose the bare, harsh core. Rising from the bed, he shuffled into a bathroom with white tiled floors and walls, a porcelain sink with gold faucet, a bathtub with gold clawed feet, and a rain shower. All modern, yet it had a touch of the Twenties about it. Old chic. How this had been built, he had no idea, but for someone of Aurelia's power, it was probably a mere trifling thought to conjure out of stone.

He undressed and stepped beneath the showerhead. It didn't have taps but she'd explained how it worked. He'd detected her demure pride. She came across as austere, but these touches belied a little craving for pleasurable things. The beds were that, the curl in her hair (when it wasn't tied back), and the bathroom with its fluffy towels and opulence. She'd allowed herself to become the mountain but couldn't mine all the diamonds.

Water set at the right side of too-hot cascaded down. His skin pricked at the massage, the brand no longer stinging, the scab having formed, and he lost himself beneath the flow. For a moment he wasn't sharing a home with witches and vampires. For a moment he wasn't there to feed his rapist. For a moment he was simply a young man having a shower.

He lowered his head, opened his eyes, and spat out the water.

What bullshit!

He didn't want to be nothing. He was meant to be something. An immortal—and one of great power. And he was not there as some passive feedbag for Olivier to bury his snout in. He was there to make the vampire suffer as much as he could.

And he'd be there when the bastard died.

He scraped his hands through his hair, soaped himself, and rinsed. Exhaustion may have dogged him before, but it gurgled down the drain. The pain dulled to a constant, muted pressure behind his eyes that he could ignore. He stepped out from the flow, which stopped immediately, dried himself with one of those luxurious towels, and conjured new clothes. Faded jeans and a black T-shirt were all he needed. He looked at himself in the mirror, eschewing the serious, forlorn look that had fallen over him, and reverting back to the self-assurance he'd shown when he'd first met the vampire.

Olivier can be controlled. Olivier can be overcome.

He repeated the mantra inside his head, ignoring the slight pinching at the corner of his eyes. He breathed in, his chest rising; meanwhile, his belly rumbled.

He conjured a simple meal of eggs and bacon, and wolfed it down, not realizing the depth of his hunger. Once nourished, it was time to put his strength to use.

He walked out of the room, and the polished stone cooled the soles of his feet. Silence surrounded him. No one wandered the lonely halls of Aurelia's lair. He descended to Olivier's dungeon. The room Aurelia kept him locked in wasn't at the bottom of the tunnel, but he couldn't mistake the oak door marking the entry. He paused, contemplating letting his scent drift to the vampire, then leave and keep him waiting, salivating, hanging to rot for another day.

When had he learned to think in games?

When had he lost his nerve?

He cracked his knuckles and unlocked the door.

"I knew you couldn't keep away."

Olivier's voice purred and rubbed against him despite him still being pinned to the wall. He hung like it was intentional, a workout he was trying so he could maintain that hardened physique. His head cocked to one side, his lips kicked up in one corner. The muscles along his shoulders bulged with the effort of keeping himself tight as if he were about to spring off the wall.

Oberon's gaze flicked from one restraint to another.

"Like the cuffs, do you?" Olivier grinned. "Figured you were into kink."

He turned his back to close the door, hiding the way his

throat bulged with the effort of swallowing. The lock slid into place, trapping them in together. His thumb dragged over the door's grain, its ridges sharpening his attention.

"You talk a lot of shit for someone stuck to a wall." His voice came out as level as it could under the circumstances. He was surprised at its calm.

"And you talk tough for a coward."

Fire flared in his chest and his hands sparked. What coward would share a room with his rapist?

Olivier's eyes shone gold, and his mouth widened in an exhilarated smile. "Going to try to fry me again? You're not much of a quick learner. You can't hurt me, no matter how strong you think you are."

"And you think the way to get my blood is to piss me off? I could easily let you starve. No one would give a shit."

The predator glared at him, no smile now. "If that were true, you wouldn't be here. So, don't fall under the misapprehension that you matter, or that you hold any power *whatsoever*." His voice stalked around the stone room. "I may be the one bound to a wall, but you're going to feed me."

"You look well fed enough. I could wait until you're hanging there like a dried-out husk."

"Then leave."

He opened his mouth to shoot something back, but the words jammed.

Olivier smiled a knowing smile. "It's okay. I know what it's like to enjoy the euphoria that comes from having another in your power." His voice dropped down to a clear and crisp whisper. "I know it intimately."

"I am nothing like you."

He laughed hard and loud and long. "What do you call this?" He rattled the chains. "Looks a lot like torture to me."

"I'm not your torturer."

"Of course you are, you smug self-righteous piece of shit. There is no difference between you and me. What lies do you tell yourself to make you do her bidding? What justification could there possibly be?"

"You raped me!"

Olivier's face shrugged because his shoulders couldn't do it for him. "You can't rape the willing."

The vampire's words detonated the pain buried behind his eyes. Light exploded out of his hands as he darted forward and pressed them against Olivier's chest. The power charged into what little passed for his heart, chasing Olivier's bellows out of his throat. The vampire's roaring filled the room, but it did nothing to obliterate his own torment.

He withdrew his hands and marched across the dungeon. His heavy breathing matched Olivier's labored efforts. Frustration galloped through his body, searching for a way out, pushing against his fences to break free and take this awful, bone-crushing shame and hate and despair with it.

He paced until Olivier's cackling lassoed him.

"The lady doth protest too much, methinks."

Oberon sneered at him. "You're a monster, Olivier."

"So I've been told. Why don't you come up with something more original?"

"How about: You're going to die, and no one will mourn your passing?"

He snorted. "You'll be in the ground long before me and forgotten as soon as the dirt hits your coffin. Tell me: after I was done with you, who picked you up off the floor? Who did you call?"

"We're finished." His hand touched the handle.

"No one. I've seen your type before, witch. The loner.

The cocky one who thinks they can have it all, be it all, when really, they're a scared little prick desperately trying to fuck their way to relevance. And then I come along and relieve you of those delusions. It would have been better for you if you'd died. But at least this way I get to see the results of my work. I get to know the pleasure of beating yet another self-important nobody who couldn't even rustle up a friend to scrape their bleeding, *pathetic* corpse off the carpet. You have the nerve to come down here and deny me what you were ordered to do? Thinking you have a spine? Thinking you have a choice? That you can build yourself into something strong enough to cower in my shadow? You should be grateful Aurelia chose you. You should be *ecstatic* that you get to present me with your otherwise worthless blood. Because if you're not here to feed me, what's the point in you being alive?"

He stood through Olivier's torrent. He hardened himself against the rain and the hail and the hurricane that blew out of the vampire's mouth and twisted his face into a grotesque mask befitting the evil of his words. Some of them got through and struck the tender parts of himself, but he tensed and withstood their brunt. This was not happening to him. This was happening to someone else. He stood in their place because *they* weren't strong enough.

When he didn't respond and Olivier's words ceased, the vampire sneered again, a look of contempt that had even less effect than his words. "Get out of my sight."

He could have gone but that would look too much like a master dismissing his servant. Summoning a twelve-inch blade in his right hand, he advanced on Olivier.

"I said get out." Uncertainty fluttered in Olivier's eyes as they glanced off the blade.

"You think my blood is worthless? Let's see how long you last without it."

He raised the knife above his head with both hands and plunged it into Olivier's chest. Blood gushed out of the wound and splashed onto the floor. His hands still locked on the blade, he widened the hole with a wet and bone-crunching leverage, resisting Olivier's bucking. He opened the gash in his solar plexus until it was ugly and red and jagged, and gave a final shove, embedding the knife in Olivier's heaving and grunting body.

He backed away, the blood pouring out and painting the floor. Olivier cursed him with a flood of words, but he couldn't make them out over the hiss of white noise in his ears. With a shaky hand, skin dripping scarlet, he fumbled on the door handle and exited the dungeon.

The door closed and locked behind him, and he heaved his breakfast onto the stone floor. When nothing else came, his hearing returned. The smell wafting up from the mess on the floor burned in his nostrils. He inhaled the stink of his trauma, Olivier's muffled cries behind him. He clenched his fists to squash the panic. It couldn't help him. It hadn't helped him when Olivier had raped him. Magic hid the evidence of his weakness, and he ascended the dungeon to seek the mountain air and blow away the stench of his failure.

XII

THE WITCH HAD STABBED HIM. *ACTUALLY* STABBED HIM. IN the mother-fucking-chest! Olivier had been hoping to goad the little bitch into doing something reckless that might open an opportunity, but he hadn't expected him to open a bloody hole in his torso.

What power to inspire such hate!

His lungs scraped against the metal edge, his skin suckering around the wound. He wasn't worried about dying from it; he'd endured worse. Though perhaps, just maybe, a little, he had steeled himself against the strike. The witch wouldn't have killed him; he didn't have it in him. Maybe a little anger, a little hurt that would push him to do something violent, but not kill, not murder. That wasn't him.

Still, getting stabbed wasn't exactly pleasant and he'd had enough of it over the past few weeks. Thierry's attack had been the greatest, even more painful than what the Duke had put him through.

He shifted, rolling and lengthening his shoulders and caving in his chest in an attempt to evict the knife. But the knife wasn't the real problem; it was the loss of blood. The last time he'd fed from the witch hadn't been enough to replenish all that he'd lost. He'd been too hasty and played it too strong. He'd suffer starvation until the shit decided to come back. He had to get it out or else, when the witch showed up, he'd be too weak to drink.

He pulled on the chains then pushed, stretching the bonds as far as they could reach. He'd have to work harder on the witch if he hoped to get out of there, preferably before Aurelia collected him.

He raised and inflated his chest, twisting to dislodge the blade. It sliced with every move, some worse than others. More blood ran down his stomach and down his pants. Some soaked into the already stained fabric; the rest dribbled down his leg and onto the floor.

His blood.

Wasted.

He writhed. A nick this way, a gash that, the wet meaty sound of his flesh tearing bringing back memories of when he'd meticulously carved out a fur trader's heart on the shores of Hudson Bay. He'd cut out his tongue first and stoppered his mouth to keep the screams down. Pinning him to the dirt had been easy; extracting the heart pure bliss. He'd removed it, warm and beating, holding it lovingly in the palm of his hand. So red and succulent. He devoured it, owning the heart just as the trader had tried to win his. Good times.

After uncounted hours, his convulsions eventually unhooked the blade, and he thrust and panted, heaving his torso forward, using the wall to brace himself until finally, this *kitchen utensil* clattered to the floor.

He sagged, the ache in his shoulders more acute with his body weighing down on them. Slowly, minutely, his skin stitched together, but that healing act, which used to be so simple, sapped even more of his waning strength. He let himself hang.

Meanwhile, inside, the beast padded around its cage.

XIII

"Is that all clear?" Aurelia looked from face to face, checking that each of her four followers understood what they were being asked.

"So we're certain, keep the redhead alive?" With hair so pale it was almost white, Viktor was the squad's leader. A scar ran down the right side of his face, long since faded from a war long since won. He wasn't the only one to bear them, but his was the most visible and drew her attention to his silver eyes.

All four of the squad were dressed in black clothes that hugged their athletic physiques. The ammo belts, guns, and knives strapped to their bodies were seemingly quaint when they had magic at their disposal.

"Absolutely. If she's struck, heal her. This is a capture mission. Sinara is the goal, and this acolyte must not die."

"Understood."

The other three witches nodded sharply. None of them smiled, none had the light-hearted air around them that some of her other coven members projected. These witches were soldiers, and she'd chosen them long ago because of it.

Viktor and Moroni had both been generals fighting on either side of world wars; Larissa served as a spy and rebel leader, and Felix a paid assassin. The four, once trained in magic, had gravitated towards one another. She'd once believed it better to spread their skills around, but efficiency came from their teamwork. Taking them from Thierry and Carn and replacing them with others had been a calculated risk.

The mission laid out, it was time to move. She held out her hand to Viktor and Moroni, then the others joined and closed the circle. Loic had pinpointed the witch—twenty-eight-year-old Rafferty Jones—to a farmhouse in rural Montana, but having never been to the exact location, they had to travel to somewhere near.

Felix took them to the outskirts of Salt Lake City before they traveled on foot north-east across snow-covered plains and skirting mountains. They pushed hard. Covering a lot of ground in a short space of time taxed them, but they didn't complain. Their eyes locked on the horizon, drawing them towards it and their prize.

Nearing the valley where Rafferty and her allies had based themselves, Aurelia called a halt before they crested the hill. Endless stars studded the sky, shedding enough light on the ivory Earth below for them to make out the farmhouse nestled in the valley. A porch surrounded the two-story dwelling. Beside it sat a garage and then, some distance from the main house, a barn. Lights shone out of two windows on the house's top floor, meanwhile a porch light illuminated the door. Smoke twisted out the chimney.

Aurelia brought her fingers up to her lips and cast out her breath. The air turned white as it dissipated, drifting across the valley like a ghost stealing through the air towards the house. A hundred yards from the building white turned to red, spreading like a crimson gas to pinpoint pits and traps, and outlining the shape of the shield. It was far enough away that those inside would be alerted by anyone passing through it.

Hours of night stretched ahead. Aurelia gave orders for the others to rest and restore their strength. They returned no arguments, huddling together in a makeshift tent, warmed with their magic and body heat.

While she watched, the lights inside the house turned off in one room, then on in another. She was too far to decipher passing shadows, let alone determine which one was Rafferty's.

Did she know what she held in her belly?

Impatience scrambled inside her, making her neck ache. She twisted and cracked it for some release, but she was anxious to start.

But start what?

Blowing the shield wide would create problems, but sneaking through would be impossible. Establishing a perimeter might be the way to go? Or she could pen them within their own traps? How to take them without losing them, defend themselves without Rafferty dying?

Suddenly, lights burst on in the house until the whole place glowed. They were about to find out. But it wasn't just the lights. The wooden boards on the sides of the house radiated, and then the roof. She leapt to her feet. Was every light on in the house? Were they summoning something? Was the whole place on—

The roof exploded in a jet of flames, sending planks of wood and roof tiles high into the air. The eruption reverberated loud enough to reach her, while flames rolled out of the house, burning through the front wall. Her mouth dried at the sight of it, and she was halfway down the hill before she knew what she was doing. Viktor shouted to her, but she ignored him, passing through where the shield had stood, preparing herself for an attack that didn't come. The shield had fallen. Whoever had set it, had been killed. She prayed that it hadn't been Rafferty.

Heat pulsed out of the building, and flames smothered the chill in the air. As she approached, the fire sucked back into the house then was gone, replaced with a glimmer coming from within. The blackened beams and wood panels smoked where they had been extinguished. Embers pulsed like demon eyes watching from the shadows. Sweat froze on the back of her neck.

She headed towards the entrance but paused when a shield of shimmering light slid in place above her. Glancing over her shoulder, Viktor and the others spread out. She stepped onto the porch and walked to the remaining bottom half of the red charred door. She commanded it to open, and as it widened, it unhinged and clattered to the floor.

Her hearing and sight strained for the slightest flicker within the dim light, or for the tiniest creak of unsteady floorboards. The house showed remnants of what had been a home. Lumps of charcoal or oily grease that were once furniture; paintings on walls mostly burned away. Above, much of the second story had been obliterated. In the stillness of the winter air, the house had been rendered void.

She picked her way through the debris, down a hall and into what had once been a lounge room. In the center stood the witch.

Rafferty—young, russet-haired, and scrawny—stared

at her trembling hands, but as Aurelia's foot scraped across the charred floor, her head whipped up. Aurelia raised her palms.

"Easy," she said, holding her power on the very edge, ready to strike the witch senseless. Rafferty's wide eyes and opened mouth belied her shock. "What happened?"

"I… I… The flames… They came out of nowhere… I've never felt…" She looked back to her hands, eyeing them as if they'd release another font of terror without her prompting. And then she frowned. "Who are you?" Her Southern drawl curved on the question, like she already knew the answer.

Rafferty took a step back, steadying herself rather than preparing to retreat. Recognition burst in her eyes.

"You know who I am."

"I would have thought you'd be smart enough not to come here, after seeing what I did to this place."

"I'm surprised you haven't made a run for it yet," she said. "Only Xadrak gets to kill his acolytes."

The witch swallowed hard, the wicked sneer falling.

"I can protect you though. If you come with me."

"What makes you think I need *your* protection?"

"Uncontrolled releases of power that destroy your brethren?"

"Xadrak will overlook the death of a few second-rate witches when I offer him your head."

"That's not going to happen, but either way you're coming with me."

"I don't think so." Rafferty thrust her hands forward.

Aurelia summoned a shield around her body, throwing an arm up to protect against whatever attack she had levelled at her.

But none came.

Taking Rafferty's moment of confusion, Aurelia unleashed her power and struck the witch's head, knocking her unconscious. Aurelia caught her as she went down and lowered her limp body to the floor. Her hand hovered over the witch's belly, ready to probe for the life that she knew to be growing inside her.

An explosion from outside tore her attention away. Viktor rushed in, one quick glance taking in the witch. "Time to leave."

She hissed. Extracting the new life would take time, care, and quiet—all things she'd struggle with while a battle raged.

"Can you hold them off until I get out of here?"

"The others can. I'm coming with you."

She opened her mouth to argue but he cut her off.

"There's no telling what help you'll need."

She grabbed Rafferty's hand and held the other out for Viktor's.

He whistled, a harsh, high-pitched sound that cut through the air. A pre-determined signal. Another boom. Flames painted the sky. Shouts from too many voices. She should help, but Viktor's grip locked onto her and he punched them through the ether. Howls followed. Claws swiped at them, but with a blast of her own power, they fell away, and the three—four—of them escaped.

VIKTOR'S PENTHOUSE APARTMENT OVERLOOKED CENTRAL Park, a multi-million-dollar view that many would kill for. Open plan, it featured little more than a utilitarian chrome kitchen, a table and chairs, a sofa, and a king-size bed. Some furnishings covered the wooden floorboards, but the walls were bare.

It was house, not home. A place to rest and practice his skills. One of the rugs was more worn than the others, placed as it was in the middle of the room centered with the balcony. A Persian rug of red, gold and blue, with worn patches, one almost threadbare in the middle. Aurelia imagined him sitting cross-legged, meditating, scrying, experimenting, while the city below twisted in its mortal turmoil.

Viktor had been dedicated when she began his training. His military background provided only part of the discipline he displayed; the rest came from his determination to be the best fighter, the strongest witch, the most lethal weapon in her coven. For all that his home was empty, he needed this space, to hold it against the tide of evil rushing towards them. He'd been one of the few to receive Sinara's power when it became available, and he was more than worthy of it.

He carried Rafferty to the bed and lay her on the right side. He checked her breathing and placed his hand on her temple, ensuring she remained locked down. Aurelia's gaze focused on the acolyte's belly, but she couldn't touch it. Not yet. A weariness had stolen into her, borne of the traveling and the fight and the contemplation of what she'd have to do next. And she was still shaken by what she'd seen.

By rights, Rafferty should have been able to battle her. She may not have won, but at least she'd have been able to fight. But it was as if her power had been snipped at the source, the flow stoppered where once it had surged. Had that been Sinara's doing? Was her mother able to exert her influence already? Whatever had happened, she was relieved they'd been able to retrieve Rafferty with relative ease.

The next part, however, was going to be the true test.

"I don't think I can do this now."

"Rest," Viktor replied. "I'll keep watch."

She scratched the back of her hand. The sooner she extracted the fetus… Then what? The only option was to take on the pregnancy herself—she'd more or less resigned herself to that—but was she ready for it? Wouldn't it incapacitate her? Her coven needed her, but who, other than her, was a better vessel?

Viktor gestured for her to take the other side of the bed while he placed a chair beside the acolyte. The chair frame disappeared beneath his muscular bulk, and he sat like a warrior in repose, ready to fight at the slightest command, ready to defend at the merest suggestion of attack. She climbed onto the bed, uneasy at lying next to Rafferty while she slumbered in false sleep.

"Don't worry, Aurelia, you're safe."

She rested her head on the pillow, looking at Rafferty, then drawn to Viktor's form behind.

"Will the others be all right?" Guilt scolded her for resting while he kept guard. She was the leader; it wasn't acceptable for her to get tired, yet the softness of the pillows and the quilt smoothed away that resistance a lot faster than was appropriate. She suppressed a yawn. When was the last time she'd slept more than a few hours?

"They'll be fine," he said without pause or defense. "They won't come here in case they lead someone to us. They'll return to the vampires now that this mission is complete."

"Would you prefer to be with them?"

"And miss this?" His silver eyes shone with an intensity that made her shiver. "Plus, you shouldn't have to go through this alone." At least she had the good sense not to blush. More than forty years they'd known each other, as recruiter and recruit, as teacher and pupil, and as general and soldier. He was a warrior in love with battle, nothing more.

Another yawn came, this time too strong for her to fight. "Let's hope it's worth it."

He returned her smile with warmth.

The memory of it followed her into slumber, and she rested as she hadn't rested in a very long time.

XIV

The lock clicked, the handle squeezed, and the latch retracted allowing the subtle extraction of stale air to mix with fresh when the door opened. Olivier's mouth watered.

The beast scrabbled at the gate, its claws scraping over him, trying to dig its way through to where its nose led. Little energy remained to control his hunger and all he could hope was to swallow his anticipation and hide from the witch how primal he truly was. Not that the little bitch had been right, but he'd always struggled to control himself when the time came.

There'd been so few times over the years when he'd been forced to stay his fangs, but they'd been there, serving as some sort of test, even though he shouldn't have had to undergo them. Morality, self-restraint, purity through austerity: hideous fallacies he'd spurned for the weaknesses they were. Yet now, here, starving, he wished he'd mastered his brother's self-denial.

He kept his head down as the witch's bare feet shuffled on the dusty floor. He focused on the knife where it lay sheathed in his dried blood. His nostrils flared at the scent of the fresh source. He would not look up. He would not let the witch see him so enthralled by something as readily available as blood. He poured everything into the knife.

It vanished.

Into his field of vision appeared a wrist.

His head snapped up, careful to keep his features smooth in the face of this…trick?

He looked from the witch's eyes to his wrist and sneered. Something about the way he held it, like he was doing him a favor, splashed his insides with acid. Though his shoulders ached, he pulled himself back and arched high enough to peer down—and keep away from that flesh.

"Is that your attempt at an apology?"

He wanted to bite but that's not what he must to do. Acquiescence, debasement, that's what the witch needed, or he'd remain shackled.

"That you think you deserve one is conceited even for you." He withdrew his wrist and hid his arms behind his back.

"Quickly offered, quickly withdrawn. Anyone ever tell you you're a cocktease?"

The witch blinked; it was rapid, but he caught it. The witch wasn't there because he felt guilty. No remorse pleaded in his eyes.

"If that's your attitude, I guess I can leave you for another day. You might actually be tolerable to be around if you're too weak to talk." He spun and fled for the door.

The threat of having to go even one more hour without blood pushed him to speak.

"Stop."

"What was that?"

"Stop. Please." Each word was hard wrought and

dragged from bedrock. He could barely push them past his teeth.

"Why?"

"You know why."

"I want to hear you say it. I want to hear you say you *need* me." His voice floated on a sea of pettiness.

Olivier navigated the storm that brewed in his chest. He'd lead the witch to dash himself against the rocks. "What did Aurelia offer you to do this?"

"Do you want blood or not?" the bitch asked hurriedly.

"It must have been something big."

"Yes or no?" He held his arms rigidly by his side, punctuated with clenched fists.

"Are you sure she's going to give it to you? She was never very trustworthy with her promises."

"Last chance." The muscles on either side of his throat tensed.

"You can posture all you want, but we both know you're here under orders, and you're not going anywhere until I've drunk. You think you can bargain? Let me loose and we'll see who gets out of here with their head still attached to their torso."

"You're cornered and you know it. You've lost." Empty words.

"And what about you? Serving one you hate, no free will of your own, a walking vending machine. You haven't got the nerve for this job. I smelled it on you the first time Aurelia brought you here, urging you to carry out her plans because she's too weak to do it herself. So, she gets you, already broken, already pathetic, but you can't do it. You're not strong enough, you never were. And to think I've been offered *your* blood. I'm surprised it's strong enough to keep *you* upright, let alone keep *me* alive. I could drain ten of you and still not be satisfied." The more he roared, the more the tempest enveloped him, and he shouted, hoping to destroy him now they were stuck together, hoping to break the witch completely and rescue himself on the flotsam and jetsam of this battered and broken soul.

"You want to see how weak I am?" His hands unfurled.

Olivier braced as the scent of oranges saturated the air. Ropes of white light whipped from the witch's open palms and struck his chest with a pain that torched his skin and blinded his sight with a flash.

"Aurelia said I had to feed you, but she didn't say how."

The light dashed to his wrists, his ankles, his waist and neck. All lassoed him, burned through his flesh until he thrashed from the scalding touch. The more he struggled, the tighter and more agonizing the restraints became. The one around his neck seared through to his spine. He shook from keeping his screams locked deep in his belly. His abs tensed until they shuddered, but he kept his eyes locked on the bitch's straining face.

"That all you got?" he grunted.

The witch's lips pulled back to expose clenched teeth. The ropes flared, sizzling into his flesh. He raised his open hands then snapped them shut and yanked them back towards his body. Olivier's back arched painfully, forcing his chest to bulge. Joints cracked and he yelped before phantom hands grabbed the top of his skull and forced him to stare at the ceiling. Ghostly fingers curled around the edges of his mouth. He bit back at the invisible hands, but their grip scorched his lips and cheeks, and the fingers burrowed deeper to pry his mouth open.

"You'll get my blood, Olivier, but on *my* terms!"

He would have replied if he could. He would have told the witch to burn in hell, that he couldn't do this to him, couldn't force him. And the witch would get tired eventually. He'd seen his displays of weak power before. They were bearable. He should have been able to wait this out, to flex his strength and shatter the witch's hold on him, but that wasn't happening, and then there wasn't time.

The witch slashed his wrist and held it over his gaping mouth. Blood poured out of the vertical gash and pooled at the back of his throat. He drowned in it, gasping, until he swallowed it in desperate, ragged gulps. He wanted to spit, but the taste, the sustenance, the *need* was too strong, and he took it all.

Hunger didn't care how it was sated.

The blood did its work, invigorating his aching muscles and bones while trying to heal the injuries the witch wrought. A minute passed, or ten, or merely seconds, pain distorting time until the flow abruptly stopped. The restraints withered, and the witch disappeared from his line of sight, panting as he slunk away.

Olivier's shoulders howled at the change in position and having to again bear his weight. What he wouldn't give to be able to stretch them properly. But then he'd be free and within reaching distance of that throat.

How dare he manipulate him like some doll. How dare he *force* him to drink. He growled a low rumble that poured endlessly out of him. He looked up, expecting to see that face of triumph, but all he got was his back as he hurried from the room. The door slammed and plunged him into darkness.

And he waited for the touch of those hands to fade.

XV

THE DOOR SHUT BEHIND OBERON, HIS HANDS SHAKING TOO much to be able to close it without the handle rattling. His skin vibrated with the expenditure of power, his head light from the loss of blood, but the tremors worried him the most. Strength and sickness sparked up and down his body like electricity jumping between pylons. He couldn't control it.

What had he become?

He raced up the tunnel and then, given the choice of returning to his room or fleeing the place altogether, he chose to flee. Hame's voice chased after him, calling his name, but he kept going, out of Aurelia's lair and off the edge of the cliff. He dove through the ether.

He struggled to keep himself together as he pitched to and fro. He fumbled for an exit, picking the closest location he could think of, and plunged into a bitter sea. The ocean clapped over him as he came to form in the water. After the emptiness of the ether, its weight slammed him. His lungs locked to keep himself from drowning, even as the screams punched his straining windpipe. He kicked to the surface and gulped air.

The shores of the far side of the island of Hydra lay a few hundred yards away, a place he'd visited and loved for its bleached stone houses. But he wasn't ready to swim ashore; nothing awaited him there. This was just a convenient stop on the way to his breakdown.

It had been so easy to force the vampire to do what he'd commanded. His magic had fed on his vengeance, boosting it to work something powerful. The more he'd pushed himself, the further he'd been willing to go. Holding Olivier in exactly the way he wanted, compelling him to feed when he didn't want to… Sick mixed with salt in his belly.

This was Olivier's doing. He hadn't been able to rise above what the vampire had done to him—rise above the rape—and had sunk into the swell.

Thank god the water wasn't still because he couldn't bear to see his reflection.

He lifted his wrist out so he could see where he'd made the incision. It had healed without leaving a scar, but it itched. New flesh or guilty conscience? Seeing the vampire's mouth stretched that way, seeing the muscles in his neck and shoulders fight, had brought a flush of warmth far removed from this chill.

Yet when it was over…

He spat out the salty Aegean water. What was he going to do? What he'd done to Olivier could easily be called justice. But it hadn't filled him with the satisfaction he'd expected, not in a way that lingered, that healed. All he'd done was sink to Olivier's level and wallowed in the base mud where the strongest suffocated the other. He had no desire to keep breathing in the shit.

But he couldn't let it go.

He swam for the shore. He cut across the surface of the water, his muscles relishing the chance to exercise. He breathed in, he breathed out, and settled into a rhythm that had him rocking with the waves. Choppiness gave way to calm. He'd been fighting against himself for too long. Olivier responded to force with force, attempting to destroy everything that threatened him no matter how big or small.

To rule, not to be ruled.

There was another way.

Trying to break through that massive ego would be a challenge, but it was the only hope he had of healing. The vampire's wicked laugh echoed inside his head.

He kept swimming, drowning the sound and leaving it to drift. He couldn't walk away from the vampire and what he'd done to him. The fangs had sunk too far into his flesh. But he could repair the damage.

Leave it behind.

The voice wasn't Olivier's. He recoiled from the plea. No person alive could blame him for wanting revenge. He had to break Olivier completely, tear apart that exterior to reveal the black heart in his chest, reach in and *squeeze* it until it slowed and beat at half the speed, half the vitality.

Perhaps then the poison would be expunged.

Perhaps then he'd find some peace.

Perhaps then he could again face the world.

His feet planted on the empty beach's rough sand, and he walked out of the water as the icy water cascaded down him. The wind cut into him, freezing his skin, and he shivered. With a burst of steady power, the water evaporated from his clothes, skin, and hair, leaving him dry.

But the chill remained.

He nurtured it until it encased his heart in ice. He'd

need to keep it safe because what he was about to do was going to require a heart as hard as diamond.

The heart of a vampire.

II

THE WORLD NEEDED A LITTLE MADNESS

Present Day

I

Aurelia's eyes opened to a gray morning. Rain spattered onto the skylight and the balcony. Rafferty slept, but Viktor's chair was empty. Aurelia sat up, smoothed back the hair that had worked free, and wiped her mouth for any spit that had dried around her lips. A pressure buzzed inside her head.

Where are you? Hame's voice entered.

I'm with Viktor. We have Rafferty and Sinara. Do you have any news?

Carn and Thierry are fine. They located another couple of Xadrak's witches, there was a close call with Gabriela, but Alex healed her. I directed them to another acolyte, which will hopefully be worthwhile. I think we're going to have a problem with Oberon though.

What's he done? Aurelia's eyes unfocused and she stared into the middle distance to scry. Olivier hung in the dungeon, blood splashed on his bare torso and around his mouth, but he moved.

He fled after feeding Olivier. I don't think he's stable, Aurelia. Is he really the best choice?

He'll have to do. Her vision shifted, and she watched Oberon asleep in his room in the mountain.

He's not communicating.

He's not there to chat, Hame. He's there to feed Olivier.

Yes, I know that but—

Have you found the key?

His thoughts paused and the intensity lessened. *Not yet. I'm working on it.*

Keep focused.

He didn't respond. He knew what he had to do—and she'd questioned his commitment. *I didn't mean it like that, Hame.*

You're right. Back to work. I'll talk to you later.

And he was gone.

Viktor appeared with two cups of coffee and offered her one.

"Good morning." He smiled and sat next to her on the bed.

"Did she give you any trouble?" She inhaled the smell of the coffee, freshly brewed and pungent with rich spices.

"None. How did you sleep?"

"A little too well." She sipped the hot liquid. "Comfortable bed you've got."

"Haven't had any complaints yet." Those eyes were a little too intent.

She was not used to being so unguarded around the soldier; their interactions always having been professional. Though, if she were honest, she'd been too clouded in her misery to notice anything otherwise. The prickly distance between her and Hame, and the constant tension with Carn, had sapped away much of her willingness to let others get close. Zoe, Zach, and Mira had managed it and found their way through her defenses, but Viktor… Well, Viktor had been a general. He knew what it meant to lead. Distance wasn't luxury but necessity.

Rafferty hadn't moved all night. Her chest rose and fell at steady intervals, her face and body remained relaxed. The magic worked better than any anesthesia. And they needed this unconsciousness for what would happen next.

"Are you rested enough?" he asked, his voice as smooth as vintage port.

"I am. Are you? You must be tired after keeping vigil." She imagined him at night on the edge of the battlefield wrapped in a fur-lined coat watching for enemies while his men slept. Wounded, of course, and waiting to be sent to die on the front line, but nevertheless keeping watch. She shivered as if she stood there with him.

"I'm fine." His voice kicked her out of the daydream. "I'm ready for whatever you need."

She drained the coffee and ignored the fantasies his words conjured. "Then we should begin."

She handed him the cup then came around the bed to stand by the unconscious Rafferty. Having slept, Aurelia's mental barriers had strengthened and the world, though dreary outside the apartment, had thrown off the weariness of the night and embarked with new energy. She could face this challenge. She pushed back her sleeves and placed her hands on the witch's belly.

Fire danced within. Tongues of flame burst and coalesced in the darkness; the power must have overwhelmed Rafferty. But for all its tumultuous and raw force, the fact that her mother was so close stung her eyes.

"Is everything okay?" Powerful fingers touched her arm.

She nodded. Her throat closed to any useless words. Instead, Sinara's awareness reached out and acknowledged her, bringing recognition and love, and an eagerness to connect. Her knees quivered, and she braced herself against the side of the bed. They were going to survive this, survive Xadrak and the madness he brought, now Sinara was there.

"How do we start?"

Uncertainty was so foreign on him. "Are you sure you want to help, Viktor?"

He forced the doubts to submit to his will. Hard not to find the strength of that appealing. Like his lazy grin.

"Well, not every day I put a baby in someone, Aurelia."

Again with the fantasies…

She swept past him into the other room, mostly to disguise the sudden flush billowing up under her collar. He followed, and she ran through their approach. They discussed it, interrogated it, modified it with each retelling. They'd have one chance.

Collaborating with Viktor was easy; they fought no battles over who was right or wrong. He respected her judgement, offered suggestions when he thought of a different—and better—way. When they finally had a working method, they repeated it again, questioning all their assumptions, before running it through with their actions.

By the time they were ready, hours had passed. They grabbed some food, but her appetite wasn't strong, nerves unsettling her stomach, the impatience and the trepidation crackling and sparking.

Finally, they were ready.

She lay next to Rafferty, then placed her hands on her own belly. Her womb had long lain dormant, her flow ceasing soon after it had begun. All those eggs locked within her six centuries ago. Were they still viable? Could she have mothered generations? While not too late to do so, the thought had never appealed. She'd had her brothers, her coven, and her mission. No child could have competed with all that, just as she'd been a natural second to her mother's work.

Though surely not second in her affections, nine-year-old Aurelia argued from deep inside.

It mattered little. The practicalities of it had decreed child-rearing was not for her. Until now. Of course, this would be no ordinary pregnancy. The birth of this child was merely a means of bringing Sinara fully into the world. She would not see the babe grow. Sinara would emerge out of it, leaving nothing for her to coddle. Or raise. Or inspire.

It would be best if she thought of it not as a babe, but as an egg.

Her heart and mind separated, and she set herself to the task. Even though she was not touching the acolyte's stomach, Sinara's anticipation swirled like a storm on the horizon. The change in pressure, the crispness to the air. How much help would Sinara give in her transference and ascension?

Slowing her breath, Aurelia formed a triangle with her thumbs and fingers. Even through the blouse, her hands' coolness tightened her skin. Gradually they warmed and heat traveled through her abdominal wall and into her compact, oblivious uterus. Her awareness and her power delved inside to coax it from its slumber.

At first little changed, like slipping into a tepid bath, but as the temperature rose and the rhythmic pulse of her magic quickened, her stomach cramped. Insistent and strong fingers dug into her, deep inside where she couldn't reach. She kept her hands from massaging her belly, and instead gnawed her lip as she was pulled and prodded. A sharp tear arched her back, and Viktor asked if she was okay, but she couldn't answer. She had to concentrate, hold strong against the pain as it hacked her insides. She bore down, grunting and delving inside, deep where her slumbering womb was compelled into wakefulness.

Sweat cooled her forehead while embers burned in the hearth of her belly. She was ready.

Viktor's anxious stare was the first thing she saw when she opened her eyes.

"Viktor, I'm fine."

"You didn't look fine. You looked in agony."

"The trials of motherhood." A joke but she didn't laugh.

And Viktor didn't smile. "Do you want to rest before we try the next part?"

"No, I want this over with." She'd meant the transfer, but it wasn't until she'd said it that she realized they still had a long way to go. Who knew how quickly she could bring the pregnancy to term? Then again, the sooner she started, the sooner Sinara would enter the world.

Then would come the next battle.

Viktor didn't question her. Instead he came around and lifted her head, holding a glass of water to her lips and carefully pouring it into her mouth. She lay her hand over his and looked into his eyes as she downed the lot. His focus burned her while the ice-cold water washed away the residues of pain that had lingered and refreshed her for the next trial. He blinked and the scar on his face wrinkled as he smiled and took the glass away. She propped herself up and thanked him.

"My pleasure." He stood slowly and returned to Rafferty's side.

Heat flushed through her body. Her skin tingled where he touched and where she yearned for him to touch. She blew out a steady stream of air.

Focus, woman!

She wiped an imaginary drop of water off her chin and shifted her attention back to the sleeping acolyte. She had no guarantee the way they were doing this would work, but when she put her hand on Rafferty, she shivered with her mother's encouragement.

In this she was not alone.

She pulled her shirt off over her head, while Viktor slashed through the fabric of Rafferty's T-shirt, exposing her still-flat stomach. Aurelia had not the shame to cover her own breasts from Viktor's eyes, but neither did she position herself for his attention. They had a job to do. When she shivered and goosebumps rose on her skin, within a second Viktor had increased the temperature in the room. Other than that, he didn't acknowledge her nakedness.

"Are you ready?" they asked in unison then laughed, perhaps a little too hard. His shoulders lowered, and he held his hands a little looser over Rafferty's body. They looked in each other's eyes, and then he nodded, closed his eyes and breathed. Gratitude struck her chest. If he hadn't been there, she doubted she could have done this.

She raised her own power in readiness to bend it to her will, holding it at bay until the moment when she would accept her mother's precious new form and introduce it into her primed body. When Viktor opened his eyes, the air sang electric. A pale green light, promising healing and life, pulsed between his hands with each heartbeat, until it expanded downwards and into Rafferty's body.

The witch shuddered in her slumber, but Viktor remained rigid. Pure concentration, pure focus, pure dedication. The light shone brighter and the color deepened, sliced with red streaks. Seconds passed into minutes as she watched this part-healing and part-theft. Nobody moved.

The light pulsed and changed as he delved deeper inside, unhooking embryo and sac and placenta.

Gold tendrils reached out of Rafferty's stomach. Threads of sparkling light rose, first as mere wisps, then growing in thickness, in certainty, as they reached upwards towards Viktor's hands and the source of his healing power. They twined around his fingers, burrowed into his palms, and overtook the green and the red that he'd provided.

As the last of the green light winked out, he raised his hands slowly, rotating them then, rising out of Rafferty's stomach, through the skin came a ball of golden light that at its center burned incandescent white. Viktor's hands held Sinara and everything needed to transfer this new life into her.

He offered her the glowing orb. Whereas before he'd been serious and severe, now he smiled, a serenity that belied what they had done. He handed embryonic Sinara to her.

With trembling hands, she mirrored his posture and slid her hands in place to cover his. She opened her power slowly, reaching out to touch this new source. Sinara's power shot out and into her, reaching full circle to the power she'd bestowed.

The connection sealed in place and she gasped. Sinara's presence coursed through her hands and body, and with it a fervor to become one. It urged Aurelia's hands to retreat, and Viktor slipped away leaving the orb in place. It belonged to her, and her breath hitched in her throat. She brought it towards her body, towards her bare belly and pushed it through. Her flesh tingled at the intrusion, then buzzed as it greedily accepted more. She pushed until her hands lay flat on her belly, and she'd absorbed all the light. She maintained the flow of power, encouraging the necessary parts to knit to her uterus, to position the placenta and lock it in place, to encourage it to feed on her blood and nutrients.

A rod of pure white burst through her body, from her feet and out, to her head and out, suffusing every cell, every molecule. The bonding worked on the physical, an immediate shift in her strength, in her heart jumping to push blood further around her body, to accommodate a second life.

But more than that, the coupling with Sinara brought with it power far greater than ever imagined. Even with her lineage. Even with her mother's gift. Sinara opened herself wide to this link, giving freely of every part of her essence to make her strong, healthy, and ensure their mutual survival. She breathed in the power with every breath, then breathed it out into the world. She floated on the light, her body tingling and rising on a high so pure.

While no thoughts came, no words with which to communicate with her mother, a wave of joy flowed through her, and tears streamed down her face without her making a sound. Her heart swelled beyond physical possibilities, so big it could consume the world.

Together again.

11

Sinara's presence hummed through Aurelia's body and stirred her out of a comforting rest. The emotions raised when receiving her mother's new form had eased, yet the remnants of it wouldn't be hard to stir. A pleased acknowledgement greeted her as she came to consciousness before her eyelids fluttered open. Morning again, though this time with blue skies. She looked for Viktor, but she was alone.

Rafferty's body had gone too.

How much of Sinara's power had the witch felt? Had she experienced anything beyond horror at her own strength that surged from nowhere and burst through so uncontrollably? Knowing how aware Sinara was, it seemed logical that Rafferty had been ignorant. The destruction of her allies purely for Sinara's necessity, same too the cutting off of the witch's source at the right moment. To possess such strength then be denied...

She sighed. Sympathy was not anathema to her, even for an acolyte.

She sat up, the bedcovers falling to her waist, and picked up her shirt where Viktor had folded and placed it beside her. Slipping it over her head, she ran her fingers through her hair and retied it into a ponytail.

Pulling back the blankets, she got out of bed and walked into the other part of the apartment. Viktor sat on the rug, exposed to the waist. His back bore long pale lines punctuated with what once would have been holes. He didn't have many, not enough to call him disfigured. In fact, she appreciated them more than expected. Her fingers itched to touch them. If she didn't know better, she thought the baby bounced with amusement.

Baby.

She scoffed. It was nothing more than a collection of cells. Even if those cells were self-aware. The sooner she brought Sinara to term…

"Did you sleep well?" His words snapped her out of her reverie.

"Uhhh…yes, very well. And you? Where's Rafferty?"

He twisted and the muscles in his back shifted in beautiful motion. "I got rid of her."

One less difficult decision to make this day.

"Thank you."

"It's what I do." All six-foot-two lithe strength and grace rose in front of her. "Do you need anything?" He walked past her and to the kitchen, the gunpowder scent of him wafting past her as close as if he'd touched her.

"Something filling."

Jesus…

She cursed her thoughts and urges as they conspired to distract her from what they had to achieve. It would be better if she left. Then he could join the squad again, and she could focus all her energies on growing the baby.

Alone.

But she couldn't muster any enthusiasm for such a plan. She slid her hand low on her belly. She wanted

Viktor with her; protecting her, protecting the life he'd helped to save.

He made them breakfast the hard way. She rarely cooked old school, but his pleasure shone through the way he cracked an egg, whisked it with a fork, and then his attention, that same focus he used with everything, on making sure the bacon and tomatoes and fresh coffee also came out perfect.

Her stomach growled.

He served them both, everything arranged to accentuate its color and appeal even more to her starvation. Her fork hovered over the food, torn between wanting to shovel everything in at once and to preserve it for as long as possible.

He laughed. "You sure you're hungry?"

"Starving." She speared the food and once the first morsel touched her tongue… Decorum be damned. She ate steadily and Viktor did too.

They chatted, settling into a rhythm that swung from the mundane—if anything in their lives could be described as such—to the plans they had for the battles ahead. She preferred to talk about what he did when he wasn't fighting acolytes. Hearing how he embedded himself in the city, from the seedy happenings in nightclubs to the museums and theatre and fine food that the city offered. She had not been much for museums or art or culture, having seen so many fall, having felt so distant from them all, separated as she was with Hame and her brothers. Perhaps she had missed out.

Then again, she abstained so that others didn't have to.

Keeping Xadrak in check, guiding her brothers, slaughtering evil had been all she'd known for some time. What would happen when they finally banished Xadrak?

If…

"Are you alright?" His fork rested on the side of his plate, and he placed his hand over hers. The scrape of his skin scratched something inside her and looking into silver eyes had her longing for what usually came before a shared breakfast. But a dark future amassed on the horizon.

Even this warrior could fall.

She smiled away his concerns and returned to eating, finishing off the plate with a speed that verged on disrespect. But they needed to hurry, they needed to start so they could finish.

She downed the coffee. Viktor matched her and they returned to the bedroom. She kept her eyes forward, lest he detect what was really on her mind. His body was already a little too close to hers. She stood at the foot of the bed, taking a moment to compose herself. Why was it so hard to swallow? They had a task to complete. They were both dedicated to their mission yet…

Climbing onto the bed, she lay on the right. Something about being where Rafferty had once been twisted her stomach. The bed sagged under Viktor's weight, pitching her towards him. He steadied her before she steadied herself.

"What do you need me to do?" A seriousness stole over his features that had her cringing from her wayward thoughts. Over half a millennium old and acting like a stupid girl with a crush. She matched his businesslike approach.

"You place your hands on mine and pass your power through to me." She laid her hands horizontally across her belly while he rested his on top. Even without the magic, his palms ran hot. Sinara's awareness whirled at greater speed, reaching up to brush them. Three, not two, would be involved in this work.

"You channel your power through to me, which I'll

fashion and pass through to grow the fetus." She had wanted him to be directly involved but she couldn't take the risk—however small—that his thoughts might stray, or they might not match with hers and growing the baby required precision and a singular purpose.

"Will I be strong enough to give you what you need?"

Yes. Always. "Every bit counts."

"Then take everything I have." He smiled and his hands burned.

She closed her eyes but couldn't fight her own grin. A few deep breaths and a lot of mental manipulation later, her focus settled deep inside her, sensing the life growing in her womb. Sinara was nothing more than a few cells, a consciousness yes, but that was more to do with Sinara herself than the presence of another awareness. The demoness had been attached to this little collection, but she needed space, she needed to enter the world fully for when Xadrak came.

Xadrak had been born to Earth many times, yet only one had allowed him to enter this world close to his true form. She believed that he'd been brought in second, latching himself onto another soul and its shell rather than being formed together. Sinara had gotten there first. And she was going to be so perfectly twinned with this body that her power could flow easily, she could emerge as bodily as Xadrak would attempt through Peter.

At least that was the plan and the hope.

"Ready."

Her skin vibrated with Viktor's power, first a tingling before heat intensified and agitated, scuttling along the back of her hands. She reached out with her energy, rising up to twine with his, golden threads interlacing with silver and forming thick ropes. Then she was no longer reaching but *there*, one with his power.

Bound together she gathered her magic, tapping into the deepest sources she could access, dragging on the power of the Earth and sky and, yes, even Sinara's. Amassing such energies into a reservoir that she could draw on, she held in her mind the singular thought of growing this baby as quickly as possible. She wanted to steel her body for the massive drain this would take, but restricting herself, holding herself in fear and apprehension, would stunt the working. She had to act as a channel and deny her own worries. Her body hummed with the power, drawing on all threads, each one she was aware of, each one wrapped together, and then she smashed the dam.

Power that had been welling up reversed and flooded into her, lifting her body up, but Viktor forced her down. Her body cracked and fizzed, the working turning into claws that grabbed and snatched at her body's nourishment. This wouldn't be slow. This wouldn't be gentle. This stealing, this claiming of her body for another's, done at such a speed, rent her apart.

Life—that greedy motherfucker—needed her for another.

She ground her teeth until her temples throbbed. Her hands stiffened, and Viktor's pressed hers. Life writhed. Twisting on itself as cells divided and multiplied, as her body was depleted of its strength and grew Sinara's new vessel. Power flowed, healed and replenished her yet still the draining continued.

Sinara attempted to comfort her, but the trials drowned her mother's soothing. She had to concentrate too hard on restricting the flow enough that she could maintain it, while holding back her own discomfort and restore her ailing strength. She had not the mental space nor the fortitude to accept her mother's concern. Her power was enough.

On and on the conjuring fed and starved her, thrown from one extreme to another, as the fetus took on form and expanded within her until the power thinned, the flow trickled, and her world shrank to the darkness of her womb and the life beating within. She had to keep going. There was still so much growing to do, but the power dripped to nothing. A voice called far in the distance; words muffled as she scrambled for the energy to return.

"Aurelia!"

Her body spasmed as her name burst through and the connection severed. She tumbled down into a black world, and consciousness fled when she hit bottom.

III

Olivier salivated over the approach of his food; a deep yearning that had him cringing. His hunger slunk back from what was about to be placed in front of him. He growled. He would not let the witch see him shy from this. He'd been through enough hell to not go through this too. He'd faced stronger men in his lifetime and always come out with their throats in his jaw.

He thought he'd had the witch, had already crushed him, but it hadn't been enough to take him and belittle him. He had to go further, had to be subtle. He'd seen that once the rage dulled. And as much as he hated to debase himself, the witch's ego required it. His psyche was built on shaky ground already and one misstep would bring him tumbling into his outstretched arms, ready to be torn apart. The witch kept returning. That had to mean something.

But when he entered all Olivier could remember was being manipulated however the witch wanted. Olivier wanted to drink, wanted to feed, but on his own terms.

"I don't want your blood."

Oh, he'd feed forever if he could. He'd give anything to sink his fangs into that neck again. He should have drained the fucker when he had the chance, but he had chosen to posture instead over his supine body.

Smart move, Olivier.

The thought slapped his mind. He needed to do better, or the witch was dangerously close to unsettling him.

"I've got my orders to keep you fed and strong." He stopped in front of him and held his hands in front of his crotch.

"We both know why you're here. You can't keep away from me."

"Don't flatter yourself."

"I knew seeing me tied up got you going, but you took it to another level the other day." He leaned forward on the manacles. "You're here for more."

"Bondage doesn't do it for me." Arms crossed over his chest.

Button. Pressed. Olivier smiled.

"You can lie to yourself if you want, but I've seen that look in plenty of men before. I know what grabs their balls and seeing me at your whim crushed yours."

"I'm not you."

"You're not even half of me."

"And grateful for it."

He flicked his eyebrows. "You said it. You might think you like holding the rope and swallowing the key to the cuffs, but that's because you've not come to terms with your real purpose. You're not the one in control."

"And neither are you. Look where you are. Look at what you are forced to do. You're an impulse, Olivier. A primal need dressed in flesh. You're not able to control yourself any more than you're able to control the world around you." The witch inched closer, stood right in front of him. "You don't matter."

His chest tensed, steeled itself against the drumming in his chest. What would this witch know about him? What could he know of what he'd been through? What would he know of the hole inside himself where Thierry used to be?

"Look where they've put you. Aurelia doesn't care. Your own twin doesn't care."

Olivier flinched, and the witch's eyes flared. *Control yourself.* He couldn't let on about Thierry, about how much it still—

He didn't need them, didn't need any of them. The witch might have scratched old wounds, but he wasn't about to tear them open. He kept his mouth closed.

"If you mattered, you'd be with them. They'd be happy to have you around, but all your posturing, all your terrorizing—" the witch clicked his fingers, "—is just so much noise."

Wrong. He'd done what he did because that's what he was made for. That's what he was destined to be.

In control.

In charge.

Indomitable.

The world needed a little madness, a little terror to keep it spinning, grease it so they could all carry on as they wished knowing death waited for them.

"That's why you do what you do, Olivier." He stood close enough for the blood to tantalize. "You think it makes you important to them. You think that if you're the worst you can be then they can't help but notice you."

He should lower his head. He had to let the witch believe he was beaten or else he'd never get out of there. But the witch was wrong. So wrong.

"And where do you fit into all this?" he hissed.

"We're not here to talk about me." The witch took a few quick steps back. But the hook wouldn't dislodge that easily.

Olivier twisted it. "That's because you're nothing. You're inconsequential. You're a fuck and feed that I used. Discarded. You're lucky I let you to live. Most don't get that. Then again, bad lay, bad aftertaste."

"It wasn't a lay, it was rape, you fuck." The witch's eyes widened.

"The only things worth having are those you take yourself."

"Like Thierry?" Those two words broke out of the witch's mouth like a cracked whip. They stung Olivier's heart, and his eyes narrowed to slits.

He had to get control of himself, but the witch kept poking, kept digging into those tender spots, trying to find a way in. If he'd drunk his fill, he would have had the strength to resist.

If he'd been free…

If he could feel Thierry…

If. If. If.

"What would you know of it? What would you know of our history? My brother is even less of a friend to witches than me."

"Liar." His voice dripped venom—seductive, deadly.

Olivier closed his hands into fists, his wrists bulging against the manacles.

"I don't need to know it all. I can see what effect the mention of his name has on you."

"You have no comprehension of what he means to me."

"Don't you mean *meant*? Past tense? Because he's not here. He's left you to rot. He couldn't care less what happens to you."

A dull blade carved his brother's name into his heart, each sloppy stroke cut his chest into a bloody mess. But he'd suffered worse and no one had noticed.

"Says the inked up little boy who thinks he's a man. The loner. No one scrambled to your aid when I drained the blood from your body."

The witch brushed it aside. He thought he was winning. "You know why Thierry left you behind? Why he wants you dead?"

"Thierry will return. He always does." He leaned forward. "And then we'll feast together on your insides."

Dark hair shook. "You have no idea the trauma you've caused, do you? You stampede through the centuries thinking it's all yours to do with as you wish, with no punishment, no karma."

He tipped his head back and peals of laughter stripped out of his throat. "Who is there to punish me? I may be in a dungeon, but I am not dead. I don't suffer. Unlike you, bound to the will of others, locked in here with someone you despise." He let his eyes glow with fire. "I've transcended you. I did centuries ago. I am the pinnacle of fucking creation, and you're nothing but slime desperate to catch a ride on my boot."

"You're mad," he whispered. "You really don't have any idea."

The witch straightened, puffed his chest, and that putrid stench stole into the air. Its tendrils scrambled across his chest, into ribs and pulled tight on the muscle. His eyes lit up, they *sparkled* with what? Glee? He was happy about this. Bordering on ecstatic. The laughter and the righteousness abandoned Olivier and cowered in the deepest darkest corner.

"Get the fuck away from me," Olivier snarled. "Get out!"

The fuck shook his head and smiled, and it was a smile that turned the skin on the back of his neck clammy. The witch opened his arms, the tattoo along the inside of his forearm flashing with the light that shot out of his hands.

Aut inveniam viam aut faciam.

The light slammed into Olivier's forehead so hard his skull rebounded off the stones. But when he opened his eyes, he was in a room splashed with blood and staring at a body tied to a chair.

Reiner…

The whore had been dead for two centuries but seeing him again, even if dead, he almost snarled.

Almost. This wasn't *his* memory and something greater swamped the jealousy, and he flowed deeper into his brother's mind.

Grief crushed him and forced him to beg at the knees of his beloved Etienne-returned. An empty hole gaped where Reiner's heart used to be, torn out by Olivier, that monster, that brother.

Why did he have to do it? Why couldn't he have let him have this slice of happiness, this sliver of hope?

Oh God, Etienne was gone again, and he may never find him. Centuries of missing him, of having to watch himself follow Olivier's terror, of sinking closer and closer to Olivier's depravity in the desperate hope that he'd lose himself completely. He'd even felt it, felt it the way they used to share things when they were mortal. The bond always there.

Why couldn't he understand they weren't meant to be with one another?

And Etienne, who had been the right one for him, taken again as he was taken then, and condemning him to this wretched, tormented existence.

Howls ripped out of the depths of his being, all for this lost love, this lost hope.

"I had to."

He attacked Olivier before the words were fully out, propelled by such a desperate hate that it spurred him to a greater urge for destruction. He could sunder the world with that loathing. He rained down blow after blow on his unworthy brother.

Olivier tried to speak, but he'd not listen to his brother's justification of this heinous act. He struck his cheek, his jaw, his chest, anything to cause as much injury to Olivier as he'd dealt him.

"I hate you for what you've done to me."

Though Olivier heard his brother's thought-scream as words, he broke beneath Thierry's utter hopelessness. He'd never escape this life of endless blood and torture and torment, all while his brother, who professed to love him, lapped it up, sucked at the bloody teat of the Devil for nothing but chaos.

The fight continued inside and out. They burst from the room, even as Olivier still hung in his chains, tumbled down stairs that hadn't existed for a century, into the hall, moving, fighting, punching. Thierry trying his best to obliterate his brother and destroy the expanding despair.

It thundered out of the long-lost past, gaining speed, gaining ground, pounding into him. No matter how fast he tried to evade it, hungry maws bit at him, ready to rip him apart. What he would have given to feel Thierry as deeply as he once had, but this… This was too much. This was far too much.

He closed his eyes and reared back, twisting in his chains. He had to break out, but the wretchedness closed in. He wrenched his shoulders in an attempt to shatter the bonds, while the fit rose ever higher out of his belly, up his throat. He tilted his head to keep above the snapping jaws.

No, he hadn't done that to Thierry. Thierry had betrayed him. All he'd tried to do was protect him, to keep him safe, to protect him from that…that…

"Whore!"

The witch stumbled back.

Thierry's blind suffering drowned him, and he kicked to free himself from the worst.

"You think you know?" he screamed. "You think you understand what it was like to watch him and know that the one person I loved in this whole fucking life couldn't stand me? I did it all for *him*. I did it all for *us*. And he betrayed me!"

Spit flew from his mouth as he strained against the shackles.

"Let me loose! I need to be free. I shouldn't be here. You have to let me free."

The witch blinked, took a step back and then another. The fucker was going to leave. He couldn't. Not before releasing him.

"Don't leave! You did this. You and all of them did this to me, and you don't get to shy from it. You don't get to ignore me, lock me away in the dark, and carry on as if it's what I deserve."

Hadn't he suffered? Hadn't he been forced to do the unthinkable? He'd done everything he could to keep his brother safe, to keep him *alive*, but it had never been good enough. Thierry just moped for that lost life, that awful fucking putrid life, where all they'd done was survive. Henri. The abattoir. Fucking *Carcassonne*. All the while he'd made the best of it, tried to squeeze as much joy out of the steaming shit that had smothered them. Then came the chance to have it all. To live the finest lives. To have the power over life and death.

And if the witch thought he could use some cheap mind trick like this then he was sure as fuck going to stay put and see it through.

To see his side of the story.

To understand why it had been like that.

Why *he* had been like that.

What had been *his* Genesis.

But the coward retreated and twisted the handle on the door. He couldn't go. The screams in his mind would never stop if that door closed again. As much as he hated the fucker, he needed to have someone to rail against, to not turn on himself and tear himself to shreds.

"You're weak!" he boomed. "You can't even finish what you started. You see me here in hell like this and you run from it. There was a moment I thought of turning you into a vampire, but there are enough feeble fools in existence that to have you living for an eternity would be more than the world could bear."

He lied. He'd never make another like himself. He'd never lessen himself the way his maker had and allow himself to be torn apart by his dark children. But he was desperate and the more he shouted, the more he could rise above those emotions engulfing him.

"Look at you, ready to run from the slightest sign it's getting hard. They'll rejoice when I snuff you out."

But the witch ignored him, the door opened and closed, and he was left alone to brace himself for the stampede inside his chest that brought the shivers and the tears and the horror out of his throat and quivering on the verge before breaking through him and out of him in a storm of howls. Even as they poured forth, the despair sunk its claws into him and latched on for dear life.

God, why couldn't it let go too?

He sobbed and wailed into the darkness the witch had plunged him into where even Thierry couldn't reach him.

IV

Power as harsh as ice water flooded Oberon's veins
and smashed into the wave of Olivier's hysteria and
violence. The vampire's muffled screams bellowed at his
back while he tried to compose himself. He hadn't wanted
to do it that way. He'd wanted to give some perspective,
but he'd lost control and unleashed Olivier's endless
perversion.

His hands wouldn't stop shaking.

Seeing what Thierry had seen, feeling the loss of both
brothers, of looking into a gaping bloody wound: Olivier
had done that. The smell of blood burned in his nose. He
hadn't meant to go with him, not like that, but he'd slipped
and been dragged into the stream of memories.

He'd had to end the spell. He brought back pity, for
Thierry, for himself, and the sadness that Olivier wouldn't
admit the harm he'd caused—and never would.

With the walls between them, Oberon's heart rate
eased, leaving sickness sloshing in his stomach. He needed
a shower. He needed to eat. He needed to be anywhere but
near the fucking vampire.

Rushing up the tunnel, he crossed the chamber to the hall that led to the bedrooms.

"Glad to see you're not leaving again."

He turned at Hame's voice. The red-headed oracle, half hidden in shadow, leaned against the archway to the left, arms folded across his chest.

"And if I did? I'm not a prisoner too, am I?"

Hame held up his hands and shrugged. "You're free to come and go as long as you're safe. We wouldn't want any unwelcome visitors coming in after you."

"Is that what you're here to warn me about? Seen something?"

"Just a guy who looks like he's on the edge."

He walked over to the oracle. "Tell me, if you're an oracle, why do you let bad things happen? Why couldn't you stop all the awful things Olivier did? Why couldn't you —" His voice broke over the rest of what he was about to say.

"I can't see everything, and sometimes bad things have to happen."

"You're useless." Oberon headed towards his room. He'd rather lock himself away than spend time with someone who had the power to avert disasters but chose not to.

"How many people did you let die in Perth?"

His head whipped round. "What?"

"How many? How many suffered while you did nothing?"

"How can you— I never hurt anybody."

"But how many did Olivier and Thierry kill while you knew of their presence in the city?"

An icy finger scraped the back of his neck. "She…she told me to watch."

Hame wrinkled his nose. "You didn't have to follow her

orders. You could have disobeyed. You could have intervened."

"I did intervene! I offered my assistance, and I got violated for my trouble."

"So, if you'd done nothing, maybe that wouldn't have happened."

His mouth gaped. "You're blaming *me* for getting raped?"

"No, but what I'm saying is all actions have consequences, whether intended or not, and shit happens. I could choose to open myself to all the prophecies, and alter as much of human history as possible, yet bad things will always occur."

"Then it's all futile. Why not close yourself off completely?"

"Because this is *my* choice. To work with Aurelia to defeat Xadrak. To save what I can for myself and for the ones I love. It's mercenary, but it's the only way to survive."

"Yeah, well it sucks, and you can justify it all you want, but the fact is you could save far more lives than you have, but you choose not to." He wanted to be alone in his room, but the hallway had never seemed longer and the walls never closer.

"I'm sorry for what Olivier did to you, Oberon."

It hurt to breathe but he forced it.

"Fuck off." He sliced the air with his hand. "Condolences are easy, Oracle. Words don't matter. It's what you do that counts."

"And what are you doing with Olivier?"

"Making him pay for what he did while I've got the chance."

"And that will make you feel better?"

"It's a start."

"Oberon, I—"

The oracle's words cut off with a strained gasp and mist clouded his eyes. Hame's face slackened like time had stopped and he started to fall. Oberon rushed to catch him, sinking beneath the big man's heavy weight and laying him on the floor.

"Hame!"

The oracle's pulse butted against the fingers he'd placed at Hame's neck, but no amount of shaking and shouting could wake him.

V

Aurelia woke with Viktor's hand pressing down on hers and his head slumped on her shoulder. Drained of her power, she could barely wiggle from under his weight. And if she was so weakened, what had happened to him?

"Viktor?"

Her voice cracked on his name. She cleared her throat; the minute movements racked her body with shivers. She endured them and writhed enough to move his head and squeeze herself out from underneath him. His hand slipped off hers and fell. She couldn't hear him breathe.

Mustering what little strength she had, she turned on her side to watch his chest. She dropped her hand on his sternum. He was warm. His chest rose slowly. He slept. The flooding relief pushed her onto her back, and she lay as close to him as she could and stared at the ceiling.

How much had she taken from him? How near to death had she brought him? And had it been worth it? She focused on the life inside, finding Sinara's awareness, pleased, growing.

A wave of nausea rolled through her, bringing with it

the smell of rotting oranges, that sickly pungent aroma that Olivier harped on about. As it rose, so did her bile, and she hurried to lean over the edge of the bed and hurl the undigested remains of a breakfast that seemed from days ago. It hit the floor with a wet splat. Not finished with her yet, she threw up twice more before she was able to lie down again, the smell bad, the taste worse. She needed to get up, but even that verged on impossible.

The stench became bearable then forgotten. Viktor slept still and she dozed, restoring her strength. She hooked onto a scrap of her power—or was it Sinara's?—and used it to repair and strengthen herself. And eventually, when hunger fought hard to make itself known, and the awful draining had eased, she was able to sit, then stand. She let Viktor rest. His face still held that same alluring intensity. She wanted to kiss him, but she pulled away.

If she and Viktor kissed, it wasn't going to be with the tang of sick on her tongue.

Careful to avoid the mess on the floor, she dragged herself off the bed and shuffled into the bathroom, turning on the shower and undressing. Hot needles speared her body, piercing the fog that blanketed her. She washed her hair, running her fingers through her black locks, then down her body. She touched her breasts and flinched, their tenderness making her wince, withdraw, panic. It wasn't prominent but something was there, something *different*.

Awake, she slid her hand over her belly and massaged its hardness. She'd always been taut and slender, but... There *was* growth. There *was* expansion. The spell had worked faster than they'd expected. Elation bubbled up inside her at finding such progress.

Invigorated, she hurried out of the shower, dried and dressed, brushed her teeth, and removed the evidence of her sickness. She hunted the kitchen for food and devoured whatever looked appetizing and ready to eat. The more she ate, the hungrier she became. Filling the endless pit inside her body, her power rebooted, a spark of electricity that twinned with her mother's shared joy. This was working.

Sated, she returned to Viktor, eager to continue their working. She wouldn't ask him again to give so much; that had been selfish on her part. If it hadn't been for him, she would have drained herself to death and taken him with her. She needed him to keep her grounded. And she'd been wrong to invest so much energy at once, her body could not keep up with such an avalanche. She could, however, keep up a constant stream, at a lower level, but over a longer period of time.

She rested her hand on Viktor's chest, and a rivulet of power traveled down her arm and into him, revitalizing and healing. He stirred, murmuring in his sleep, and twisted beneath her touch. His eyelids flew open and he was sitting.

"Are you all right?"

She smiled. "I'm fine now. I'm sorry for what I did to you."

"Don't be. I survived and I've never felt part of something so huge, even when I received Sinara's power. It was just so—" He blushed. "Forgive me. I got carried away."

Her heart warmed before the cold crept in. "I'm glad it didn't frighten you, or break you, but I can't let you do it again."

"Why not?" He withdrew his hand quickly, and his eyes drifted to her belly. "Didn't it work?"

"It worked fine. It worked well, but the way we did it isn't the way it should be done. It's too risky." She held up her hand. "Not just for you but for me as well."

"But you need my help, don't you?"

"Yes, but I don't need your power."

"I'm here for you to use, me *and* my power, to make this as quick and painless for you as possible. I am *your* warrior. Why won't you use me?"

"Because too much power will kill me. The way I did it before, yes, it worked, but I drained myself too much. I drained you, and if you hadn't shaken me free, we would have both died. It can't be done as fast as I'd hoped."

"Then drain us all. Take me. Take Moroni and Larissa and Felix. Use all of our power, every last drop."

"My body can't take such rapid changes. Please, Viktor, I know what I'm doing. I wish there were another way, but it must be done slower than we'd planned. You're helping me more by keeping me safe than by lending me your power."

Conflict warred in his eyes, of wanting to give everything as a soldier should but coming up against these orders and her reason.

"I want to spare you pain," he said.

"There is no pain. And what pain there is, is mine to bear." She stroked his cheek. "You are my warrior, now be my guardian."

She kissed him, and the electricity as her lips touched Viktor's short-circuited the need for more talk. He resisted, his lips refusing to yield, but as embarrassment that she'd got it wrong clutched her throat and she was about to withdraw, he opened to her. His mouth responded with a hunger that matched hers. She leaned into him, and his hands rose to cradle her head. She wanted his body against hers, to be held in his strong arms and crushed in his embrace.

She pushed him back against the pillows, their lips staying connected as he reclined, and she straddled him. Her body aligned to his length, his hands firmly caressing her back, her fingers spearing through his hair. He hardened and she ground herself there, eliciting a grunt from him, and he broke from her to kiss and stroke her neck.

She shivered, at once trying to escape the pleasure he gave while desperately wanting more of it. Rearing back, he rose with her, hands and lips exploring, searching, unfastening until they were naked.

All the glory of his darkened and scarred body pressed against her ripening and demanding form. How she wanted him inside her. How she wanted to smash through the decades of calcified affection and stunted desire.

Her fingers gripped his hair and pulled, forcing him to submit to her control. She looked into his eyes, seeing willingness and burning lust. She opened her mouth to tell him what she wanted, but a voice intruded inside her head and killed the words before they reached her throat.

They're dying, Aurelia! They're dying!

"You can't go!"

Viktor's shouting wouldn't stop her. Aurelia gathered her clothes and hurried to dress, while Viktor—beautiful, naked, *willing* Viktor—demanded she listen. Hame's voice echoed inside her head, the remnants of a prophecy that crashed into her, the flow of the names of the dead—of her coven—being slaughtered by Xadrak's acolytes left her ears ringing and metal on her tongue. She had to stop their demise, or she'd be left with no one. They weren't just her militia; they were her friends, her family. She was supposed to protect them. And she was about to—

"Aurelia, listen to me!" Viktor grabbed her arms. His hands on her made her itch and she reached for her power. "You can't help them. You have a job here to do."

"What's the point of doing this if they're going to die? I made a promise to—"

"The only thing you promised them was power. They knew what they were getting involved with. They're fighting for you."

"They'll die!" She broke free of him.

"Leaving now is a distraction. You must stay and finish what you set out to do. I will go. I will warn them."

She stopped, her body swaying from the imbalance. "But I need you here."

"Then they die."

He'd dressed, the moment of lust long past and leaving a stain of guilt down her gullet. He awaited her order. He expected her to be the leader. That's what she was, but, when so many lives depended on hers, she wavered. She resisted the urge to crouch in the corner and hug her knees close, protect her belly, and wish it would all go away. Coming so close to success, why did she hesitate?

Because there's so much to lose.

She massaged her forehead, pressing the skin against her skull until it hurt. When did she fall? When did she weaken?

"Give me your orders, Aurelia." No condescension studded his voice. As always it hummed with his respect and devotion, even after seeing her like this. He considered her a warrior too, not just their leader. He fought because she fought.

She let her hand drop, and with it her indecision fell. "Warn them. Tell them to stand down and hide."

She gave him the names of the witches Hame had seen die and where they were. Carn's group would be attacked, but Hame would have warned him first. Then there were the others, sent to attack acolytes whose locations had been gathered through coercion, perhaps a subterfuge of

Xadrak's as he laid a trap of his own. Mira had gone with them; she had to be told first. At least Zoe and Zach were still holed up safe with Peter. She gave him what other information she could and hoped that would be enough to save them. And then she'd have little to do but stay and grow fat.

"What will you do?" He was about to walk out the door.

"I will do what I must to see this end before more blood is shed." The steel had returned to her voice and suppressed the churning nausea.

"I'll return before long." With a smile and a nod, he was gone before she could tell him to come back to her alive.

VI

OBERON HAD MANAGED TO GET HAME ONTO THE BED, BUT the oracle remained locked in prophecy. Unable to do anything, he watched. His fingers bunched at his mouth, pulling at his bottom lip. Where was Aurelia?

The door burst open and he jumped from the chair to face a blond giant who strode in and pushed him aside. His clothes had been ripped, dried blood splattered across his body and face, but none of this seemed to bother him.

He was there for Hame.

"How's he doing?" The man picked up one of Hame's hands and held it in his fist. His other hand pressed against his chest, gently resting over his heart.

"He's… He's out of it. Who are you?"

"Carn." As if that was enough to explain his sudden appearance.

"Why are you here?"

"Because he warned us to get out and come back."

"Us?"

The sound of feet at the door turned his head, and he looked at a face he'd never thought he'd see again.

149

"Oberon?"

"Alex? What… I don't under—"

But his confusion at seeing a past one-night stand drowned in the terror of seeing Olivier standing behind him free of his cell. Both men's mouths bloodied, their clothes singed and torn, and the vampire glaring at him from the doorway.

He couldn't stop staggering back a little.

"Who are you?" the darker vampire asked.

Oberon's brain rebooted. This was Thierry. But what the vampire was doing with Alex, he couldn't yet—

Both mouths stained with blood.

His stomach twisted. "When did this happen?"

Alex wiped his mouth with the back of his arm, not that it did much to remove the smear. The last time they'd seen each other Alex had been doing an entirely different thing with his mouth.

"You reek of my brother." Thierry's eyes narrowed. "Where is he?" A threat rumbled through his words.

"He's in the dungeon but—"

Thierry disappeared down the hallway, doors slamming as he scoured the chambers in his search.

"You can't get to him," he shouted after the vampire.

But Thierry didn't answer and continued on his useless quest. The door would hold. Meanwhile, Alex Roche was far from home.

"He turned you into a vampire?" His forehead didn't have enough muscles to frown at this and make sense of it.

Alex rubbed the back of his neck. "To save my life."

His eyes bulged. Had this happened while he was busy watching Olivier in Perth? Had his focus on one brother led to Alex falling prey to the other? One more failure to add to the heap. Hame had said bad things happen, but even the oracle had tried to protect someone other than himself.

Alex took his silence for disapproval. "You wouldn't understand."

"Try me."

"Hey!" Carn snapped. "If you two want some sort of heartfelt reunion, would you mind fucking off elsewhere?"

"Do you want help, Carn?" Alex asked.

Carn shook his head and waved them off. Oberon jerked his chin towards the hall and Alex followed, closing the door and leaving Carn to minister to the oracle.

"I'm sorry you got suckered by Thierry."

Alex folded his arms across his chest and leaned against the wall. "It wasn't like that. I love him."

Oberon's eyes were in danger of leaping out of his skull. "What? Because he saved your life? Last time I checked you were pretty good at healing yourself." They'd never discussed it during their brief fling, but Alex's abilities were obvious.

"I'd passed the point of no return."

"You're telling me."

"Look, Oberon, you and I are nothing to each other. We never were more than a one-time thing, so I don't need to explain this to you and I definitely don't need your approval."

Alex walked away.

He refused to chase after him, but part of him wanted Alex to stay. His was the only slightly friendly face he'd seen in what felt like weeks. "I'm worried about what you've gotten involved with."

Thierry's muffled rage swept through the lair.

Alex stopped and turned. "I could say the same about you. Why are you here?"

Did Alex deserve answers? Were they even worth

anything? How much did he already know about the portal and Thierry's part in it? "There's this witch called Aurelia—"

"We've met."

Of course.

"She needed my help with Olivier." He swallowed hard over the vampire's name.

Alex came closer, a cautious look behind him. "What kind of help?" he whispered.

He couldn't think of what to say but before Alex could see that, Thierry emerged out of the tunnel and wrapped his hand around his throat and slammed him against the wall. The vampire's eyes glowed burned umber, and he exposed his fangs.

"Let. Me. In."

Olivier's face loomed in front of his vision, the memory of being held like this attacked from the inside. He tried to break free, instinct making him grab hold of Thierry's hand, believing his magic couldn't help him before adrenaline pushed him to fight. His power exploded out, flinging Thierry across the hall. The vampire was down, but Oberon readied two balls of light and crouched for another attack.

"Don't EVER touch me!" Oberon bellowed.

Thierry rose to his feet and sneered at him. "You'd protect that *thing* down there?"

"From someone trying to kill him? Yes!"

"I'm not going to kill him. He's practically unkillable. I do, however, want to beat the ever-living shit out of him."

"Then take it up with Aurelia, but he's my responsibility, and you're not going to hurt him."

Thierry's lips thinned. They twitched like he was holding back from sinking his teeth into something. Or someone. "You'd let me in if you knew what he'd done to me."

Oberon reached for the quickest weapon. "Like killing Reiner?"

Thierry flinched. "How do you know about him?"

"I've seen it. I've seen what Olivier did." But that didn't absolve Thierry from turning Alex into a vampire. As far as he was concerned, they were twins in every way.

"Then you have some idea what happened to Alex, only this time I managed to save him before Olivier ripped out his heart."

His magic sputtered and died. Olivier had caused this too? He'd assumed Thierry had bitten Alex and then took misguided pity on him.

"That shut you up. Well, go and ask him about Etienne. Ask him about our early life together, then we'll see how strongly you stick to your orders." He walked away and opened the door to Hame's room.

Olivier had done worse to Thierry? He wasn't sure he could handle seeing more.

Alex lingered. "Don't judge him too harshly, Oberon."

"It's hard not to after what's happened to you."

"I've found something strong and eternal. For all the horror, for all the death and the fighting, I'm happy. And I'll do whatever it takes to make sure it stays that way."

Alex followed Thierry, leaving Oberon alone in a cold hallway, trying to understand how—in a place that included not one but three vampires—*he'd* somehow ended up being the bad guy.

VII

"Returned with more cheap tricks, witch?" The doorway filled with the scent of oranges and Thierry.

That was a master stroke, the witch's phantoms banging and shouting at the door, threatening to break it down. Magic, illusion, that's all they were. Designed to destroy him like those supposed 'memories' he'd summoned.

As if Thierry was truly capable of loving that whore.

"What tricks?" Thierry's scent intensified.

Olivier forced himself against the wall, before it weakened his heart further.

"Don't insult my intelligence. You've conjured up a ghost of Thierry, but if you think you can rattle me with that, you're mistaken."

"Thierry is here. With Alex."

Olivier studied the witch's blank face. "You're lying. And if you're not going to feed me, you can leave."

"He was pissed he couldn't get to you. Not to rescue you, of course, but to attack you. Lucky the door held."

The witch forced a chuckle. "Do you know what he said I should ask you?"

Olivier ignored him and focused on the wall to his right. Thierry wasn't there. Thierry hadn't spoken to the witch. Thierry wouldn't have left him hanging.

"He said I should ask about your origins. He said it'd help me understand why he turned Alex. It might even help me understand you."

"And why would you want to do that? So, you can justify to yourself why you're doing this? To give it a moral stamp of approval?" He snorted. "For fuck's sake, call it what it is: you want to torture me because you think it'll make you feel better."

"The more you fight, the more I want to see. The more I want *you* to see." The witch's expression shone with evangelical light.

"Your tricks didn't work last time. *Memories*." His mouth twisted around the word. "They'll be forgotten, like you."

"I'm never going to die, Olivier. That's what I get out of this, and you'd better believe I'll never have to go through what you went through to get it."

"You'd never survive it."

The witch's lips went hard and straight. "You got lucky. Instead of getting cancer, or heart disease, or cholera, you got bitten by a vampire."

"What would you know of my beginnings? You weren't there."

The witch's lips curled into a fanatic's smile. Light shot from his hands and Olivier gripped his chains and braced himself as it slammed into his head.

OLIVIER TUMBLED THROUGH DARKNESS TO LAND IN A NIGHT-shrouded forest. A fire flickered and the sound of Thierry's struggles sliced through the crisp air as their maker, Rellius, told him lies about Etienne's final moments and bit into him. The smell of the firewood mixed with the scent of fresh blood.

He stood out of the light, watching the shadows wrestle. Near him Etienne's empty shell slumped against the trunk of a tree. He'd had to kill him otherwise Thierry might have tried to turn him. Olivier couldn't allow that. And Rellius would haven't either. He'd wanted Thierry all along but mixed up the two brothers, so alike had they looked. Olivier couldn't spend eternity without his twin, couldn't bear to watch him wither and die. And he wouldn't spend it beneath the heel of another brutal father. He and Thierry were meant to be together, the two of them against the world, strong and safe. Etienne had to be sacrificed. What they'd had wasn't love, no matter Thierry's protests.

"What are you doing here, Olivier?" Etienne asked.

Olivier turned to the corpse and the scene shifted. Time flowed backwards as Thierry and Rellius vanished, and Olivier walked into the ring of light surrounding the fire. As he approached, Etienne stood. Unlike most people, Etienne de Balthas always knew which brother was which.

That's because he's only been fucking one of us.

"I could ask you the same thing."

"I'm guessing if you're here, you already know." But Etienne didn't say it with any defeat. He said it with pure defiance.

If only he knew…

Olivier had been slaughtering people all day, drinking their blood, building himself up to this kill, one that would actually mean something. He'd trailed Etienne out of the city and into the forest. Thierry would be there soon. Rellius was waiting nearby. This had to be done quickly.

"You can't have him, Etienne. He belongs to me."

"That's for him to decide, not you. I love him, Olivier. I'm not sure what you feel for him, but it isn't love."

Heat blazed through his veins, boiling the blood of the multitude he'd ingested. Etienne's would soon be added to the mix, and his lying words would dissolve and never surface again. "We're going to be together always."

"Then he'll fight you always. Thierry doesn't love you; you disgust him. The maniac, the monster. Why can't you leave him be?"

"You don't know what I've done for him. You don't know what he means to me, and I can't stand by while he makes this mistake. You're not the one for him, Etienne. It's always been me."

"We'll see about that. When he gets here, we can ask him. Then you'll have your answer, and you'll abide by it." Etienne dragged his hand through his brown hair and turned away.

He couldn't risk it. "It's too late for that. You've blinded him. But when I show him what a life we can have once you're gone, he'll realize it was meant to be me all along."

And if he doesn't, we'll have the rest of eternity together. He'll come to see that I'm worthy of his love.

Etienne's head whipped around and his fists closed. As if they could protect him.

"You're insane, to think that after all you've done, all the violence and hate in you, the control, that Thierry could love you like he loves me. No one loves you, Olivier," he spat. "It's impossible. Not Henri. Not Aurelia. Not Thierry. Ask him and you'll hear the truth."

There existed no truth greater than Olivier's sacrifice in service of Thierry's love. And to have it spurned by this…this…*mortal*. He charged Etienne, his speed faster than anything he'd managed before, and slammed him against the tree. Something cracked, possibly a rib, hopefully Etienne's spine. He stepped back and the whore collapsed to the ground, gasping for breath. He sucked in air, coughing as he did so, and hunched on all fours.

"How did you do that?"

Olivier reached down and grabbed his hair, pulling him up to stand. "If I say Thierry belongs to me, then he belongs to me."

"We always said you were a devil, Olivier, but we didn't think it was actually true."

If they believed him evil, how could they fault him when he became evil? His fangs dropped, and Etienne reared back and swung his fists. The impact made less than that of a fly landing on his skin.

"There's no point in fighting. Thierry's mine, and that means there's no place in this world for you."

"He will never be yours." The whore wheezed. "He's mine as I am his. You know that. You've always known that."

Olivier's blood bubbled, and each burst urged him to kill. "You seduced him and filled his head with lies. I'm the one who's always been there, taking the punishment so he doesn't have to. Well, now we're going to be equals as we always should have been. We'll be mighty, we'll be immortal, and then our love will have the freedom to grow into what it always should have been."

"That'll never happen because no one could ever love you."

His teeth were in Etienne's neck before he knew what happened. The artery spurted hot blood into his mouth, and he bit through the sinew. Etienne struggled against him, his fists beat on his chest and tried to push him away, but he weakened until Olivier had to hold him up to his starving mouth. When Etienne's heart stopped, Olivier sucked hard to extract the last of his foe's blood. He'd take all that affection, that love that he professed. Thierry would see that he really could love.

After all, that's what he'd been trying to show him for as long as he could remember.

He withdrew his fangs. Etienne's body slumped to the ground, and Olivier spun at the weight of his father's hand clamping down on his shoulder.

Henri's fist struck his fifteen-year-old face, and the impact hurled him across the room. He slammed against the grubby floor and skidded through the straw. Henri stomped towards him, the great hulking frame of his father rising and falling with each berserker breath. From between his father's legs, he saw Thierry pressed against the wall where Henri had cornered him. The great ox didn't know one son from another when he was in this kind of fit, but Thierry couldn't suffer for this. His twin's fear swamped him. He had to push back.

Go! Run! He shouted the words inside his head, and Thierry heard them. His brother darted around Henri and grabbed Aurelia from the other room.

"Where are you two going?" their father snarled.

Aurelia's eyes narrowed, the defiance in them making Henri roar and forget about Olivier on the floor. Thierry didn't look back, just pulled her along behind him. Henri chased them, but Olivier leapt from the ground and tackled his father.

"Leave them!"

He wasn't strong enough to knock Henri over, but slamming his whole body into the brute distracted him so his siblings could get away. Henri's meaty hand grabbed him behind the neck. Henri shoved him against the wall so hard he thought he was going to go through it.

"You little shit. You don't get to tell me what to do. You're nothing, you little maggot. Nothing."

When he thought he'd be flattened and his bones would break, the pressure eased for a second before he was thrown and slammed into the table.

Please, no. Not again.

He pushed himself back so he could run, but Henri was too fast for him. The shock of all those other memories of being pinned and fucked weighed him down. Henri's hand closed around his neck again and forced his face against the wooden table. The rustle of his tunic, the rough grabbing at his hose. He struggled. He kicked back, but his father had been dealing with pigs and cows his whole life. The defenses of one boy were easy to knock aside.

As Henri took him, he was swept back to the first time he'd been forced to suffer his father's ire. Nausea rose up his stomach at the jolt of memory, and his heart constricted at the sound of Aurelia's crying from the other room.

Thirteen-year-old Thierry hugged him from behind, his forehead pressed against his back.

"We have to stop him," Thierry whispered.

"But what can we do?" They were not strong enough to fight their overbearing father. They'd seen him punch a man and split his skull. Power hummed in those fists. They were aware of it now that Mother was gone. It had all gotten worse since then. He hated hearing Aurelia's cries, but they were stuck. He'd managed to keep Henri away from Thierry as much as possible but Aurelia... If only they'd been triplets it might have been easier.

"We could kill him," his brother said.

"They'd hang us. All of us."

"We can't let this go on." Thierry sat up and shoved back the blanket and stood. His brother was going in there, but if he did, he might never come back and that crushed Olivier more than any sound coming from his sister.

Olivier grabbed Thierry's hand and swapped places with him. "Stay here."

"You can't do this alone."

"I won't let you get hurt."

He shoved Thierry back. His brother stumbled and fell, but Olivier didn't wait. His legs shook, but they carried him into the other room. The hulking mass of his father rose and fell in the shadows. His grunts crushed Aurelia's cries. Olivier's nose wrinkled at the smell of oranges, a moment of confusion, before it drowned in the stink of his father's sweat. He ran at Henri's side and the impact shook his body like he'd run into a wall, but the attack disturbed his father enough to throw him. He withdrew from Aurelia and growled like some beast in the darkness. Oranges bloomed again and stayed as Henri's fingers wrapped around Olivier's neck and pulled him down.

"Go," he whispered at Aurelia, and she scrambled out of the room as Henri pressed him down to the straw mattress and a ripe stench smothered him.

A warmth blossomed in his chest, Thierry's relief at having Aurelia close, and he held on to that, focused on it, filled his whole world with it, while he was raped. He didn't cry. What was the point? He had to stop feeling and instead hold on to the belief that what he was doing was for the good of them all.

Thierry would understand that.

But it became harder to think about Thierry with Henri savaging him and squashing him hard against the straw mattress while his skin rubbed raw. He needed to be strong. He held onto Thierry. His hands bunched into fists, and he cultivated that rage, that hate and fury, until it was a rod running through him.

Whatever Henri did to him, however much he grunted and groaned, his unsparing hand pressing down hard on the middle of his spine until he thought it would snap, he stuck to those murderous thoughts. Henri would one day suffer for what he did. He and Thierry would have their retribution. The more Henri fucked him, the more he stoked the fire for his own pyre, and however it happened he would get his revenge. He'd bide his time until the moment was right and when he was strong enough—

Olivier will pay for what he did.

He jolted out of the hovel and scraped against carpeted floor. The thread burned his cheek. A hand pushed down onto his back, a heavy weight across his hips. Henri had him pinned, but Henri was gone. Henri was dead.

He attempted to rise, should have been able to push off anyone who'd tried to keep him down, but it was no use. Then his hands burned, the carpet singeing, and he strained to look behind him and gasped.

It was…*him.*

For half a breathless moment he thought it was Thierry because his mind bucked at the impossibility of seeing himself…feeling himself…but he couldn't deny that the creature looming over him was Olivier d'Arjou. Unfettered, snarling, his eyes golden and glowing, attention fixed on what squirmed beneath him. His hand tore his clothes until he was naked. He knew what was going to happen, but he couldn't stop it, couldn't use his magic, couldn't fight this inevitability. The sound of this other him's belt unbuckling, the fly popping. How could this happen to him? By him?

I don't deserve this. Why can't I beat him?

Thoughts tumbled over one another and names flittered through his head, chasing and devouring one another.

See what you did to me!

I can't stop this. Why aren't I strong enough?

Why is this happening to me again?

This other him bit into his palm and lathered his hard cock with blood, smeared it in between his ass cheeks, and forced a bloody finger inside. He tensed but other-Olivier pushed deeper and scoured him. He couldn't keep him out. He couldn't get him out.

Not again. Don't do this to me again.

The light shifted, and he was back in the hovel. The weight bearing down on him changed. The stench overpowered him. He bucked again. And was thrown forward in time.

He was the witch, the panic rising, knowing what was going to happen, that he was probably going to die from this, and his magic, the one thing he'd held onto throughout his life, the one thing that had made him stronger than everyone else, was going to be absolutely useless in the face of this strength. He couldn't let this happen to him, couldn't let the vampire get inside him. He was meant to be stronger than this.

But he could do nothing. The vampire *was* stronger, that was it. Brawn kept him down, a hand splayed across his back kept him compliant. He fought when the vampire forced his way into him, just as he'd fought every time Henri had taken him.

No, that wasn't me. I wasn't there. That was YOUR memory, not mine.

He had to struggle; Henri wouldn't let him take it quietly. He needed to dominate, needed to fight. The bastard knew Olivier would rather lie there, that it was easier to accept this fate, to let him ride him until he was spent, and go on planning. But Henri punched him and rattled him, told him to fight back so he could see him bested. The burning pain of being ploughed against his will, being torn up and threshed.

After a while, Henri didn't notice when he stopped fighting.

Did you see when I stopped fighting, too?

He hissed. The thought wasn't his. But it was. He stopped fighting. He couldn't feel it. His body had gone numb and his mind had drifted. He was aware of the vampire riding him, but he'd retreated deep inside behind protective glass. He could see out. Could vaguely hear it, but it was still out there. Happening to someone else.

And all that inhabited this space with him was a cold fury, a murderous wish that he would never conquer him again, that he would never be weakened to this state again. He'd have his revenge even if it used up his last breath.

The glass cracked when Olivier bit into his shoulder, but it was like being in a car that had plunged into the bottom of a lake. The glass withstood the pressure for a while, but eventually it caved, and water gushed in. He stayed behind, let the water drown him. He'd have to wait to fight back if he wanted any chance of destroying the monster.

The vampire left, slunk off to wherever he went.

Like Henri used to.

Disgusted with his son, disgusted with himself. A kick to the ribs on the bad days. Ha, like *that* was a bad day. As if they weren't all bad days. But it didn't matter by then. He'd left his mark, had defiled him, had taken and shown him that the strongest always wins.

He'd tried so desperately to not be Henri. He'd seen

how Thierry looked at their father with fear, freezing when their father's face flushed. Is that why he'd turned away? He'd tried to protect him, protect them all, but he'd succeeded in turning himself into a monster, replacing the one they had. Fighting Henri the only way he knew how, with absolute strength and ferocity.

And Aurelia hadn't been grateful for his interference. Did he expect gratitude? Perhaps she thought he deserved what he got after all the times he made her cry as a child. He'd wanted her to hate him so she wouldn't feel guilty that he'd taken the abuse for her. Maybe she didn't even remember. What did it matter?

The memories—his, Thierry's, the witch's—retreated and he was forced back into the dungeon. His hands bound. Footsteps shuffled on the floor as he steadied himself, his breathing ragged and forced. The witch was looking at him, he could sense it, but he kept his face downturned. The fire had been doused in a cold ooze that dripped down the length of his torso. He couldn't bear to see the triumph, to know that the witch knew it all, knew all that he'd kept buried with a stake through its heart. And seeing his accusations… Well, he had no wish to see them either.

Nausea hovered. Centuries of chasing after Thierry, desperate for his love at the same time as fighting the world, fighting his brother, fighting himself when it had all been for nothing. He'd done this to himself for nothing more than hope. He'd deluded himself that Thierry's recent betrayal with Alex had been just his acting out. Underneath it all, he'd been so sure that Thierry loved him above all others.

Despite the evidence.

All for them. All to save them.

Used. Abused. Discarded.

None of them realized it. Or if they did, they didn't care. He'd never asked for their thanks, but he'd be lying if a bit of credit wouldn't have helped.

But monsters aren't allowed to be heroes.

How many lives had he destroyed to fill the hole that truth had torn?

One of them was standing in front of him.

That was rich. The only person to have seen what he'd been through, the one person who might understand, he'd burned completely. This little exposure had been the witch's revenge. It should have made them even, though he knew from experience he'd never be forgiven. His sins were endless. He could never be redeemed. No one thought it possible, so no one bothered.

Words bulged in his neck, a stone swallowed and lodged. If it worked itself loose, then maybe he would be free. But the pressure was too great, and it was too jammed in. The tears backed up behind his eyes, straining, the pain building inside his head. Wrung out and wretched, he let himself hang. He should have been fighting to stand, to face the foe who'd attempted to—

The witch approached, the blaze of his body that much closer, but still he couldn't bring himself to look. He turned further away. He sought something to fix on, but he had no strength. He drifted, his mind stumbling from memory to memory, year to year, every heartache, every shame. The bodies of men and women and children he'd left in pieces behind him, the blood he'd drunk in an endless need to slake his greatest unquenchable thirst. Eyes and hands that pleaded with him, words that defied but also begged, cries as he, the cruel Reaper, dispatched them without a care. Because why should he care? That was life. There was nothing in it for him, and there was nothing worthwhile in it for them. Each one weighed down on him, dragging him deeper and deeper into the still, murky darkness where screams couldn't be heard. Sinking beyond where anyone could reach him.

Bergamot came closer but it didn't matter. Even the smell of witch couldn't provoke his usual disgust. He didn't resist when fingers brushed his cheekbone, continued through his hair and around to the back of his head. Whatever the witch wanted to do to him, he didn't care.

The witch lifted his head and pushed it towards his bared throat. Blood pumping fast, the artery throbbed. He heard it, the sound quickening his heart. He inhaled the scent of sweat and blood, and his stomach growled.

No.

He reared back, throwing his head like a horse fighting its bridle. He wouldn't drink from this one again. He'd already taken too much and given nothing in return.

"Drink, Olivier." The commanding tone in the witch's voice forced him to look into those earth eyes. He couldn't be doing this willingly. It must be another trick.

The witch repeated his order. The chains lengthened and loosened enough for him to reach the other side of his cell if he ran. His arms and legs relaxed from their stranglehold. His aching muscles groaned at being able to move freely again, but he didn't take his attention off the witch. He backed away, trying to escape through the wall.

"I won't drink from you again."

The witch stepped closer. "Drink."

He said it so clearly, so surely. He took another step.

Olivier pushed him away. "I won't."

But the witch returned. "I am giving you what you need."

"I won't harm you again." He turned his face to the side. Why wouldn't the witch leave? Did he want his enemy's defeat to be resounding? He had won, he had seen through to the marrow and now what? He wanted to suck it out? To prove that he was nothing more than a leech, a *monster*? All those words that he'd drawn to himself to form a shield turned their barbs inwards. He couldn't bear them any longer.

But the witch wanted to see him torn apart absolutely.

"Drink." He closed the tiny distance between them again.

Olivier shoved him harder, enough to send him across the room, but not hard enough to cause injury.

I will not hurt him.

But the witch came again.

"What do you want from me? I have nothing left!"

Still the witch came. "I am giving you my blood, freely and willingly."

"Then you're an idiot."

The witch grabbed the sides of his head and held him still. "For fuck's sake. Drink!"

He wrestled with the witch, attempting to throw him off, but he had empowered himself and wouldn't budge. The intensity of his stare, those brown eyes harder than a mountain, defied him. Olivier scrambled to avoid those eyes, but they transfixed him.

"I forgive you."

The witch couldn't mean it. Not after what he'd done. Not after what had been thrown at him. But even if it were a lie, he couldn't deny the sledgehammer to his chest that those words wrought.

"I cannot be forgiven." He looked into eyes that no longer accused, that no longer burned with the vengeance of the wronged. His throat strained. If he spoke any louder, he'd break.

"I forgive you."

"No." To be forgiven meant he'd have to change and

become better than he was, but after so long that was too hard. It was already hard enough to deny the blood in front of him.

"I—"

"No!" Olivier roared.

The witch smiled, but it wasn't a mocking smile, it wasn't a leering grin of triumph. It was built with kindness, a joyful, cautious smile. One he'd not seen in a long time, if ever.

"I forgive you."

The dead wood that was him split and revealed a trace of green center. Olivier's vision wavered as relief spiraled through his body. What a blessing to be forgiven. He breathed in the sweet smell of oranges, and his body shook. Oh god, he couldn't cry. Not him. Not here. He sucked it back, restrained it as emotion fired through him. All the despair and the joy, the regrets and the shame, flowing through him in their own way.

But before he could weep, the witch took his head and pressed it into his throat.

"Drink," he whispered again, "and heal yourself."

His lips stayed closed for a second. He was not worthy of this, but the hunger, the need, the gratitude overcame him, erupted in his jaw and prised it open to free his fangs. With all the self-restraint he could muster, he popped Oberon's silken skin. The witch tensed and sucked in his breath at the piercing, but his hand, instead of pulling him back, pressed him down.

Sweet nectar flowed over his tongue; a parched riverbed doused with the first rains of the season. Caramel and roses bloomed in his nose as his mouth filled with the witch's freely given blood. He swallowed it as more pumped in. He lapped it hungrily, the thick liquid filling his belly as he thirsted. Solace washed through him, such joy at being so fed, so replenished. He hugged the witch tight, pulled harder on his veins, inhaled his scent of sweat and earth, loving the way the witch smelled, the feel of his body against him, of warmth, of willingness.

He drank.

And he drank.

"Olivier," the witch finally whispered, his voice shaky.

But he didn't hear it, not consciously, remembering it when he found himself sucking hard against a flailing pulse.

"Oli—" and then nothing.

He snapped out of the fugue, Oberon's limp body in his grip. Panic stampeded across his chest.

"No, no, no, no, no, NO!"

He lay Oberon on the ground, kneeling behind him, about to shake him, but he knew intimately the despondent thump of a heart near death. Unresponsive, Oberon's eyes stared at nothing.

Oh god, what had he done?

He raised his wrist to his mouth, ready to bite, but stopped.

Is this how I should repay his gift?

Oberon would loathe him for turning him into a monster. That would be the last resort. It would come soon, but he had to try something else, something he'd never do for himself. Crouching on all fours, Oberon's blood giving him renewed strength, he inhaled and with the entire force of his voice, roared for Aurelia.

VIII

After an eternity of falling down, Oberon ascended, rushing out of his body and into a new space… Though it wasn't new at all. The muted gray and violet triggered his memories and fear, freezing him in place, locking him into an endless purgatory.

He couldn't see anything—he was barely there himself—yet he spun, or at least he thought he spun, but then he was looking in more directions at once than should have been possible. Or *would* have been were he not on the astral and on the brink of death. Suddenly facing one way then instantly the next, he searched, not caring how it was done, just that he could do it, that he could prepare for anything that snuck up on him.

Like a demon.

Last time that woman had turned into a demon. But hadn't there been two of them?

Olivier had drained him then as he had now, and he'd drifted and found himself lost. She'd called to him and, when he returned to his body, all he'd known was that he could never die again.

Which is why he'd come to Aurelia and agreed to feed Olivier and act as his guardian.

No, he'd come for revenge because of what Olivier had done.

And had done again.

But it was different this time.

Did Olivier care that he'd drained him? Had he been wrong to give him his blood? Had Olivier's remorse and sorrow all been for show?

No. He'd felt what Olivier had felt. That couldn't be faked.

While he couldn't hate him for causing this, he sure as hell didn't want to stick around. But he had no way to get back. Last time… What had happened last time?

The realization slammed into his head. Sinara had rescued him. Aurelia's mother, guardian over them all. Dead. And he was where…

Where Xadrak ruled.

Alone.

His mind darted as he did, searching in the distance on all sides of himself for anyone. Should he travel? If he went up, would he die? If he went down, would he be lost? What was he going to do?

He couldn't die. He had to return. He was meant for something. Sinara had made sure of that, that's why she'd sent him back. That's why she'd protected him from Xadrak. She'd… Yes, that's what she'd done. She'd shielded him while an army attacked her. He saw it all around him again, the recollection summoning ghosts. The terror at being surrounded by evil shook him. She'd said it wasn't time, that he was needed. She'd called him a key.

The key.

His heart seized, silencing the beating, and stopping it from alerting others to his presence.

No, no, no. Not him. Not the thing they were looking for. Not the one they were going to use and destroy. He couldn't die. Not like this. Not like that. He quaked. He looked at his hands and they quivered as well, their outline becoming fuzzy then fading even more until he blended into the nothingness and reformed in sharp lines lit with violet light. He shook his head and his human form returned. Would dying now be preferable to dying later?

But he didn't want to die at all.

"Don't go."

He hissed at the sight of Hame standing in front of him. He solidified again before something broke off him like a sheet of ice separating and plummeting into the ocean.

Then another and another. He was breaking faster, growing weaker, the fear requiring too much energy to keep him there.

Hame held out his hand. "We need you."

"I won't be used again." He stepped back.

"You won't be used. You'll be helping us, helping the world. It's what we've all been made for, even you."

"I don't want to be a sacrifice in a war I never asked to be a part of."

"You will survive this, I guarantee it."

"Don't believe him." A voice growled from behind. The sound of bones crunching under foot jittered through his body. The world turned dark. Hame shrank.

He didn't want to turn, but as the thought came, he faced the demon. Oily black skin covered muscles and talons and horns. More of himself shook loose. He wouldn't get the chance to be used; he was going to die there and then.

The demon wasn't as big as he'd been before, standing only a head or two taller, but he sucked all energy towards himself. He drew all the hope and good thoughts in. More pieces of himself disappeared.

"He can't guarantee anything," the demon rumbled. "Liars and idiots, the pair of them, him and Aurelia."

"And what can you offer anyone other than pain and death?" Hame shouted.

"I don't need to offer anything." His clawed hand opened, and black light shot out and ensnared Hame. He struggled but the bonds wrapped tight, and Hame's face twisted in agony. The demon turned his glowing eyes back down.

Oberon faded. This is what the demon wanted. He wanted him dead so the key couldn't be used to banish him. Xadrak advanced, opening his mouth to reveal jagged blackened fangs. He retreated but couldn't move fast enough, could barely move back a single step without buckling.

"So weak and terrified. Like Olivier."

He was unable to make a sound, but Hame's screams may as well have been his own. Paralyzed, he watched as the demon's claw descended towards him, heading for his neck, and the triumphant look on his gnarled and horrifying face shredded him even more. The demon was going to kill him, and all his scheming had been for nothing.

He braced for the final shattering of his soul and the rendering of his connection with life.

The claw touched him, and he hurtled down, down, down…

IX

Too many screams. Aurelia strained to concentrate on growing the baby, while her heart urged her to listen to the cries of her coven. Even Olivier's mad howling wanted her attention. But she couldn't relent. She was doing this for them, for all of them.

For two days she'd stayed behind while others risked their lives. Her belly popped the day before, rounding with the hardness growing inside her. Sinara, whose power circulated through her body stronger now, aided her as much as she could, providing what comfort she could while demanding more.

She had no way of knowing when she'd be big enough. Perhaps the next day, considering her growth rate, but that was a guess. She was impatient for it. And Viktor's silence didn't help.

A sense of knowing came through from Sinara.

"I know, Mother. All will be well. Have faith. Stay the course. But is it too much to ask that for once things go easy?"

Bemusement rippled through her. She continued the

flow.

But the flow was easing. Her mother's involvement reduced to a fraction of what it had been. Her own power was almost drained, but she barreled on with it, thinking it was needed.

And not wanting to believe that the time had come.

She poured more of herself into the working, but Sinara closed her off completely. Cut from giving more, the power had been snipped at the source. And the bottom of her compressed and squished stomach dropped. Sinara would be born soon. Her baby would be born soon, and she'd be—

Hame's terror-streaked thoughts smashed into her and forced her to her knees. He'd been caught. Xadrak had him. But through his babbling terror, she heard his message.

Oberon is…the key.

Then he was gone.

She raced down the connection—relieved that there still *was* a connection—but he'd slammed her out. Wherever he was, she couldn't go. Not to his mind, not out there on the astral where Xadrak had trapped him. But she could return to his body.

And Oberon…

To think the fucking key had been under her nose the whole time.

They finally had it. She had all the pieces.

She rose off the ground but as she stood a knife sliced through her stomach, from the inside out, and cramping brought her back to her knees, gripping her belly and silently shrieking.

No, this can't happen now.

She needed to get back to them. Spasms lessened before they returned. Was it labor? Was there something else? She cried out, not from the contractions, but from being stuck there, where she couldn't rescue Hame and ensure Oberon's safety.

Xadrak knew. He had to know. And that meant he'd come looking for the three pieces, using every means possible to get them so she had to—

Pain spiraled through her, and she reached out for anything to hold onto and crush in her hands. She reached forward.

And Viktor's hand gripped hers.

She squeezed, looking up into his eyes, his face smeared with dirt and blood and his clothes shredded. He was there.

"Hame's been taken, but we've found the key," she grunted.

"Damn the key. I'm more worried about you." He helped her up slowly and walked her around the room.

Her blood hummed with the need to do something, to lend her aid, but even standing brought with it too much agony. She couldn't go anywhere. Helplessness crushed her. Again, she was useless, not where she should be. At least Oberon and Olivier were safe, and they were better staying where they were.

Olivier…

His howls.

Oh, god!

She swung her sight to the dungeon. Oberon at Olivier's feet, not moving, drained of blood, remains smeared across Olivier's wide mouth. He roared like the insane monster he was, and he'd just destroyed their chances of defeating Xadrak. She had to get there and get there now.

But as she banished the vision, her head swam, and nausea swamped her. She fainted into Viktor's waiting arms and pain chased her down into unconsciousness.

X

Oberon's breathing got shallower. Soon it would stop altogether. But Olivier maintained his screams, his fangs bared ready to gouge open his wrist if Aurelia didn't come soon to rescue him.

Hurry, Aurelia!

He watched the jerking rise and fall of Oberon's chest, and as his time ran out, he raised his wrist to his teeth and stopped screaming long enough to bite into his flesh and rip open a hole. His blood bubbled up into his mouth then he pulled his arm away to—

The door burst open, his manacles tightened, shortened, and flung him back against the wall as a blond witch entered.

"Help him!" Olivier shouted, not caring who this was. "Heal him!"

The witch rushed over, followed by that whore. Thierry hovered at the entrance, stuck. So, he *was* there. He *had* heard him. Not that it mattered. But while Thierry was barred, his body slamming against a solid nothingness as he tried to get at him, the whore and the witch approached Oberon's body.

"Don't turn him!" Panic whirled through his body at the young vampire being so close. He struggled against his bonds, wanting to get nearer to help, to save him from that fate. Oberon would never want to become one of them.

They ignored him as they sank to their knees and placed their hands on Oberon's body. Was he still breathing? Had they come too late? Filtering out the distraction of Thierry's snarling at the doorway, he focused on Oberon's chest and watched for any change in his breathing.

Concentration lined the brows of the two men working over Oberon. Why had he taken so much blood? Why had Oberon offered himself? But he'd been so relieved at such willingness that he'd lost himself in it. Unable to stop. Wanting to drown himself. And all he'd succeeded in doing was bring Oberon once again to the gates of death.

"You're a disease, Olivier," Thierry snarled from the doorway.

He ignored him. Or he tried to.

"How many more of your messes will we have to clean up?"

"Thierry, you're not helping," the blond witch barked.

His brother paced. At least he was free to do that. He would have done the same but for his shackles.

"Come on, Oberon," Alex whispered, eyes closed, body crouched low, and the muscles in his neck straining. What from? The blood? The effort? If Alex bit him—

Oberon's lungs expanded like large bellows.

He breathed.

He lived.

Olivier slumped against his manacles, legs and arms slackening as the tension broke.

I haven't killed him.

Since when had he ever been relieved about that?

"Let's get him upstairs." The witch wiped the sweat from his brow, a whiff of violets drifting through the air. Alex scooped the unconscious Oberon into his arms. Whatever power the young vampire had, he poured it into Oberon's resurrection.

"Thank you," Olivier whispered, but the two men didn't hear him, or if they did, they ignored him. Shunned him. After all, he'd nearly killed Oberon.

"Will he live?" he asked, louder this time.

"Thanks to Alex," the witch said. "If he'd died, then we'd all be royally fucked. The sooner you've served your purpose, the better."

His skin went cold; the hairs on his arms and the back of his neck bristled. What did he mean by that? What were they going to do to him?

And who *was* Oberon?

But they had no time to answer. The witch was impatient to be gone.

Alex carried Oberon away; this would be the last time he'd see him. Not that he had any right to claim him, but the potential loss, of not knowing what was going to happen next, had him straining to keep his eye on the tattooed witch as long as possible.

Like a piece of him had been taken.

Alex and that other one left the dungeon and, before the door swung shut, Thierry's brow knitted in a question unasked. The door clanged shut, and Olivier was left alone with the smell of spilt blood and the oily stain of guilt dripping down his spine.

XI

THE WRITHING AND PUNCHING INSIDE AURELIA'S BELLY brought her out of the darkness and to a late-night New York lit with city lights that hid the stars. She brought her knees up as far as she could in Viktor's large bed and hugged herself until the latest wave passed. It came quickly and went quickly but she fortified herself for the next. Every part of her body ached, her hair wet with sweat and the worries of Oberon rushed in, impatient they'd had to wait. She scried for him, finding the witch asleep on a bed, his neck healed and with Thierry and Alex watching over him. His chest rose and fell steadily. Her held breath burst out of her, ugly and heavy but welcome, and she fell back on the mattress.

He lived.

All three pieces were in one place.

Another contraction took hold and she curled up on her side, calling out as it surprised her. Viktor appeared and rubbed her back. Whether magic or his simple touch, she unwound and stretched a little, but she didn't have long before another contraction came, and soon after that another, and another.

"It's coming," she croaked.

He pulled back the covers and helped raise her, stuffing pillows behind her to support her back. She dripped with sweat, her hair plastered to her scalp, but the time was here, all too soon but not soon enough. She wanted this done with but no, she refused, it couldn't come yet.

"I don't want to do this." She pleaded with Viktor as if he could do something about it. "It's not time. How can it be time?"

Another contraction. And this time even more painful, even stronger than before, bearing down through her, the baby wanting out. She screamed as it broke her apart, fighting against her wish to keep it in and stop it from destroying her.

Whatever it was, human or demon or both, sunk its claws into her, using whatever it could find to gain purchase, its nails digging in and ripping chunks out of her. Scream after scream after—

White flooded the world. She winged out of her body, taken away from the mess and misery. Not of her own design, she rose away from the pain, vaguely aware of her body left to do the work, going through the motions, but that was so far away it mattered nothing.

A hand touched her shoulder and she turned to her mother, not in the guise of the demoness but as she'd been when human. Elaine with her raven hair and brown eyes, her short, solid stature.

"I'm proud of you, my darling." Elaine's arms opened.

She dove into them, and they enfolded around her, so real, so *there*, and so comforting. Sinara had been with her throughout the pregnancy, but it had been muted and abstract. What it would have been like to have Elaine there to hold her hand, to wipe her forehead, to kiss her and guide her through this. To share another of those moments that they'd never had.

Aurelia held on harder. "What should I expect? What will happen next?"

"Birth will drain my strength and as I fully enter the earthly plane, I will need a little time. Time to adjust, time to grow."

"But we don't have any. We need you. Xadrak could come for us any day, now he knows Oberon is the key."

"It can't be helped."

"And for how long am I meant to be a nursemaid?" She couldn't bite back her disappointment. She needed Sinara to show them what to do, to *fight*. What could she do with a crying babe? Still, she didn't pull back. This would be the last time she'd see her mother's form like this, would be the last time she'd have such a bond and easy connection between their emotions. It stripped her raw.

"It won't be as long as you expect, but you need to think of my protection first, not of running into battles that put you in danger."

A strangled cry escaped her lips. "But I've been so absent. They need me. They're dying."

"They are stronger than you know. They know what they're doing. Have faith in their abilities and in yours as a leader. You don't need to do everything yourself. Lean on Viktor. Lean on Mira. Lean on Zoe. They will keep you strong. And soon, I will be there to aid you."

She had no other words to say and filling the air with them was a waste of precious time. Elaine's body shifted, signaling even this moment had come to its conclusion.

"Ready?"

She held her daughter and kissed both cheeks, a smile on her face, a look full of pride and love that broke Aurelia's heart as the vision faded and she returned to her body to give birth to their savior.

XII

OBERON JOLTED AWAKE TO THE ANXIOUS INTERROGATION of Alex's sparkling blue eyes. The vampire smiled to reveal bright white fangs. The sight sent Oberon scurrying up the bed. He tried to calm his rapid breathing but being in the same room with the young vampire—alone—brought him to a panic.

"Good, he's awake. We can leave." Thierry's cutting voice sounded from the corner.

Not alone, after all.

Alex sighed, his eyes shining with preternatural light that mesmerized. Olivier's golden eyes had that allure too. Maybe it was a vampire thing.

"What happened?"

"Olivier nearly killed you."

"And Alex saved you from your own stupidity," Thierry said.

A chill skittered up Oberon's spine, raising goosebumps in its wake. The room was dimly lit, and Olivier's twin sat in shadow.

The memories pressed behind his eyes. Hame finding

185

him, telling him he was the key, *knowing* it as he'd known it the first time he'd died but forgotten. Then almost dying, being shredded by the demon's claw. But now he was back.

Did they know?

"Ungrateful bastard," Thierry muttered.

He should thank Alex, but his throat sealed tight. He looked to the door, expecting Aurelia to burst in and drag him to the dungeon to be imprisoned.

"Don't worry, he's locked up," Alex said.

He frowned. "What?"

"Olivier. He's still chained to the wall."

"I wasn't worried about him."

"Oh." Alex looked down at his hands in his lap.

Thierry leaned forward in his seat, and his face emerged out of the gloom. "Alex saved your life and you look at him like he's diseased. You'd better be nicer, or I'll take it personally."

He hadn't intended to offend Alex and of course Thierry was right. If he could understand what had made Olivier the way he was, and even forgive—

His body stilled and inside his chest a question echoed.

Had he forgiven him?

He probed for some emotional sensitivity, a flinching around his heart, a sickness in his gut, but he didn't find anything.

He had forgiven Olivier, before and after being drained of blood.

If he could do that, then Alex, who had done nothing to him, deserved his respect as well.

But he didn't need a friend.

"If you don't like it, Thierry, you can fuck off," he hissed. "I've had enough of your brother to last me an eternity, I don't need you aggravating me as well like the second-rate copy you are."

Thierry approached him so fast that Oberon slammed into the headboard. He struggled to keep the vampire's face in focus, and instead his gaze darted from one fury-filled eye to the other.

"There is no comparison between me and my brother." His voice rumbled. "He's insane and vicious and devoid of anything good. That is not me."

"So you think."

Alex sighed. "Let's go." He tugged on Thierry's sleeve, and the vampire's eyes flashed red. But Thierry's hate didn't affect his heart; Alex's weariness and sadness on the other hand…

It couldn't be helped. They were the ones who'd survive this, whereas he was going to be torn apart. Hame had—

"Where's Aurelia?"

Miraculously, the vampires stopped. Thierry ignored him but Alex turned. "We don't know, but until she comes back, Carn says you're not to leave the lair."

"Why?" Unless Hame had got a message through to Carn that he was the key.

Alex hesitated.

Yeah, he knows.

"They're the orders. Carn can explain."

"Where is he?"

"He's with Hame. Something's wrong with him so maybe give him some time."

Then they were gone.

As soon as the door closed, he jumped off the bed, an ache shooting up his legs and back from having been thrown out of the astral and into his body. He ripped off his stained shirt and pants, summoned replacements, and dressed. He touched his neck where Olivier had bit him, wiping away flecks of dried blood. The puncture marks had closed.

So much for *jamais encore.*

He cracked the door and stuck his head out into an empty corridor. Muffled voices came from down the hall. Thierry? Carn? He didn't hang around to decipher the sounds. It would either be about Hame or about him and what was going to happen to them all next. At least Aurelia wasn't there. She'd have the answers, but the way Hame had pleaded with him on the astral, he didn't want to hear them. Would the oracle be alright?

He couldn't think about it. Instead he suppressed the nausea sloshing around in his stomach and hurried away. The mountain's exit beckoned. To hell with their dictum. He'd leave if he wanted to. They weren't going to use him like they'd use Olivier.

He ran down the tunnel to the exit, and darkness enveloped him. He walked through the pitch black until a dim light at the end guided him out—and back to where he'd started. A wrong turn? He tried again, his pulse quickening as he sprinted in and returned to the spot he'd left. No exit. He might not be locked in the dungeon, but he was trapped.

Frantic, he tried to blast his way out with magic, but it made no difference. In and out, back to the beginning, locked in a perpetual loop controlled by another's whim. Running but getting nowhere, his breaths getting shorter and shorter as he kept getting spat out into this prison.

He and Olivier had more in common than he thought.

He could pour more of himself into breaking the spell but that would alert Carn. Would it be better to play dumb, stay behind, and wait for an opportunity?

Or maybe he didn't have to escape at all.

He wasn't the only piece to the puzzle.

He hurried down the tunnel and flung open the door to Olivier's prison. The vampire shot up at his appearance, his eyes shining and his mouth widening in shocked pleasure.

"You're okay!" The chains rattled as Olivier repositioned himself.

His heart paused and he halted at the threshold. Having a vampire pleased to see you was not typically a good thing. "Yeah, Alex saved me."

Olivier's half-smile crashed. "I'm grateful they came to your rescue, but seeing them again…"

Whatever he thought about Olivier, he had to put it aside. This was about his own survival. He hurried up to the vampire, the chains and manacles warning that what he was about to do was not a good idea. But what other choice was there?

"I should ap—"

"Do you know what they've got planned?"

Olivier shut his mouth over his apology and some of the arrogance returned to his eyes. "More torture as far as I know. But the blond witch said something about you being important, like losing you would be a great tragedy."

Olivier sounded like he didn't believe that. Perhaps what they'd shared was cast aside, and Olivier was the best actor the world had ever known. The blood stuck to his mouth and chin would be enough evidence of that. How could someone once so noble turn into something so twisted? Everything about him drew you in, sweetness and light, soulful brown eyes, an attractiveness that verged on the painful, and when his eyes were soft and his mouth relaxed, he was just a dark-haired beautiful man that could make him feel—

He reached up and used his thumb to rub away some of the dried flakes below Olivier's bottom lip. His hand was steady, but his heart thrashed, intensifying under Olivier's searching gaze.

"What are you, Oberon?"

His hand froze and he forced himself to step back from unsteady ground. Would Olivier use him to save his own ancient skin? Or was he safe from the vampire? He had one way of finding out.

He summoned his strength and released his power. The chains slackened, manacles opened, and Olivier landed free on the ground.

"What are you doing?" Olivier hesitated.

"They're going to use us and I'm sick of it. But I can't leave so I want you to try."

He flinched. "You're letting me go? Aurelia will make your life hell."

"She's going to anyway, whether you're here or not."

"Is this a trick?"

"I'm done with games, Olivier."

He took a few steps forward. The air between them filled with heavy possibilities. "Aren't you frightened?"

"I trust you, or at least I want to. What's the difference?"

Olivier's eyes narrowed. "What do you want from me?"

He paused. There was the slightest chance that Aurelia believed locking Olivier in the dungeon would be enough.

"All I want is for you to try to escape. I don't know whether you can get out or not—it's only a theory—but if we don't try, we're going to be waiting around for our fate. Aurelia will come back, and that will be it. I've seen what we're up against. I don't want to be a part of it."

Olivier's tongue rolled over his bottom lip.

"Please, go. I don't know how much time we have."

"It won't work," Olivier stated with a surety of

someone adept at making plans. "And if it does, they'll find me as soon as I step outside."

"I never pegged you as someone who'd give up so easily. Not after what I did to you."

"And I never thought you'd be willing to help me considering what I did to you."

Oberon glanced away, finding it harder to breathe than he did a moment ago. What had seemed like a good idea while swapping memories was now tarnished with idiocy. Could what they have shared neutralized Olivier to the point where he was no longer a threat to his safety?

But this isn't about Olivier. It's about me.

If Aurelia or her enemies didn't have all the pieces, then his own life would continue for as long as possible.

"We can either argue or you can do what I ask."

Olivier looked at him for a long time. Locked in this limbo, Oberon wondered if he'd made the right choice after all. Should he have tried harder to escape on his own? He'd be able to hide himself better than Olivier could— not that the vampire wouldn't put up a fight. But Aurelia was distracted, Carn too, and that might give them the time they needed, time he could use to figure out how to get out of there and ensure he wasn't used as another pawn.

"Well?" he asked.

"So I've got this straight, you want me to escape because it'll mean saving your own skin?"

"Isn't that what you'd do?"

Olivier chuckled. "I suppose. And there's the added bonus of seriously pissing off my sister. But you'll get into trouble."

"Do you care?"

What they'd shared was one thing, but he was giving

Olivier his freedom. He expected the vampire to not give this a second thought.

Olivier bit his bottom lip, but his eyes crackled with unspoken thoughts. He spun and walked through the door. That was enough of an answer. Oberon hurried to keep up.

Olivier strode up the tunnel, his arms tensing as he opened and closed his fists. Would Thierry come looking for him? Would Olivier leave without seeking revenge on his brother? The risks mounted the higher they climbed, but he hoped he could direct Olivier.

They reached the exit without incident, but as Olivier stood staring into the darkness, he raised his head and sniffed the air, caught on a whiff of something, perhaps Thierry, or Alex, or the scent of magic. He inhaled and closed his eyes, his muscles bulging as he stood rigid to the spot. His jaw clamped shut. He fought but he couldn't stay to fight.

Oberon touched his arm, and Olivier's eyes flicked open. They stood locked as the vampire glared down at him, all menace and hate pouring out of amber eyes. Oberon didn't flinch. He didn't back down. He held on and defied Olivier's gaze until it eased, and he relaxed and bowed his head.

"Hopefully this is goodbye."

"Yes," Olivier said. "Hopefully."

He lingered. Remorse? From Olivier?

This might not work.

"Go," he said, "before they know you're gone."

Olivier slipped away. But as he disappeared, the draw to stay by him worked doubly hard, pulling stronger than it ever had. Olivier's charisma, that magnetism that drew people to their dooms, magnified, despite the voice screaming inside his head that Olivier had to leave. Never had Olivier's pull been that fierce. There'd been attraction, curiosity, and allure. Natural for a beautiful man enhanced with vampirism or whatever, but this time… This time he felt Olivier wanted him.

Don't go, he imagined he heard, but it could have been a hangover from what he'd done to the vampire. Sharing that much had already knocked him off his equilibrium, he should have expected more, expected worse.

Still—and he'd die before he admitted it aloud—there were worse things than wanting to be in Olivier's arms.

And they would all come to pass if the vampire didn't leave.

Oberon forced himself to stay put to make sure Olivier didn't re-emerge, holding onto a breathless hope. An earthquake rumbled through the rocks and shook the mountain. He steadied himself as his breath shuddered inside his chest. Aurelia's spell had detected her brother's attempt to escape. He backed away as Olivier came rushing back.

"What the hell was that?" Olivier said.

"I… I don't know. An alarm?"

The mountain shook again, then paused, before more bone-rattling vibrations rolled through the home.

"I guess that's—"

They stopped at the shouting from Carn, Thierry and Alex as they ran down the hall towards them, their faces lit with shock, and their eyes widening at seeing him standing with Olivier. Another attack, stronger than before, cracked the roof and he looked up in time to see it crashing down. He was going to be crushed. He raised his arms to protect himself. Olivier grabbed him and pulled him out of the way, carrying him back down the tunnel towards the dungeon. Slumped over Olivier's shoulder, falling rocks sealed them off from Carn, Thierry and Alex.

Olivier ran while the mountain broke apart. Someone was trying to get in.

Oberon cast light for Olivier to see, and they burst through a door at the end as more of the roof crumbled and dropped stones on his head.

They entered a white-walled chamber. Olivier placed him back on his feet and spun to guard the door. "Please stop that blood," he growled.

Oberon's hand shot to the back of his head and came away wet. He grimaced, healed the wound, and wiped his bloody hand on his jeans. He surveyed the room, spotting a dagger on an obsidian altar. This was Aurelia's inner sanctum. He grabbed the hilt and his sweaty palm buzzed. The presence of magic eased the tremor in his hand but didn't stop the world shaking. He searched for another way out, but they were at a dead-end. He would have to make their own exit.

"I smell sulfur," Olivier said.

Brandishing the blade, he pulled Olivier back towards him and cut a circle into the air. Blue light poured out the tip to form a perfect sphere above, below, and around. Olivier's nose twitched.

Oberon enhanced the shield with sigils to protect them from physical and magical attacks. The last sigil locked into place as a head-sized chunk of rock plummeted towards them. Olivier forced Oberon to the ground and shielded him with his body, but the rock rebounded and slid off the defenses. Safe, Olivier helped Oberon to his feet.

"Thanks."

Olivier's mouth hitched up in the corner.

Would Olivier protect him given the chance to save himself?

Questions for later. He had to focus. While the destruction became more violent and he crouched to lower his center of gravity, he imbued the shield with invisibility, expending enough energy to mute their appearance. A glance wouldn't reveal their presence, but a studied look would cause someone to look again. They'd have time to get away, but he wasn't planning on sticking around long enough for whoever it was to bash their way down there.

He drew on more of his power, tapping into the earth, Aurelia's past workings, and the magic in the blade, and redirected it inward. He held it in readiness to travel. Fixing a location in his mind, his grip sought and tightened on Olivier's hand, and he tested the edges of Aurelia's protections, finding the thinnest resistance.

Hovering between going and not-going, his pulse quickened as the assault intensified and his breath held until a mighty crack split the mountain apart. The earth and stone convulsed as rubble and boulders tumbled from the sky. On and on and on until the mountain opened, and Aurelia's protections fell.

Light poured in. Olivier roared at something unseen. Oberon shoved through the failing defenses, and they hurtled through the ether.

III

ALWAYS THE FUCKING SACRIFICE

Present Day

I

With the baby suckling at her breast, Aurelia cast her sight far to the east and strained to do nothing as acolytes tore apart her home. The torture Xadrak inflicted on Hame must have been enough to extract its location. They cracked the mountain into pieces, their grubby hands ready to plunder its secrets as granite and gneiss erupted. She did nothing as thirty acolytes destroyed what had been the seat of her power for six hundred years and swarmed inside to steal her brothers and the key.

Viktor begged her to tell him about the horrors she witnessed, but she kept silent. She froze her tears in the cold darkness, vaguely aware of the rhythmic tugging at her nipple.

The acolytes vanished inside and emerged empty-handed. She followed her brothers as best she could as Oberon—untested, impetuous, important Oberon—took Olivier out of their prison and out of the hands of their would-be captors. But then, try as she might, clutching the baby closer and harder to her, she could find them no longer. They had vanished and their trails masked. Where had they gone?

The baby unlatched from her breast and cried. Relaxing her grip, Viktor offered to take it—her—and she raised the babe into his arms. Defeat wore her down and pushed her into the bed. She stared off at nothing, listening to Viktor shushing the baby even though she made no noise.

She scried for Carn and Hame, Thierry and Alex, but they were hidden from her sight too. Had they been taken or were they cloaked? Her body slumped with more weariness than she'd ever known. Her body had worn thin with time and become brittle. One touch and it would fracture. Exhaustion welled tears in her eyes, but they refused to fall. She refused to *let* them fall. She had no proof either way where the pieces of the portal had gone.

In that ignorance grew hope.

She told Viktor what she'd seen and like a true soldier he didn't react. He listened and analyzed, yes, but he wasn't shocked. He gave no useless platitudes that would have made her throw something.

"What do you want to do now?"

For one second she hated him. It was a bomb peppering her body with its shrapnel. She didn't want to give orders. She was beyond being able to think clearly yet she was still expected to lead, all while he waited with the baby. All that despair and anger filled one tiny moment that nearly shattered her.

But it didn't.

It tested and strengthened her. And she had a choice.

"Summon everyone. They're to search for Thierry, Olivier, and Oberon."

Hame suffered in Xadrak's claws. He was still there, distant in the back of her mind, and sealed off. She'd rescue him if she could. But even as she thought it her eyes fell on her mother-in-child-form in Viktor's arms. A fist crushed her heart, the wet flesh of it strained and broke.

Viktor nodded. He handed her the baby and kissed her, his hunger pushing against her, stirring her, responding to her fire, her drive for action. She didn't want him to leave, worried she'd do something rash without him to steady her, but that was an excuse to keep him safe. He needed to hunt, he needed to be her sword-arm. If he survived…

"We'll win this," he whispered to her. Taking her free hand in his, he kissed her fingertips and left.

Seemingly unaware of what was happening around her, the baby settled and drifted to sleep. She'd barely had time to look at her. She was such a tiny thing, with a few wisps of dark brown hair on her crown, a face not yet grown into but sweet and soft. So helpless.

How much longer before Sinara took her rightful form?

And then what would happen?

The babe she'd given birth to would vanish and be replaced with a demoness, the one on whom they'd pinned all their hopes. That's why she'd bestowed no name on her. To call her Sinara would humanize her and make her long for the babe once she was gone. Any other name and she may as well carve out her heart.

Rest. Grow. That's all Sinara could do.

But while that was easy for the babe, for Aurelia it felt impossible. Sleep fought to claim her, but her mind resisted, and the panic burbled inside, making her jump. The names and faces of those she loved flashed through her head as she scried for them, checking on those who were still safe, and hoping to find those who'd been taken.

II

HANDS GRABBED AT OLIVIER AS HE AND OBERON whiplashed through a soupy grayness, Oberon's hold the only thing keeping him together. Fingers passed through him, snarling faces leered at him, and he lashed out but struck nothing and found he was made of nothing too. But he was aware that whatever *was* there wanted them.

Oberon's strength and maneuvers helped them evade capture. With each swipe, each lurch and frantic flinging of their bodies sideways, Olivier became more mindful of his uselessness—and of the danger he posed to Oberon's survival. If their enemies took him, the witch would have a greater chance of escape. He inched his hand out of Oberon's iron grip, but the witch mashed his knuckles together, and he ripped them through faster.

And then they were out.

Their bodies whole.

Their hands unfastened as they came out of that nowhere place. Olivier tumbled to the parched earth and crouched ready to attack anything that followed. Oberon grunted behind him. He turned to help the witch, but he was already raising himself onto his knees. He held Aurelia's knife in both hands above his head and plunged it into the earth.

Light erupted from the ground. The creeping shadows of dusk fled as a blue fire formed a dome around them and expanded to take in a circle of giant gum trees and a darkened cottage. The light shone as bright as a baseball stadium for a night game, burning out the browns and greens and grays of the Australian bush. It smelled ready to burn.

Seconds passed before the light faded. Pinpricks of glowing dust fell to the dirt, and the scent of oranges lay so thick they could have been in an orchard.

Oberon hunched, panted, and rested his head forward on the earth like he prayed to Mecca. Olivier touched his back.

The witch flinched. "I'm fine. Give me a minute."

He didn't like waiting, something about seeing the witch trying to catch his breath and trying to rise. Unable to help. Watching again as he was fading away. Only this time wasn't like when he'd drained him in the dungeon. As much as that memory urged him to take action and carry the witch into the house to rest, he refrained. He'd seen the wariness in Oberon's eyes when the shackles had fallen. Instead he searched the night, imagining where the invisible boundaries stood, and watched for any disturbance to signal they'd been tracked.

"Where did you bring us?"

"Somewhere safe." Oberon struggled to his feet, using the knife as support before pulling it out of the ground and walking towards the cottage.

Was he expected to follow? Or now that the immediate danger had passed should he seek shelter elsewhere? Stepping outside the protection of the circle might bring enemies from either side.

"There's nowhere else you can go," Oberon called back without stopping.

Being told he couldn't do something almost made him want to do it. He could leave, that's what he wanted to do, wasn't it? Be free?

But where would he go?

He followed the witch into the cottage. To his right was the family room with a couple of couches, a rug and coffee table, and a TV. Beyond that, a kitchen with a table and chairs, appliances, everything you'd need to survive out in the middle of wherever this was. More rooms deviated off the hall with a bathroom down the end, into which Oberon disappeared and closed the door. A few seconds later the shower started.

He wandered through the house, poking through drawers and staring at photos of Oberon with people he presumed to be parents. A mother, a father, all while he was quite young—yet still possessing a cheeky cockiness that had followed him through to adulthood—and then a few with an older woman—a grandmother?—but they were the only obvious personal touches. Otherwise the clutter was nondescript: books and board games, a few old magazines, scraps of paper, and a collection of pens in drawers. Dust covered everything.

The largest bedroom had a double bed, and the wardrobe was empty apart from a few coat hangers. The other room was smaller with a single bed covered in a quilt with that ridiculous blue train on it. A shelf of books, a cupboard with some clothes—for an adult, rather than a child—and stuffed with cricket bats and wickets, a football.

The shower turned off, but he didn't hurry. If Oberon

thought he'd observe some sort of sanctity of privacy, he hadn't been paying attention.

This had once been a home, and despite the length of time that had passed, it was safe enough. The question they had to ask though was for how long would it conceal them?

The bathroom door opened, and Oberon's damp feet padded over the floorboards down the hall. Olivier closed the cupboard and turned to the wet-haired witch, dressed again in black jeans and a blue T-shirt. Meanwhile, Olivier still wore the blood-stained trousers he'd had on going into his imprisonment.

"Have a good look around?"

"Would you rather I didn't?"

Oberon shrugged and dried his black hair with the towel while walking into the living room. "I've left some clothes for you in the bathroom."

Clothes could wait. "Are you going to explain what happened back there?"

Oberon dropped onto the couch, the dust puffing into a cloud as he hit the cushions. His skin looked even paler. "How much do you know of Aurelia's plans? What she's been up to for the past few centuries?"

"I didn't think she had a plan." He lowered into the opposite seat.

Oberon shot air out his nose. "If she'd known what I was, she wouldn't have put the two of us together. Not yet anyway."

Olivier leaned back, extended his arms out to the side and let his hands dangle off the edge. Oberon's eyes brushed down his bare chest on their way to his own hands resting on the towel in his lap.

"You're not making much sense, witch."

Oberon twisted the end of the towel, rolling and

unrolling it. "You, me, and Thierry are part of a portal that opens a doorway to a world where demons live. One of those demons is here. He's named Xadrak and he's Aurelia's enemy."

Olivier's hands curled up, and he flicked his fingers against the pads of his thumbs. "Sounds like I should meet him. Aurelia told you this?"

He nodded. "Aurelia wants to use the three of us to open this portal and send Xadrak back to where he came from."

The heat in Olivier's blood raised, and he dug his nails into the palm of his hands to cool it. Aurelia's machinations, no matter how clumsy, always brought out the need to feed and he had no chance of satisfying that. "I'm guessing we don't get a say in this."

"I think Aurelia has plans to keep Thierry alive but you and I…" He smoothed the towel over his lap.

"So that's why you were so keen for me to leave. If she doesn't have all of us, we can't meet an untimely end. And the ones who attacked us? They want us dead?"

He raised his head and his expression had turned matter of fact, cold. "I suspect they want to use us, too."

"We shouldn't stick together then."

"If you leave, you'll be found in no time, whether by Aurelia or someone else. If I leave, you'll be found anyway."

"We're stuck together?"

"Until they find us. And they will. Before now they didn't know what I was, but they'll never let me go back to my old life."

"Have you known all along what you are?"

"No."

He expected Oberon to say more, but instead he held his stare.

His sister…

He was the ruthless one, but how cold-blooded she must be to enact her schemes?

"I won't let them use me." Olivier surged to his feet and paced the small living space. Waiting. Not fighting. He couldn't stand it.

Oberon gave a short, harsh laugh. "You think it's that easy? You have no idea what you're up against. They won't stop until they've put us to their use."

He stopped his march. "What if you die first?"

"That's not part of my plan." Oberon stood. His heart beat a little faster.

Olivier stepped closer. "But at least you'd go out the way you wanted."

The witch's eyes narrowed, and the room bloomed with magic. "I will shackle you again if I have to or leave you to fend for yourself."

Olivier chuckled and brushed his semi-threat aside. He leaned against the side of the fridge. "Just asking. You did offer to be my donor, after all. I figured you had some sort of death wish."

"You knew why I was there." His voice stayed level. The witch either didn't hate him after all or he was on a whole other level of control. Oberon might have offered him his blood in some unwise act before, but with witches and demons after them, maybe he had changed his mind.

"And now? You've got me where you want me. A more powerful foe wants to make me their bitch, so you could easily turn me over to some greater terror. If anything, I have more to fear from you than you from me."

"Is that what you want? Fear?"

If that's all there is.

He shrugged. "I've known little else."

"Well, let me put it in language you understand. It's more beneficial for you and me to stay alive and together."

"Why not send me somewhere and escape yourself?"

"Because I think you've been through enough." Oberon walked towards his bedroom.

Olivier grabbed his arm hard enough to pull him to a halt but gentle enough not to break it. "You think because you've seen my past that somehow explains me? I'm still the same guy I've always been, and if you think I won't sacrifice you to save myself, then you're even stupider than you look."

Then why wasn't he using Oberon to secure his own freedom? It wasn't because it had the stain of futility across it. Something else was going on. The idea fluttered to the back of his mind, its tatters catching on thorns.

Oberon didn't answer. Instead he looked from the hand clutching at him and up into his eyes. Utterly unreadable. What was buried in the witch's deep earth eyes? Fear he knew. Hate even better. But what was this? Why wouldn't he save himself? The opportunity was there; it was the least Olivier expected after what he'd done.

"What do you want from me?"

"I don't want anything, Olivier." Oberon extracted himself, went into the other room, and closed the door.

Oberon's words hollowed out his heart and drained it of the percolating poison.

He wanted nothing?

Nobody had ever wanted nothing from him.

Not his help? Not even his suffering?

Was it indifference?

That was always the worst. His siblings' contempt had been comforting in its intensity, but when Thierry cast him aside after he'd slaughtered Reiner, that had brought him low enough to consider ending his own life. Then he'd been rescued with a newfound awareness of his twin's inner connection, but that had gone, and he couldn't tap into that animosity.

And here he was alone with a man who wanted nothing from him.

What was he meant to do to change that?

III

Aurelia forced her eyelids to stay open. When had she last blinked? Scrying for her brothers and Oberon, for Carn and Viktor, for any of her witches had stripped her of her everything but the will to keep going. The suckling babe had also taken its fair share. She caught flashes of Carn and Alex, but the others…

Hours passed before the door to Viktor's apartment burst open and in hurried Carn with Hame cradled in his arms.

"The bed's through there," Viktor directed as he followed behind.

Aurelia struggled out of the chair. "Carn!"

He brushed past her.

Hame hung limp in the witch's arms, but she couldn't see any wounds on his body. Everything that was happening to him was happening to his mind, and those scars would be worse than any physical injury. She made to go to Hame's side, to stroke his fiery hair and weep over what was happening to him.

"Aurelia, where is he?"

She turned at Alex's voice. He was alone.

Her pulse quickened, a thousand hammers beating her heart at once. She stared at the nothing behind him, hoping Thierry was playing his invisibility trick, annoyed that they'd been put in danger, but the air was just air.

"What happened?"

"You tell me!" The vampire's face had hardened since she'd last seen him. "We were supposed to be safe, but they attacked us and pursued us." His hands shook and his fingers curled into claws before closing into fists. The veins popped on the back of his hands, and blood seeped out to drip on the floor.

She reached forward to touch his shoulder.

He shrugged her off and paced the room. "They took him. I don't know how, probably because there were so many of them and only one of Carn. And here you are nursing a fucking baby!"

Her heart yielded to the hammers. She should have been there. She should have saved them.

"Watch your tone," Viktor said behind her and the steadiness in his voice kept her standing.

Alex bared his fangs. "Watch my *tone*? Fuck my tone." He jabbed his bloody finger at her. "I'll watch my tone when she brings Thierry back."

"Your shouting at her won't help."

"No? Then maybe I should go and search for him myself. Be better than sitting around with people who don't give a fuck about him beyond his purpose as a magic door." He sneered at them and made for the exit.

The door slammed shut before he could go through it. "It won't stop me," Alex said.

Viktor moved, but Aurelia moved faster. "Alex, please, don't go. My people are looking for him. It's better if you stay."

He hung his head. "That's not good enough."

"It has to be. They want Thierry alive as much as we do, but you… They wouldn't hesitate to destroy you. And that would wreck him."

"I can't sit here and do nothing!"

"We're not doing nothing. Do you want to know why I'm here with a baby? This is Sinara. She is the one we've been waiting for."

He scoffed. "What's she going to do? Puke on them?"

"I know you're scared, Alex. We all are. Even me. But this is the best place for you. Letting you go out there would be a distraction we don't need."

"Rescuing Thierry is a distraction?"

"Think about it. What could you really do against their magic? He'd want you to be safe."

"So what? We wait twenty years until she grows?"

"It won't be that long. In the meantime, we'll search for him and for Oberon and Olivier. If the acolytes get them too, we're in even deeper trouble."

"How do you know they haven't got them already?"

She had to lie, or he'd be out the door if she said she was taking it as a matter of faith. "I saw them escape."

"Then why haven't you collected them yet?"

"They… They don't want to be found."

"Oberon always was a smart one."

"Yes, well, he's made a dumb move because instead of coming to our protection he's at an even greater risk of being snatched by Xadrak. I hope for all our sakes he doesn't do anything stupid."

Or let Olivier kill him again.

"I hope he never shows up." He pushed past her and went into the bedroom where Hame was resting.

Carn and Viktor were looking at her, and a pressure built within that threatened to snap her in two. Her eyes fell to the babe staring up at her, silent. The expression wasn't blank but consoling. The pressure eased but the fatigue remained. She was being crushed by the defeat they'd suffered. But they had to push on. While Thierry mattered, the chances of rescuing him were slim.

Oberon and Olivier, however, were still unknowns and the greater prize.

Viktor came close to comfort her, but she feared she'd shatter if he touched her.

"Bring Mira and a squad you trust. I want them scrying for Olivier and Oberon, and ready to launch as soon as we know where they are."

With no lair left to her, this apartment would have to be her command center.

His eyes softened and he gave a small nod. As he walked past her, his hand brushed hers then he was gone. Tears burned in her eyes, but she forced them back. Exhaustion couldn't have her. Too much was still at stake.

IV

WHEN SUNLIGHT BURNED THROUGH OBERON'S SLEEP, memories of the night before swooped to fill the gap the nightmares had left. He was awake—unsteady and woozy but pushing through as he pulled on gym shorts and crashed from the bed to the doorframe to search the other rooms for Olivier.

The cottage was empty.

Heart thundering and sweat springing from his brow, he wrenched open the front door and hurried onto the verandah.

Olivier sat on the top step, looking at the forest.

Oberon sighed in relief—too much relief—and sagged against the door. Thankful the vampire hadn't done the stupid thing and left the protection of the circle; he would have preferred to not have to go through the heart attack of finding that out.

"You expected me to run?" Olivier was dressed in the jeans and blue shirt he'd left for him.

"Why didn't you?"

"You asked me not to."

He couldn't hold back the short, harsh, and verging on hysterical laugh. "You never do anything anyone tells you."

"Then consider yourself honored."

Oberon walked the few steps to where Olivier sat and hugged the post. The bush clicked and chirruped in the rising summer heat, the smell of dried eucalyptus leaves and hot earth warming childhood memories of holidays with his family. One hundred-foot tall Jarrah trees surrounded them, while shrubs fought it out below for space and sunlight.

"Have you been out here all night?"

"Most of it. When I wasn't watching over you, I was out here."

He watched? "See anything?"

"Only animals. An owl lives in that tree, and a possum in that one."

Olivier pointed but there was nothing there. Looking at the trees reminded him to renew the shield. He stepped past Olivier, who rose to follow.

He stopped and gestured for Olivier to remain. "I'll be right back."

"I want to see what you do."

"There won't be anything to see."

"I want to come along anyway. You're not the only one who gets to make unreasonable demands." Olivier's eyebrows raised to punctuate his argument.

Oberon laughed easier this time. "I don't think asking you to stay so I can keep us safe is unreasonable, do you?"

"Depends on one's reasons for doing so." His eyes narrowed and a smug grin appeared on his face.

The vampire wasn't going to catch him out that easily. "And what do you think my reasons are?"

Olivier smiled, like he was keeping a secret. It was infuriating.

"You can come, but don't interrupt."

The vampire trailed behind him, picking his way through the undergrowth so carefully he made no sound. Meanwhile the dried twigs and grass crunched and speared his bare soles. His awareness of Olivier, like the pain in his feet, faded as his attention turned to the work he had to do.

When they'd arrived during the night, he'd poured an enormous amount of his energy into strengthening the protective shields that already existed. But the working had been a stopgap measure, and he had to reinforce the wards.

He walked to a tree that stood to the east of the house and gathered his power. He didn't need Aurelia's knife for this. He delved inside himself, reaching down into the Earth and pulling it up while harnessing the energy from above to channel and mix within himself.

He hummed with the power, the warmth of it shimmering up and down his body. He held up his hand and faced his palm to the tree, releasing an invisible stream of power—unseen but not without its effects buzzing in the air around him. He traced a sigil in the air in front of the tree, then walked the edge of the circle to the tree that stood in the north. He drew the sigil again then moved west, south, and back to east. A perfect circle surrounded them and rose into a dome above and descended below. Feeling it connect at all points and offer complete protection, he stamped the ground to seal it.

Olivier leaned close and inhaled. The skin on Oberon's bare back tingled at having the vampire so near, at once ready to jump away, while also wanting to lean back. The brand on his shoulder itched beneath real or imagined focus. He forced himself into the cottage.

He grabbed a shirt from his room and released another stream of power to cleanse the house of the musty smell and the dust. Bright, clean, and homey, like it used to be but tended with magic rather than love.

"Have you come up with a plan yet?" Olivier took a seat at the table in the kitchen.

"Have you?" He leaned against the bench. "You're the one who's been awake all night."

Olivier drummed the fingers of both hands on the table. "I still think killing you is the best chance for my survival."

He shook his head and picked up the kettle. "You've tried that a few times. I don't think it's going to work."

"Are you really not frightened of me anymore?"

The purring in Olivier's voice tickled the back of Oberon's neck. He paused with the kettle held under the tap, ready to fill it with water. What did Olivier want him to say?

"If you wanted to kill me, I'm sure you would. I'm still wary of you, but I'll save my fear for the demons." He turned the tap.

"Aren't you afraid I'll drain your blood again?"

"Last time I offered it to you."

"What about raping you?"

His heart slammed into his throat, and he gripped the handle hard as he shut off the water. "You'll never get the chance again." He plugged the kettle in and flicked the switch. When he turned around, Olivier was smiling at him, a smile that broadened into something wicked.

Had he taken his words as a challenge? Would he have to keep watch? He'd forgiven him, hadn't he? But did that mean he shouldn't worry about falling prey to him again?

The sooner they separated the better.

Right?

Olivier, perhaps sensing the conflict he'd fought in his head—those entrancing eyes divined too much—leaned back in his chair. "How do you think they're going to use us?"

"Considering we've got two vampires and one human, it's likely you and Thierry will have to drink my blood."

"How did you figure that out?"

"Just a hunch."

"We could refuse."

"They'd make you."

Olivier rubbed his sternum. "What do you think will happen to us all, when it happens?"

"Obliterated, I guess."

"Except for Thierry. Aurelia always had a soft spot for him."

"What did you do to her to make her hate you? I saw what a sacrifice you made to save her from Henri."

He shrugged. "None of us likes to be beholden unto others." Olivier fixed him with a meaningful stare that reached into his stomach and gripped his insides.

He moved through the uncomfortableness and took the seat opposite the vampire. "But after that? You must have done something."

"Why do *you* think she hates me?"

His finger drew little lines on the wooden tabletop, counting the tit-for-tat of the family's lives until he came up with something. "Because you didn't do it for her. You did it for Thierry and she knows it."

Olivier pursed his lips and tilted his head quickly to the side like he was parsing the suggestion. "Sounds good enough. It was all so long ago."

"And yet here we are. Time didn't make you hate each other less."

"That's the burden of immortality. What else would I have to keep me warm in my endless years? Whereas you —humans, I mean—don't have the luxury of holding grudges, or at least you shouldn't. It wastes your pathetically short lives."

"You're telling me you weren't the same when you were human?"

"I suppose. Perhaps it's unavoidable. We know we're going to die so we hold on to whatever we can to make life that much more meaningful. What do you hold on to?"

The kettle boiled and the button clicked. Oberon got to his feet and filled a mug with hot water, drowning the summoned fresh coffee grounds and releasing the rich aroma. He sat back at the table and wrapped his hands around the mug, holding them in place while the sides burned his palms.

He sipped his drink and swallowed the bitterness. "I help others a lot." Charities, volunteering, domestic violence victims in shelters, a little magical justice when it was right.

"Really?"

He sat back and crossed his arms over his chest. His thumb landed on the Ô. "What's that supposed to mean?"

"From what I saw of your life there weren't many people in it. A sterile apartment. No friends at the clubs. Who came to your rescue when you were dying on the carpet?"

"You keep focusing on what you did to me. Why?"

"Because I don't buy it." His fist slammed the top of the table, spilling Oberon's coffee. "I don't believe that after what I did to you, you can so casually sit there and not want to destroy me."

His heart jerked inside his chest. He gripped his arms tighter. Olivier worked on fear, on reaction.

Keep still and he might calm down.

"Is that what you'd do?"

"I wanted to. Not you, not now at least, but when my

father raped me, not a day went by that I didn't want to torture that motherfucker into insanity." Olivier's lips curled into a snarl and his fingernails clawed the wood. "He took everything from me. He destroyed me and then made me what I am."

Softly. Gently. "I know."

"That's right, you were there. *That* was your vengeance. Did it work out the way you intended?" His hands turned into fists.

"I'm sitting here with you. What do you think?"

"I think you and I aren't the same, and that being raped has had different effects on us. It turned me into what I am today, whereas for you I don't know. What did it do to you?"

It's done. I don't need to give this to you again.

"You were there. You saw it. You felt it."

"But I don't understand it." His fists fired open as the words shot out of his mouth. "I know about the powerlessness, I felt that, I couldn't believe it, this destruction, all because someone stronger than me decided that's what they wanted, but after that… Why are you not trying to kill me?"

Olivier's eyes searched for a hidden answer he'd already been given. The blood should have been enough. Maybe it was never enough.

"Because I forgave you." He whispered the words, but though they were quiet, they didn't shake.

"It's not possible."

"Believe it, don't believe it, but I know why you did it." He got up from the table and carried the cup to the sink, tipping the remains of the coffee down the drain. He rinsed the cup and left it to dry on the side. He turned back to Olivier's intense gaze. "I know you've been little more than an impulse fighting against perceived threats your entire life, so you can come out on top, but that's not me. Sure, I wanted you dead. I wanted to feel like myself again, but I understood then that even you raping me wasn't my fault, and it didn't change who I was." He scratched his head and shook out the strands, dislodging the memories that were threatening to bind him. "I couldn't bear the hate. It helped being able to understand you. It helped knowing why you are the way you are. But it was knowing that the only way I'd feel like myself again was to forgive you for what you did and let it go."

Killing him would have only helped a little.

"And you think I should forgive Henri for what he did to me? What Aurelia and Thierry have done to me?"

"What would have happened if you had?"

"Henri would have kept raping me."

"But eventually he stopped, didn't he?"

"When he believed I liked it. When it was more than rape, and it bordered on fun, on appreciation." He laughed, but the sound was off, discordant, and squeaked against Oberon's back teeth. "That messed him up."

"And if you'd forgiven him?"

"Never." He glowered and his top lip twitched.

"*But if you had*. Would you have lived a different life? Would you have had a happier life? And what if you forgave Aurelia and Thierry?"

"They'd never forgive me. They'd still use me."

He hurried back to his seat, leaning forward close as Olivier leaned back. "But would you still fight if you forgave them? If they no longer saw you as a threat, would you have the kind of relationship with them that you once wanted?"

"I'm not the one to blame," he snapped back. His finger stabbed at the table. "They've always had their secrets and their plots and their hate for bad old Olivier.

It's easier for them to paint me as the monster because it absolves them of their guilt."

"But what if they no longer saw you that way? Wouldn't it be harder for them to destroy you if they had to see you as something other than a monster, as something human? To see you the way I see you?"

Olivier's bottom lip dropped. He paused before looking away.

Oberon breathed again.

"It'll never happen."

"Why?"

"They won't listen."

"So, you'll let them hunt you until they capture you and die fighting because that's the way it's always been?"

"I don't see you offering yourself like some willing sacrifice. You'll fight until your last breath."

"And what if I did hand myself over?"

"You wouldn't."

"*But if I did?* It would be an easy thing. Oblivion has its benefits."

And if it meant saving the world, maybe it wouldn't be so bad.

"Then I'd stop you."

"Why?"

"Because you don't deserve it."

He scoffed. "Since when have any of your victims deserved what you did to them? Did I deserve what you did to me?"

"I've had enough of this." Olivier got to his feet, pushed away from the table, and walked towards the front door.

Oberon followed. "You can't leave."

"What does it matter to you if you've already given up? I may as well bring them raining down upon us, and we can have this all finished within minutes."

Olivier wasn't stopping so Oberon made the door close and bolt in front of him. Olivier pulled up short and spun, his eyes hard and levelled directly at him. "You think a door will stop me?"

"Wait. I have to understand."

"No, you don't. You've already seen enough; I have nothing left to show you."

"Why do you fight who you know you truly are?"

He laughed hard and bent over, mania flashing in his eyes. "I'm a killer! I'm a sadistic murderer who's slaughtered thousands of people for nothing more than my own enjoyment. Whatever redeeming features I once had have been fucked out of me and drowned in the blood of innocents so don't think I'm worth saving because I'm not."

He advanced and the glowing red in Olivier's eyes, the descended fangs and the hands primed ready to claw forced Oberon to retreat, primal fear scattering through his blood. Olivier wouldn't attack him, not again, but the closer he got, the smaller that inner voice became.

"And if you want any hope of getting out of this alive," Olivier said, "then you'd do well to consider me a lost cause. Use me, because that's what I'm doing to you. I'm using you to keep me safe until it's no longer feasible to do so."

Was he lying? Was he trying to scare him to protect him? But why would Olivier do that? After what they'd been through, the vampire wouldn't believe he owed him anything.

He hit the wall, but Olivier closed the space between them and pressed against his body. He glared down at him, and Oberon forced himself back to stop from blasting the vampire across the room. Posturing, that's all this was, and defending himself.

But snakes were deadliest when cornered.

Having the vampire this close, close enough to have his body against his, and his own body breaking out in sweat, offering up all those memories of once desiring him, of flirting with the idea of danger and then being unable to defend himself when it had all gone horribly wrong.

He forced himself to stare back into Olivier's eyes. "What do you suggest we do?"

V

OLIVIER HAD NO SUGGESTIONS THAT DIDN'T INVOLVE HIS fists and fangs. Frustration always made him thirsty and being close to Oberon, smelling his sweat and the cinnamon of his skin, his tongue recalling the caramel in his blood... His gums itched. Barely a day since he'd drained the witch and still he hungered. He kneaded his sternum and popped his jaw. Oberon's eyes widened rapidly before he dampened his nervousness with a bite to his bottom lip.

In another world, in another time, he'd have taken it for a sign of attraction. But that was ridiculous considering what they'd been through. He might profess to have forgiven him, but forgiveness couldn't be that easily conjured. His brother and sister were testament to that.

If Thierry and Aurelia wanted any hope of resolution —a laughable proposition—they could start with the 'I'm sorrys', then maybe he could meet them halfway. That would be an easier start, perhaps, because it was biblical, an eye for an eye, you cut off my leg, so I'll cut off your arm.

But Oberon?

No sane person could forgive what he had done to him. Olivier knew that better than anyone. It was too hard to do, but Oberon had made it look so easy. As easy as breathing. Another thing Olivier was incapable of.

What would it be like to forgive? It didn't bear thinking about—and thinking about it was too hard to bear. Yet there the witch was—and *after* offering his blood. If only his blood was the only thing he'd given.

Which gave Olivier an idea—and a distraction from the unsettled feeling expanding inside him. He stepped away. "Maybe we—"

A chasm cleaved through his chest, and he grunted from its suddenness. He looked down, but while no axe lodged in his ribs, inside, deep inside, Thierry charged in and the connection opened.

His brother. His twin.

In agony.

Knives stabbed a ring around his heart, and their blades sawed in and out with furious speed. He clutched his chest and doubled over.

"Olivier!" Oberon shouted.

Hunched over his knees, his fingers digging into his skin, he stared ahead and saw the vague impressions of what his brother saw. Shady figures watched as he writhed beneath the touch of the one who'd removed the block and drained Thierry of his blood. The veil fell. Olivier couldn't sharpen the vision, but the sensations were strong enough.

Olivier. Can you…hear me?

Yes. His mind shoved back the answer as the pain punctured him.

Come to me, Olivier.

What are they doing to you?

Please. Come. And bring Oberon.

Thierry's mind shut and the pain dulled but didn't disappear. It hovered on the edge of his nerves and sparked to remind him of the connection.

Thierry was back. And in torment.

"What happened?" Oberon's hand was on his shoulder. When had he put that there?

No matter. Thierry was calling for him. They needed each other. At last his brother recognized it. He straightened, and the witch's hand dropped.

"They've got Thierry and they're hurting him. We have to go."

"Are you insane? That's what they want."

The witch would try to talk him out of it, but he knew —all the way through his soul—that this was the right thing to do. Better than stewing in his own guilt. Oberon's eyes saw too much.

"Fine." He hurried for the door. "You stay if you want but I need to be with Thierry." If he was fast enough, he could get away before—

Oberon hooked his arm and with both hands pushed him towards the couch. He forced him to sit, then perched on the coffee table opposite him and grasped his hand. He was trying to get him to meet his gaze, but all Olivier wanted was to get through that door.

"Think this through, Olivier. You don't know if it's really him."

"It *is* him." As if he wouldn't know his brother. "You don't understand what Thierry and I share."

"You're right. I don't understand that level of dysfunction."

He ripped his hands from the witch's hold. "Fuck you. You saw what we went through."

"I saw the damage you did to him. Do you *really* think, after all that's happened, he gives a flying fuck about you?"

His gut seized from a familiar sucker-punch. "He's my brother!"

"And you killed two of his lovers and almost a third. Is that what brothers do to each other?"

There were reasons for that. Good reasons but he didn't have time to explain. This was his one chance of getting what he wanted. If he and Thierry were together, perhaps it could be made better. Oberon had forgiven him, perhaps Thierry could after all. He had to try.

"I don't care what you say. I'm going." He jumped to his feet, but the witch grabbed him again.

"Why don't we tell Aurelia?"

"No, we can't wait." She'd try to stop him.

"Please, Olivier, I don't want anything to happen to you." Oberon peered up at him, pleading, as if he actually cared.

In another time… In another place…

"You only care what happens to yourself."

Oberon's eyes narrowed. "If you mean I don't want to die, then yes, but I also don't want you to die either."

"You do." He bent and their noses nearly touched before Oberon pulled back an inch. This intimidation didn't hum with its usual satisfaction. "Deep down you do. You want me to suffer." Why else taunt him with absolution?

"I want you to shut up and listen."

"You've nothing worth saying."

"Please." The defiance in his eyes softened. "Stay with me and let's work this out together."

This was all lies. Platitudes designed to make him think he cared. Caresses and false concern. He knew the depths of Oberon's hate; he had felt it and been through what he'd been through. That didn't just go away. It couldn't. All you could do was hold on to something stronger. And, after all this time, that was Thierry.

But he betrayed you. Over and over and over again.

Six hundred years and not once had Thierry seen him the way Oberon had seen him. But if there wasn't Thierry, what else was there?

Oberon pulled him down. Olivier stiffened, preparing for some magical assault, but Oberon stared into both his eyes, begging for both their sakes.

Thierry only ever begged him to stop.

And he was about to repay the witch with destruction. Who was to say he needed the witch anyway? Maybe this could be his one consolation to what Oberon had given him. He'd get to be with Thierry and save Oberon's life at the same time.

"I'll go on my own. I know how we can do this, and you don't have to be anywhere near me and Thierry."

"How?"

"I'll take your blood, as much of it as I can, and then go to Thierry. If we need to drink it to activate the portal, then you don't need to be there at all."

Oberon hesitated and pulled back. Fear splashed across his face.

"Offer it to me like you did last time."

Oberon let go, and a chill crept up Olivier's arms where warm hands used to rest. Too late he tried to hold on. The witch walked away, his arms wrapping around himself, and his thumb rubbing against that Ô on his bicep. If Oberon said no, would he take it anyway? Was he capable of doing it again?

For Thierry?

For Oberon?

The witch studied him, warring with himself over whether to allow this sacrifice to go ahead. He could save himself but condemn Olivier. Isn't that what he'd wanted all along?

Oberon closed his eyes. "I don't want you to get hurt."

Why won't he let me go? "Keep your sympathy for someone who needs it. Give me your blood."

Oberon sucked the inside of his cheeks, his malevolent gaze bearing down on him.

Olivier wanted to hide. The shame swamped him, drowning out even Thierry's dull agony and its insistent scratching and whining and pleading. All Olivier was good for was taking—blood, love, forgiveness. But he hadn't always been like that. He'd once given everything for those he loved—and become a monster because of it. Perhaps saving Oberon from becoming the portal could, in a small way, help balance the evil.

"This is going to take a while," Oberon said eventually.

Olivier slumped under the relief that Oberon's offer released.

"If this is to work, then you'll need all my blood and you can't take that in one hit. If we had Aurelia here, or even Alex—"

"We'll manage by ourselves. They'll only try to stop me."

"Do you know what you're going to do by handing yourself over? You'll destroy Aurelia. You might even bring about the end of the world."

He didn't care. It could all burn, Aurelia with it, if it meant he got to be with Thierry.

But what about Oberon?

It wouldn't come to that. Whatever happened, Oberon would be safe. He had survived worse. And he'd never have to risk losing his blood to Olivier again.

"You can warn them once I'm gone."

"Olivier, think about this."

"We'll discuss it later, but we need to get to work." He couldn't take any more pleading or else he'd waver. The witch should be glad it was going to go down like this.

Oberon's lips closed and a deep burrow carved into his brow. How many more times was he going to lose his blood? But despite his hesitation, Oberon returned to sit in the armchair. He didn't look Olivier's way. Instead he waved his hand over the table and a needle, tubes, and plastic pouches appeared.

A knot twisted in his stomach. He opened his mouth to share his gratitude, but Oberon was already puncturing his skin.

"Bring me Aurelia's knife from my room," he ordered, and Olivier obliged.

He handed it over, standing beside Oberon as blood filled the bag. He pumped his fist to make it flow faster. Caramel and roses filled his nostrils before oranges flooded in as Oberon gripped the knife and healed his depleting supply. Olivier bit his lip and walked outside to watch the sky, the trees, the bugs.

If he didn't, he'd pull out the needle and drink.

VI

If Oberon had been stronger, he would have taken Olivier against his will and gone to Aurelia immediately. He'd had to try something else and hope it worked.

His conviction wavered as the last of the required blood drained out of him. He'd filled nine bags already. For nearly two days Olivier had skulked in the background, keeping his distance, holding each completed bag by its end as he threw it in the fridge and went outside to watch, to wait, to mourn for his lost Thierry.

Oberon clutched the athame hilt in his hand and pumped blood out of the needle in his arm. He drew on the blade's residual strength. But for all the good the magic did, each ounce of blood was an ounce of lost vitality washing out of him and sweeping them towards disaster.

Every now and then the vampire moaned or roared at nothing. He felt whatever was happening to Thierry, and he did whatever he could to distract himself.

But once the blood ran out, what then? Would he let Olivier go?

The bag bulged to capacity, and he withdrew the

needle.

"You're finished?" Olivier stepped inside the cottage.

"Five quarts, ready to go." He stumbled as he got to his feet. Olivier caught him, putting him upright and holding on to him until he was stable. He didn't let go. He looked down at him, his eyes tensing as his nostrils flared.

The blood.

He had to put it with the others, but there was something about the way Olivier held him, his hands on his back, his chest slightly pressed against his…

Too close. Too dangerous.

He shrugged out of Olivier's hold and the vampire released him. He walked to the fridge and chucked the bag in with the rest. One human's worth.

He grabbed a glass and filled it with water from the tap. Leaning against the sink, he drained the warm liquid in a few greedy gulps. He refilled and drank again and cleared out the sandpaper in his throat. Refueled, he put the glass in the sink and wiped his mouth with the back of his hand. He took a few deep breaths to prepare himself for what was probably going to be a fruitless argument.

"Olivier, look." He turned around and braced on the edge of the sink. "We should tell Aurelia. You shouldn't go in there without any support."

Olivier slinked towards him, a flowing stride like mercury personified. "I'll be fine."

"I can't let you do it, Olivier. I've got to tell her."

Olivier rushed towards him and his sudden approach had him scrambling away and slamming against the fridge. Magnets dropped to the floor. He breathed in sharply as the vampire's eyes turned amber.

"Don't," Olivier purred, sounding more tiger than tabby. "Tell her after I've gone. She can try to save us then, but this is what I want. And it should be what you want too. I'm saving you from having to go through it." He was closer, his presence charging the air.

"And when the demons come?"

Olivier shrugged and turned away.

He grabbed his arm. "I don't want you to go."

"This is best for everyone." Olivier looked at the hand holding him back.

"What about what's best for you?"

"This is it." Sadness weighed down his words.

"But he doesn't want you. What good will it do?"

He paused. "It'll make the pain stop."

"Aurelia can block it again. Or let me try." Oberon reached for his chest, but Olivier grabbed his wrists before he could make contact.

"It's not that pain." Flash of red in the amber. "It's the rest of it. I want it to stop, and this is my only chance."

"But it's not! Why do this?" He wrenched his wrists free of Olivier's grip, and the vampire's hands closed into fists.

Olivier straightened. "It's what I was made for."

"If that's true, then so was I."

"You've been through enough." The vampire turned his face towards the door.

"Sympathy? From you? Where's the vampire who fought everyone and everything because he could?" He trailed behind Olivier as he walked towards the exit. "Why roll over because you think you'll get what you *think* you want?"

"You can't convince me otherwise."

"Then I'm coming with you. I'll destroy the blood and then we'll be back where we started. Please, let me tell Aurelia what's going on." He didn't want to go near her any more than Olivier did, but with Thierry imprisoned there was less chance of the portal being opened. Olivier was going to get himself hurt. He touched Olivier's shoulder and the vampire spun round, fire in his eyes, fangs showing.

"That's not what I want." He rose to his full height so he could loom over Oberon and force him into submission.

Though shorter than Olivier, he wouldn't submit. He pushed his weight into the floor and bit back. "Fuck what you want. What about what I want? What about what Aurelia and Thierry and Alex wants?"

"Aurelia's aims and the demon's are the same, except they'll happen on the demon's schedule instead of hers."

"I won't let you go."

"It's not up to you, Oberon. I'm leaving."

Oberon prepared for a fight, but Olivier raced towards him and his arms engulfed him. The witch stiffened, but Olivier remained soft, and his own body relaxed without knowing why. There was genuine tenderness, perhaps the only tenderness Olivier had shown in a long time, and Oberon returned it. Maybe it would make a difference.

He hung on, two damaged beings holding on to something to give their lives meaning.

"I know you don't understand." Olivier's embrace tightened.

Oberon struggled to breathe, and he pushed against Olivier. "You're hurting me."

"I'm sorry, Oberon," he whispered. "I can't stay. You deserve more."

Olivier's narrowing hold compressed the air out of his lungs. Shadows crept along the edges of his vision. Panicked, power burst out of him, and Olivier grunted against the desperate force that barreled into him, but he endured it.

And the world faded as he collapsed into Olivier's arms.

VII

Olivier lay Oberon on the floor, rolled him onto his side, and grabbed the bags of blood out of the fridge. He stuffed them into a backpack and ran outside to what he thought was the inside edge of the protective circle. He gave one last glance behind him at the cottage. Oberon would live. That was the least he could do for the witch. The least should have been good enough, but he wanted to do more. Something tugged at him to stay but he ignored it. Staying behind would bring the witch harm. And two days of keeping distant made it more likely harm is what would happen. He crouched, built the tension in his stance, and bolted.

He dodged giant trees and leapt over fallen logs, propelling to the limits of his strength to create as much distance as possible between him and Oberon. The wind tore through his hair, he crossed roads and rivers, and burned all the energy he had and then more to get far away before whomever descended upon him.

He focused inwards.

Tell them I'm here. Lead them to me. Do it!

He badgered Thierry, sensing his brother's resistance, but he pushed through. The demon's acolytes had to come for him before Aurelia realized where he was. He had to keep moving because they'd never be able to catch him while he traveled at such speed. At least that's what he hoped.

Thierry's mind returned.

They're coming for you.

It came through so weakly, with such resignation, but he'd be there soon to comfort his twin then they'd be together always. Just the two of them. As it always should have been.

He broke out of the cover of trees and crossed a dried paddock. Two men and one woman appeared ahead of him, standing in a triangle and dressed in drab utilitarian clothes. He dug up the dirt in a long furrow as he skidded to a halt.

"Where's the key?" the leader said. Gray-haired and pock-marked skin and protruding eyes.

"You don't need him." He pulled off the backpack and opened it so the first one could peer in. "I have his blood. That's enough."

The leader's eyes narrowed.

"We can argue about this later, but you'd better get me to safety before Aurelia comes. I'm guessing you don't want a confrontation with them."

The woman laughed, but a side-look from the leader silenced her.

"You'll do for now." He snatched the bag out of Olivier's hand and threw it to the other man. "Do I have to bind you?"

Olivier held up his hands. "You've got nothing to fear from me."

Sulfurous magic poured out the leader's open palms

and encased Olivier in invisible bonds. He came forward and slapped a hand on Olivier's shoulder. "Kalendra, stay behind and kill any who come after us."

"Yes, Franz."

They traveled through the gray nothingness of an endless world. No hands grabbed at him this time. No jolts threw him this way and that, and they stepped out into a darkened warehouse where ahead of him stood an illuminated glass box. In a corner sat Thierry.

A chill of excitement radiated from the center of Olivier's chest.

Together at last.

Against his will, Thierry was levitated off the ground and slammed against the glass wall while the door to the cell opened and Franz thrust Olivier inside. Franz riffled through the backpack, a smirk slashing across his ugly face as he shook his head. He selected three pouches of blood from the bag but threw the rest in after him. The bonds on Olivier's wrists and around his arms fell away as the door closed.

"Why are you leaving this with us?" He picked up the bag and held it up. "It's *his* blood. You can't have enough there."

"This'll do." He brandished the pouches in his hand. "We need *him* so knock yourself out. Consider it your last meal."

Snakes twisted in his belly, their contortions knotting and squeezing their bodies to death. He should have known it would never be that easy.

Franz turned to the other man. "Take a squad. Search for the key. He can't be far from where we collected this one."

His offsider nodded and vanished. Had Oberon woken? Would he run? How long did he have? He kept his face impassive. He couldn't give anything away, but inside he howled at his own stupidity. Of course, it wouldn't be that easy.

Franz gave him a smug smile and vanished. Olivier slammed on the door, attempting to smash the glass, but it was as strongly fashioned as Aurelia's prison.

"Why did you come, Olivier?"

He rounded on his brother. "Because you told me to."

Their eyes met but Thierry's expression was unreadable. He expected to see hate in those brown eyes, or resignation at his fate, but there was nothing. If it weren't for the bond, the flood of panic over a lost love, concern for what would come next, Thierry could have been made of marble. He had to unpick his own emotions from his brother's, all except the disgust.

That was all Thierry's.

He huffed a deep breath, hoping to expel some of that putrid air, but it hung around like smog.

"You were supposed to be the one they needed," Thierry said. "The *only* one."

"Oh, I'm sorry. Did I ruin your fairytale ending?"

Hate, pure, thick, and absolute, poured through him, carrying traces of all those past wrongs and names of dead lovers. Relentless, it was impossible to hold back so he let it wash through him in the hope of finding some raft of forgiveness to cling to. The only consolation, as miniscule as it was, was that they suffered together. But even that didn't have its usual sweetness. He couldn't use it. The fight had gone out of him.

Thierry sneered. "I don't want to fight either. You're not worth it. And with any luck, Aurelia will rescue us, we'll serve our purpose, and I'll never have to look at you again."

You never saw me anyway.

Olivier crouched over the bag containing Oberon's blood and opened it. Why did they only take three? He pulled one out and rolled it over his hands.

"You drained him?" Thierry's accusations stabbed him.

"He did it himself. To save his own ass." *He tried to stop me.* "Not that it's going to do any good." He tossed the pouch at his brother, then pulled one out for himself. He hunkered down with his back to Thierry and punctured the bag.

He sucked on Oberon's blood. Stale beer and cigarettes coated his tongue. He stopped and had to force himself to not spit it out—blood was blood after all—but this wasn't Oberon's. The taste burned his throat.

The lying, double-crossing, self-serving little fucker.

Olivier had been clear he'd wanted to be with Thierry, the world expected him to destroy it, but the witch had gone against his wishes. All so he could—

The fire in his gut sputtered and died.

All so he could keep them alive that little while longer. Oberon wasn't the monster. He was. Saving the world from destruction was what anyone would do. The acrid blood oozed down his gullet. At least it was strong enough to dull Thierry's thoughts and block his hate. The curtain fell between them, and he'd never been so grateful.

When the blood ran out, the silence stretched until Thierry snipped it.

"Why didn't you kill the witch? Even without knowing what he's going to be used for, after what he did to you, why didn't you kill him?"

Nobody believed him capable of mercy or restraint. "He'd already suffered enough." Even as he said it, it didn't ring like the truth.

"What makes him so different? So different from me and my lovers?"

Olivier chewed his lip. "He forgave me."

"Bullshit." Thierry's response was emphatic and ugly. "There's not a person in this world who could forgive you for the things you've done."

You're wrong. And I ran from him.

But he wouldn't give Thierry more than he'd already taken. Some things a twin didn't have to share.

"Give it a rest. You got what you wanted in the end."

"No thanks to you."

He could have said any number of things in response: called him a hypocrite, confronted him with the sacrifice he'd made on his and Aurelia's behalf, demanded to know why he should never have wanted something for himself after what he'd done. And he could have said he'd wanted to be with Thierry so much he was willing to damn the world.

But Thierry would never understand any of it, especially not with the hate radiating at his back. Thierry would scoff and use it to attack him.

But he could say one thing.

"I'm sorry." His whispered words lanced the abscess that had grown on his heart. Those simple words carried away an infection he'd tried to ignore. It wasn't all sweetness; a sickness wanted him to gag, but he swallowed it down. "I'm sorry for taking Etienne and Reiner and trying to take Alex." He stopped talking because his heart cracked, and anything further would be an excuse.

Thierry shuffled away rather than respond, and Olivier's shoulders slowly relaxed. Thierry might never forgive him, but that didn't mean it didn't make a difference.

VIII

GROGGY UNCONSCIOUSNESS STAGGERED OFF OBERON, AND he rolled onto his back. He could breathe again. He hadn't died. He felt around his neck. He was whole and safe.

With a groan, he forced himself to his feet, wavering until he gained his balance and shuffled to the fridge. When he opened the door, the sight was as expected. The blood was gone. And he had to assume so was the vampire.

He checked the rooms anyway and finding them empty hurried from the cottage, grabbing Aurelia's knife on the way out. In the fresh hot air, he scanned for signs that Olivier remained. How far had he gotten before someone collected him? And would that have been Xadrak's followers—as Olivier had wished—or Aurelia's? Only one way to find out.

With a burst of power, he sealed the cottage and returned it to its dormant state. He had to figure out how to find Aurelia. She'd be hunkered down somewhere and contacting her would not be easy. He also had to contend with the acolytes. If they had Olivier, maybe it was already too late.

Rustling in the undergrowth turned his head. He prepared for an attack, channeling energy into the blade. The thrashing in the bushes grew louder and more violent; he crouched, his heart thumping and the hilt spinning in his palm.

Come on, you fuckers.

Alex crashed through the bush and only quick thinking stopped Oberon from blasting him.

"Oberon, grab hold." Alex ran towards him. "We need to hurry."

Without stopping, Alex scooped him up as if he weighed nothing more than a kitten and carried him out as explosions burst behind them, growing nearer, lights ricocheting off the trees and fire leaping into the sky.

"Where are we going?"

"We have to keep running. They'll get us in a moment."

He hoped 'us' was going to be who Alex expected.

Plunging into the shade and losing sight of the cottage, he prayed the protections he'd laid would keep it safe from magic and bushfire.

"Get ready!"

He held tight to Alex's body. Two men came alongside them, one grabbing Alex and the other him, and the four of them charged into the ether and away from the forest. Enhanced flight took them through the grayness unmolested seconds before they emerged in an apartment building hallway. He climbed down from Alex to stare at the two witches who'd rescued him.

"I'm Viktor. This is Moroni." He shook their hands. "How are you feeling?"

"Nervous."

He smiled. "Probably a good thing. Aurelia's not in a good mood."

Oberon cringed. "I'm sure she's going to be ecstatic when I tell her what Olivier and I have been up to."

"Where is the vampire? We lost track of him."

"If you don't have him, then he's with Xadrak."

"Damn. Look, I can only imagine what you're going through but Aurelia's reasonable." The companionable hand on his shoulder seemed sincere, but he was one of Aurelia's witches. "She's going to do right by you."

"And Olivier?"

Viktor heard the question but didn't respond.

"Thought so."

Alex gave a sheepish raise of his eyebrows. He should thank the vampire for rescuing him, but the warrior opened the door and led them into Aurelia's latest lair.

As he entered, six people in the big apartment stopped and stared. He tried to walk tall beneath their scrutiny while his stomach cartwheeled. He attempted to meet and hold their gaze, but one by one they fell away or looked further into the apartment towards what he presumed was Aurelia's direction.

Sure enough, she emerged out of a bedroom dressed in a royal blue velvet dress that swept the floor. Her hair was tied into a plait which hung down between her shoulders. The fingers on her right hand plucked the air as they hung by her side, and her face was a mask of simmering anger. Any thought he had that she'd be happy to see him shriveled.

"Where's Olivier?"

He swallowed hard. "I think they have him. He… He said they have Thierry as well."

She huffed. "At least we have you." She turned to Viktor. "Were you able to retrieve anything else of value?"

"We killed two acolytes but could not get a bead on where they came from or where the others were going."

"Well, it looks like we're in a holding pattern until someone makes a move. Neither side can—"

Now was as good a time as any to tell her the news.

He cleared his throat. "Except they have some of my blood."

He'd never seen anyone's face go as blank as Aurelia's did. Like someone had pulled the plug and the machine had shutdown mid-process. "Excuse me?"

"My blood. Olivier—no, *I* drained my blood and gave it to Olivier but—"

She surged forward, and he levitated off the ground in her invisible grip. "Are you trying to sabotage us? Have you been working for them all along?"

"No! I wanted Olivier dead, yes, but that was then, and I wasn't trying to ruin your plans."

"Then why would you do something so idiotic?"

A pack of blood-thirsty hounds would whimper at the fury in her voice; he struggled to respond.

"Look, I can explain if you'd—"

"He tortured you?"

"No. If you'd listen."

A baby cried from the other room, and Aurelia's eyes closed in exasperation. She dropped Oberon to the floor. "Bring him," she commanded as she walked away to tend to the babe.

Who had given birth? And here?

Viktor herded him into a bedroom where Aurelia and a red-headed witch tended a baby. On the bed lay Hame and beside him sat Carn, holding the oracle's still hand.

"Is he—?" He stopped as Hame's chest rose and fell.

Aurelia cradled the child and it quietened. Her baleful glare swung back to him. "You were explaining your stupidity?"

He swallowed back the rising rage. "The bond between

Olivier and Thierry returned, and Thierry said Xadrak's people wanted us both to go to them."

"Well, obviously."

He ignored her snark. "Olivier demanded to go, I refused but he suggested he take five quarts of my blood with him—" He held up his hand to stop another interjection. "I agreed but I only gave him one-and-a-half. The rest I summoned without him knowing. I didn't want him to go, but at the same time I couldn't give him everything to open the portal."

Did Olivier know what he'd done?

"I hope for all our sakes they don't have enough to open the portal."

"Are you going to rescue him?"

Aurelia licked her lips and her eyes skimmed over Alex. "We'll try." He heard the 'but' as she fixed back on him. "We might have to wait until Sinara is fully grown, then we can end this once and for all."

His heart thumped inside his chest. *Speak. Save yourself.* Aurelia's disapproval had done a good job of smothering his resistance, but he'd suffered worse and survived. He would still fight oblivion.

"Count me out."

Silence fell at his back. Aurelia looked up from the baby. "Excuse me? You're going to do what you were born to do."

"I know what you had planned for Thierry and Olivier. You'd save one but destroy the other. And I've got to presume you'd destroy me too."

Aurelia glanced at Alex again. How confident was she that Thierry would survive? What would really happen to him and Olivier and Thierry when they were no more?

"You don't have a choice." She offered the baby to the redhead.

"I do and I will exercise it." His voice strengthened. "I will seriously fuck up your plans and theirs unless you agree to my conditions."

"And what might they be?" Derision dripped off her tongue.

"You're to give us your word—and I'll bind you to ensure you go through with it—that the three of us will survive the portal and return to our current forms. I don't want to be some magical gateway for eternity, and I'm sure neither do Olivier or Thierry, so you'll make sure we're put back the way we are now."

"All of you?" She raised a condescending eyebrow. "I'm surprised you would want that for Olivier. Case of the Stockholms, is it?"

Her disregard echoed inside his chest as it tried to strike against him and bring down his resolve. "I don't condone what he's done to me or anyone, but I've forgiven him for it, and I want to see him restored. Considering what he did for you and Thierry, you should want that as well?"

She frowned. "What he did for us? He should be rewarded for being a psychopath and a murderer? For making my life that much harder?"

"For saving you from Henri."

"What lies has my brother told you?" She squinted like she was trying to read the fine print and had lost her glasses.

"No lies. I saw his past. And yours. I saw how he intervened and took assault after assault to spare you and Thierry."

She brushed aside his words, collected her braid in her hand and played with the end. "I don't have time for these sob stories."

"Call them what you will but Olivier saved you once

and you expect him to do it again, all with the same back-handed slap. And you know what? He'd do it willingly. He'd do it for you and for Thierry."

She froze mid-hair twirl. "My brother doesn't have the conscience, the insight, or the selflessness to act for anyone other than himself."

"And you are no different."

Her icy glare raised the hairs on the back of his neck. He folded his arms across his chest to heat the chill creeping through his veins.

"Those are my terms, Aurelia."

"And what makes you think you can bully me into accepting them?" She sauntered towards him. "I'm stronger and more powerful than you, I can force you and be done with it."

"Spoken like a true d'Arjou."

She slapped him hard across the face, and his cheek stung long after her hand had gone. He opened and cracked his jaw then turned back to her with a tight smile.

"If you force me, I wonder how many of your followers will feel quite so easy with being a party to it. After all, what is there to separate you from Xadrak? Or is it a case of like father, like daughter?"

She looked around at the assembled coven. Alex's hand slipped into his. The warmth of his healing power, revitalizing and removing the last of his weakness, sang in his blood.

At least Alex was an ally.

Aurelia's face grew ever grimmer, before she settled back to him. "Very well." She raised her hand.

She was agreeing! He fumbled in his pocket and withdrew the athame, satisfied at Aurelia's surprise at seeing it in his possession. He summoned his power and poured it into the blade.

"I promise to do everything within my power—" she began.

"Without subterfuge or trickery."

Air streamed through her nostrils. "Without subterfuge or trickery, to return Olivier d'Arjou, Thierry d'Arjou, and Oberon North to their current forms once their purpose as the portal is served. I promise this on pain of my own death."

In front of Aurelia's open palm, he drew a binding sigil that glowed red, blue, then white before dissipating. The binding was complete.

And he'd agreed to take his fated place as the key.

Well, fuck-a-doodle-doo.

Aurelia flipped her hand to demand her property. He gave her the knife and she stalked off.

The audience was over.

Carn looked at him with sad, hollow eyes, before turning back to Hame. Chatter resumed. Alex's hand slid across his shoulder and led him away. They stopped in front of the window and looked out over the glittering lights of the city.

They let the murmuring of the coven and the distant street noise fill the space between them. Things had to be discussed, but for a moment Oberon relaxed into the illusion that they were back in Perth. Back when they'd first met.

Alex had been sexy, intriguing, and nice as hell. They'd gone home together from the club, but they hadn't connected on a level that would have made more of a night of sweaty sex. Oberon wasn't prepared to let anyone get closer than was safe to, no matter how good they were in bed. They could have been friends if not for the secrets. What did he have left to hide?

"I owe you an apology," Oberon said.

"It's fine." He said it casually. "You don't owe me anything, Obe. We never got close enough."

"But still I… I was taking out what happened to me on you and thought that what had happened had—"

"Happened to happen to someone who happened to be me?" He laughed, and once he wrapped his head around it, Oberon did too.

"Something like that."

"I love him, Oberon." He didn't force his words. "Whether you can understand that or not."

"I think I can. And I'm sorry he's not here with you." Thierry might not like him very much, and the vampire's behavior hadn't always been fair, but Alex didn't deserve pain.

Alex stared out. "Do you think Aurelia will save him?"

"I don't know. I hope so, if not for my sake, then for yours."

"Did you really mean what you said about Olivier? That you'd forgiven him?"

"I did. What he did should be unforgivable and it probably is, but it's a hate that I don't want to carry with me for the rest of my life, however short that might be."

"I'm still surprised that you wouldn't want him to be destroyed completely. I understand saving yourself but Olivier? I've been on the end of those fangs and I've seen the trauma he's caused Thierry. Forgiveness might be one thing, but even rabid dogs get put down."

Oberon's fingers went to the brand on his shoulder. "After this I think he's going to be different. I've seen what's inside him, and it's not all dark insanity. And because I've seen it, and he knows I've seen it, he's able to see a different life."

Alex gave a short laugh. "I'll believe it when it happens."

"There's also you. And Thierry."

"What about us?"

"Thierry's got what he's always wanted, and Olivier is finally having to confront the reality that all the things he did for Thierry—misguided as they may have been—won't change the fact that he'll never love Olivier the way he wants. Not even a tenth of it, not now, not after what's happened."

"Olivier won't give up. He's tried multiple times to get rid of me."

"Yet here you are."

"I suppose. But if you think we can all play happy vampires after this is done, I think you're in for a rude shock. It really would be better, for Olivier too, if he and Thierry didn't have to share a planet."

"Time will tell. Perhaps none of us will live long enough to worry."

The scales were tipping, and he had the feeling they'd come crashing down in Xadrak's favor. Whatever Aurelia's plans, they would fail against superior strength and numbers. Olivier and Thierry would be obliterated. Him too. If Hame woke, Carn and Aurelia would be dead. And Alex… Who knew what sort of world he'd be left with and whether he'd want to continue living in it?

The waiting, the standing around doing nothing, made him itch. But he had to believe it had a purpose. Either the blood Olivier had taken would be enough to work the magic—in which case he'd made a grave miscalculation— or they'd soon have to parley with Xadrak's army and force the moment to its crisis.

Either way, there'd be bloodshed.

Though, right now, Olivier, Thierry, and he were the safest people on the planet. And when the time came, he'd be by Olivier's side.

That thought brought more comfort than he'd ever imagined possible.

IX

FRANZ'S SULFUROUS APPROACH BURNED IN OLIVIER'S nostrils before footsteps clicked on the concrete slab outside the cell. He lay on his back, looking through the glass ceiling because it was easier than looking at his brother's miserable form as he pined for Alex.

Olivier had drunk another pouch of blood and dulled his brother's emotions. The added warmth given off by the ingested blood—even if it went in cold and vile—was about the only pleasure available. Not only were he and Thierry going to die, but he'd hastened Oberon's demise too.

And to think, he could have stayed with the witch instead of running away.

"I'm sure you'll be pleased to know we were unable to locate the key." Franz stood outside the cell. Olivier could make him out in the periphery of his vision. He wouldn't turn his head to give him his full attention. He wouldn't even respond. But his heart sang. Oberon had escaped.

"I don't suppose you know where they'd take him, do you?"

Olivier kept his eyes forward. He wouldn't know the first thing about Oberon's escape plans. Or Aurelia's. Because if this lot didn't have him, she would, and she'd have squirrelled him away in some bolt hole awaiting his death. If they'd stayed together, perhaps he could have saved Oberon from that too. How long had Aurelia known what Oberon was? Had she been experimenting to see if one brother drinking his blood would be enough to activate the portal and save her precious Thierry?

He dismissed that reasoning. If she had, she'd never have allowed Oberon to roam free, and he'd already drunk from the witch before he'd shown up in the dungeon. They were all running blind.

"No matter," Franz said. The door opened and the sulfur swamped him until he coughed. He would have stayed lying down, but magic ensconced him, lifted him up, and slammed him against the glass wall. Thierry, too, was positioned opposite and pinned.

Franz came up to him and two male acolytes followed behind. One was the male who'd escorted him on his arrival; the other short, built, and with a permanent curl to his top lip. Both stood in front of Thierry. Both held short swords in their hands.

Not this again.

"Look," Olivier said. "I have no—"

Franz held up his index finger. "I *know* you don't know anything."

"Then what do you want?"

"Glad you asked."

Franz faced his men and nodded.

They lifted their swords and thrust them into Thierry's abdomen, driving them up into his torso and twisting the hilt. Olivier gritted his teeth against the mirrored pain that carved into his guts. Muted as it was, he still shared Thierry's agony. They wrenched the knife to widen the wound, and the brothers gasped in unison as the blades withdrew, slicing the skin and muscle. They held bowls beneath the gash to capture his blood and, once filled, the vessels disappeared. The men walked away from Thierry and left him to pant through the sting in his belly. There would have been easier and cleaner ways to get what they wanted.

Franz stepped aside as the men raised their bloody weapons and advanced on Olivier. He tensed his stomach as they impaled him, and the swords scorched his gizzards. Grunting against the heat, the blades shoved into him and gouged holes in his flesh. They caught his blood, with one of them stabbing him again to make the blood flow faster. Bowls full, they withdrew their swords and walked away.

Franz smiled a satisfied smile, his eyes bulging even more with a mad kind of glee. He left the cell and the door swung shut. The restraints vanished, and he and Thierry fell to the floor.

"What are…you going…to do now?" Olivier struggled to raise his torso enough to shoot Franz a defiant look.

The acolyte tutted. "If I told you, where would be the fun in that? You'll see soon enough after I see my daughter, but I promise you, you're going to love it."

Franz walked away and was soon lost to the darkness. The stink of sulfur remained in the air. Olivier pulled himself over to the bags of Oberon's blood, threw one to Thierry, and bit into another to heal himself. Who knew what strength they'd need for what came next?

X

THE BABY'S SCREAMS SHREDDED AURELIA'S DREAMS AND ripped her out of a restless sleep. She woke in Viktor's bed and searched for him in his seat beside her, but he was already across the room and scooping the babe out of the cot. His attempts to comfort the wailing infant did nothing to lessen the ear-splitting sound. She held out her hands to receive the child.

No matter how she bounced or cooed, Sinara refused to hush. The coven stirred and came to gawp. They all sensed that these cries were nothing to do with a wet nappy or hunger. She forced herself through the shrieking to find a sliver of peace.

Xadrak. Xadrak. Xadrak. Xa—

Peace turned to cold sick in her stomach. "He can't—"

She sank on to the end of the bed, and Carn took the babe out of her arms. The screaming stopped though the baby's mouth opened, and her face had turned purple. He'd saved them all from those bone-stripping screams with a shield.

Though the wailing had been silenced, Sinara's warning remained. She turned her sight far to the east and searched for Peter and his family. Her mind's eye hurried through the villa's rooms and halted at the sight of bodies everywhere. Not just Peter's but his wife's and…and…

Oh god.

Her eyelids flew open. "Mira. Viktor. Get to the villa and bring back whoever you can find who's still alive. But be careful, I think Xadrak walks among us."

Viktor, Mira, and three others ran for the door and vanished before it shut behind them. The remaining coven looked to her for answers. Oberon turned away.

"Aurelia?" Carn stepped forward, his eyes lit with a question even though he knew what Xadrak's presence must mean.

"I'm sorry, Carn. But Peter is dead. And it looks like he wasn't meant to be Xadrak after all."

A breath shuddered out of his mouth and he shook his head. "What the hell is going on?"

"I wish I knew." She rested a hand on his shoulder, but he slipped out from under it and gave her the baby, preferring to find solace in Hame's silence.

She stared into the babe's straining face as if she could read all the answers there.

If Xadrak had really returned, did that mean they were about to open the portal? Could it merely take Oberon's donated blood to join Thierry and Olivier together without a heart pumping it between them?

Why won't you help me?

How many more had she lost? How many did she have left? Viktor and Mira had to come back alive, and Zoe— dear, dear Zoe—had been spared death, though not injury. She hadn't scanned long enough to find remains of anyone else, but if Xadrak had been there, he would not have been lenient.

Mother, we need you.

The infant continued its muted screaming. Perhaps this was what they were waiting for. Perhaps they had no time left. Sinara would have to be brought forth.

Tonight.

After what felt like hours, the apartment door burst open, and Viktor and Mira hobbled in holding Zach up between them. Another witch carried Zoe. Viktor called for Alex and he was there placing his hands on Zach once they'd laid him down.

"Put her next to me here," Alex ordered until he was flanked by the brother and sister and put one hand on each.

Aurelia leapt to examine her two loyal followers, and her heart twisted. Zach's eyes had been gouged out and his stomach slashed with what looked like talons. His screams came out in strained and prolonged bursts. Zoe had fared better, but her throat was red and raw and turning purple from the crushing force of a great claw. Multiple cuts criss-crossed her body, and her right arm twisted at an unnatural angle.

"What about the others?" she asked.

"We found no one else alive," Viktor said. "Peter and Jane are dead, as are the rest of the coven. We couldn't find Diana."

The baby's arms flailed in Aurelia's grips, but the screams had stopped pouring out of her mouth.

They had to wait until Alex finished healing them, until their pain eased, and their breathing became regular, before getting more answers. Zoe was the first to rise and scrambled to reach Zach and grab his hand, kissing his cheek and hovering over his scarred, blinded face. "Oh, Zach."

A cough convulsed his body, and he shakily reached for her hand. Alex continued to apply his healing, but he wouldn't be able to bring back Zach's eyes. Aurelia's heart broke for him, and she wanted to wail and curse the demon that had done this, but that cold and calculating part of her, the rod of steel that ran through her body, made itself known and spoke its callousness aloud.

"Zoe, please, Zoe, we need to know what happened."

She sniffed, her breathing increased in speed like she didn't want to do this, that she wanted a moment to *stop*. Her wide eyes brimmed with tears.

"Ten acolytes broke through our defenses and sealed us in. They overpowered us and slaughtered Israel, Baron, Niamh without so much as a fight, then they captured Zach and I and made us watch. When I fought—" a shudder racked her body, "—they tore out Zach's eyes and said they'd rip him apart if I didn't keep still."

She wiped her cheek with her open palm, the other hand still clenched in Zach's. "Peter, Jane, and Diana were terrified and huddled together. Franz was there and he called Jane his daughter but that didn't stop him from slitting Peter and Jane's throat."

Jane was Franz's daughter?

"They collected Jane's blood and Peter's blood, and all the while Diana, that poor little girl, screamed. She was so frightened. So frightened," Zoe whispered. "They pulled out a cauldron, and five of them each dumped a load of blood into it. There were the bowls from Peter and Jane, but then they came with two others and then these pouches of blood you get in hospitals."

Oberon hung his head and muttered something under

his breath. She wanted to shake him and berate him for his idiocy, but Zoe's story kept coming.

"All the while that girl screamed and cried for her parents, but once all the blood was in, they picked her up and threw her in."

They'd focused on the wrong person. Carn had believed Peter was meant to be the vessel because that's what he'd been told. But it was the offspring of Jane and Peter, two people born of Xadrak's followers, a piece of himself secreted in each to create a suitable vessel. She'd been so blind. It had been Diana all along.

"She flailed until the blood coated her. They spoke their incantation, and she screamed louder as a red mist enveloped her. Oh god, she screamed until this terrible tearing silenced her and she transformed into the demon." Zoe swallowed hard. "He rose out of the mist in his complete form, black as oil, and the acolytes cheered."

The coven murmured, and Aurelia's eyes shot from one concerned face to another.

He's here. We're not ready.

Zoe stared up at her. "I thought Xadrak would kill us, but he offered us the chance to convert to his cause. We refused and he said we would bear witness, but Aurelia, oh god Aurelia, he…he burned the magic out of us. I…I can't feel it any longer. It's gone." She collapsed in a sobbing heap on top of her brother.

Aurelia's knees buckled, but Viktor caught her, and another witch took the babe from her arms. Three of her coven eliminated and two more without their magic. Xadrak had returned and they were greatly outnumbered.

She scrambled out of Viktor's arm and hugged Zoe as she her face in her chest.

"I'm sorry, Zoe." A giant fist mashed her heart into pulp. "I'm so sorry. We'll find a way to bring it back. We will. I'm so grateful you're still alive. That you're still with us."

She held Zoe as tight as she could, hoping to banish the pain and the horror, but the more she held on, the less comfort it conveyed.

Zoe wriggled out of her embrace. "There's more." She sniffed back tears. "He said to tell you he's ready to fight."

XI

OLIVIER DETECTED MOVEMENT IN THE DIM LIGHT BEYOND their cage, and a puff of rotten eggs followed. Franz come back for another gloat? To take more blood? His hand smoothed over his skin where the wound used to be. He flinched as his hand passed over it either from the memory or toxic residue. He'd fight harder next time and aim for the jugular. Someone had to die.

Thierry ignored him, seated on the other side of the prison and moping over his fate. He sneered while inside his twin's misery dripped acid into his belly. Misguided as always.

I should have stayed with Oberon.

"It has been too many years since I laid eyes on the two of you." A voice made of gravel and wolf howls charged out of the gloom.

The sound compelled him to turn his head, and he struggled to keep his look of boredom as a black demon, seven feet tall, with wings and horns and a pointed tail advanced towards them. His heart jackhammered inside his chest accompanied with a voice that jabbered *Danger!*

Danger! Danger! This wasn't some trick of theirs, concocting a living, breathing nightmare. This was real. His left hand —the one they couldn't see—closed into a fist and his nails dug into his palm.

Be still.

Thierry wasn't able to maintain his composure, and his brother scrambled to put as much distance between himself and the monster.

The demon stopped in front of the glass prison, and Olivier breathed out the stiffness that wanted him to play dead. Showing weakness, even in the face of this monstrosity, wasn't going to help. He was Olivier d'Arjou; he was afraid of nothing.

"I think I'd remember meeting something as ugly as you."

The demon's face contorted, whether in a smile or a sneer, he wasn't sure. Not that it mattered. It was still hideous.

"Insolence," Franz spat. "You will not refer to Lord Xadrak in such a manner."

Olivier fixed an unimpressed glare his way. "Xadrak? Sounds like a hemorrhoid treatment. Quite fitting I think."

"Always the joker, weren't you?" the demon said.

"Whatever game you're up to, I'm not playing. I've got nothing left to give you. You've nothing left to take."

Xadrak's laughter sounded like cars crashing. "Oh, we'll get to that, all in good time."

Olivier suppressed the terror, holding it down until it stopped trying to surface. "Can't come soon enough. Then I won't have to deal with the likes of you and Aurelia ever again."

"It's refreshing to see that you're resigned to your fate, Olivier. But I think your brother isn't as keen. He knows who I am, don't you, Thierry? Or should I say, who I was?"

Fake it. Olivier rolled his eyes. "Don't tell me. You're a friend of the Duke's. A brother of a countess I murdered. The milkmaid of a squire I gutted with a sickle. Am I getting warm?"

"Why don't you tell him, Thierry? Tell him what you know of me."

Olivier got to his feet and swaggered towards the demon. "Is that all this is? A game of who's the most famous? Let me think." He stroked his chin. "Did you have a pop hit in the Sixties? Did you invent the Spinning Jenny? Don't you see? I don't give a fuck who or what you are. I know we're going to die, but to be honest if living meant having to hear you speak and look at that thing you call a face forever, I'd choose death any day."

More collisions and squealing brakes. "Lucky for you, you don't have to make that choice on your own. Though I wonder if you're eager for the same fate to befall your brother." Xadrak walked around the prison towards Thierry. "I seem to remember you choosing to take his punishment as well as your own. I wonder if that's still the case."

Remember?

Xadrak opened his clawed hand and ribbons of red mist burst forth to lasso Thierry around his arms, legs and neck. The demon closed his fist and Thierry's body spasmed as he screamed wide-eyed from the unleashed spell.

Razors sliced through Olivier's skin in response, dulled but sharpening with each second. He ground his teeth until he thought they'd blunt.

Hold on, brother.

"You see, Olivier, I always knew you were taking the

punishment for Thierry and Aurelia, but it brought me greater pleasure to know it and let you keep doing it."

For all the demon's energetic vitriol, a second of cold stillness descended over the agony.

Father.

It made more sense than it should.

Thierry screamed and the sound jolted Olivier awake. "Leave him alone!"

"Or what?" The demon's eyes flashed crimson. "You'll put yourself in his place? After all these years you still want to defend him. Isn't it about time he took some of it? Doesn't he owe you that much? I would have helped ease your burden, but you always put yourself in the way."

The demon's volume crescendoed, feeding off Thierry's ongoing pain.

"I'd hoped I could fuck that out of you, but when that didn't work, I tried my fists. And here we are six hundred years later, and I'm finally giving Thierry what he *deserves,* and all you can do is *whine* at me. Useless *fucking* child. I should have bashed your brains in when you were a boy. Aurelia and Thierry too. That's what you deserved for being the offspring of that *whore.*"

Xadrak's polluted words shred the nonchalance. Spit dripped from the demon's slathering maw.

"But what's done is done and we still have our problem of Thierry here. We have time to kill before we have witches to kill, and I wonder if I should continue to torture him, or will you play your old trick and take over?"

Thierry's torment was his torment. Thierry's agony his agony. Could he let his brother take this? Hadn't he been spared so much?

But haven't I also caused him so much pain?

Could pain ever be balanced? Tit-for-tat? Thierry wouldn't thank him for it. He had never done so before.

But that didn't matter. Oberon had shown him what he had always known but refused to accept. He'd always sought to ease other's suffering out of love—but it had gotten twisted along the way. How he'd gone about it, what he'd expected in return. But he had the chance to make it right. Thierry might never forgive him for the damage he'd caused but that didn't mean intervening wasn't the right thing to do.

He would not be the monster.

Xadrak was enough.

He unfolded his arms, ready for whatever the demon threw at him. "If you want to get your rocks off torturing someone, do it to me and leave him out of it."

Xadrak's voice exploded with screeching laughter. "Olivier, you still disappoint me after all these years. I've always known the perfect way to torture you was to torture him. This way I get to hurt both of you."

Thierry's screaming stopped and he fell panting to the floor. Xadrak stepped closer. His hot breath fogged the glass.

Olivier glared up into the demon's raging eyes and hardened his heart. "I have nothing left to fear."

"We'll see about that." Xadrak smiled and his black fangs shone. He raised both claws and a red mist swept out and ensnared him and Thierry, wrapping them in a world of suffering that gripped both their bodies. Pain formed a figure-eight as it looped from inside his body to outside then to Thierry and back again. A perfect feedback of agony that obliterated his sight, obliterated his thought, but couldn't obliterate his love.

XII

"You're not thinking clearly, Aurelia," Viktor said. "If he's giving us this warning, it means he doesn't have enough of Oberon's blood. We can afford to wait."

"It's not just the key he wants. It's Sinara too," she said. "If he could open the portal with what he had, he'd still wait until Sinara was there and ready to fight him. He has to be able to throw her through."

"Won't he kill her? Won't that be enough?"

"Only if she's on Crion. Not if she's here."

"Then all the more reason to wait."

"We won't have time. He won't *let* us wait until our forces grow. He'll force our hand, and I'm tired of waiting."

"Then it'll be a short fight."

Oberon wandered away with the babe still in his arms. He'd heard enough fighting. He wanted a moment of ignorance and to forget that they were talking about him. Aurelia would try to keep her promise, but if she were dead, she wouldn't be there to try. Xadrak was already tilting the balance to his victory.

He left them to fight it out. He couldn't affect anything. He'd be taken by either side, used, destroyed. Perhaps death, once they lost their interest in him, would be the better option after all. And then he could start again in another life.

But he wanted *this* life. Even with all its horrors.

Sinara stopped crying and looked at him, as much as a three-day old baby could look at anything. Her face was beginning to fill and look less squashed. She wasn't beautiful, but there was something calming about being this close to her. He sat in a chair and blotted out the arguing between Aurelia and her coven and poured his attention into that strange face.

This was the great demoness Sinara they were all talking about. This is who they'd entrusted with their hopes. And if he could decipher the rest of what they were talking about, a five-year-old girl had become Xadrak. Meanwhile a room full of supposed adults—some older than a century—argued over a strategy of attack like kids in a playground.

He rocked Sinara, not that she needed to be soothed, but it felt like the right thing to do. His thoughts drifted around the whole shitty situation and landed on Olivier. Was he getting what he wanted by being with Thierry? Doubtful.

Alex hovered on the edge of the group, near to the mourning Carn and the sleeping Hame. His jaw was set, making the beautiful hustler appear grim and warrior-like. What had he been through these past weeks? He stayed by Hame's side to heal his weakening body, and— Oberon hoped—heal the torture being inflicted on him. Hame's body writhed and twisted from time to time, but what was being done to his mind? Would he come back sane?

All this torment because of the babe in his arms. No, not just her. Xadrak too, and his quest for domination.

Aurelia appeared before him. "Give her to me."

"What are you going to do?" He refused to hand her over.

She sighed heavily. "We're going to bring Sinara forth." She opened her arms to receive the baby.

"But how?" If he'd understood the ritual correctly, they needed the blood of the parents, plus the three parts of the portal. Xadrak had all five; they only had two.

It was looking even more likely he was going to die.

"With sheer force and trickery."

He expected Sinara to cry as Aurelia reached down and pulled her out of his arms. But the babe went…willingly? Could a child with no neck control give consent?

"I…I don't understand."

Aurelia cradled the baby with a care that hadn't always matched her words. "She's not here the same way Xadrak was. They were created differently so we're going to do things differently."

"But then what? She's here and Xadrak still has greater numbers *and* Thierry and Olivier."

She blinked at him. "Would you rather discuss strategy with an infant or a demon?"

When he didn't reply, she gave a curt nod and walked away.

He followed her and two of her witches fell in a flank behind him a little too close for it to be accidental. He sighed. *Always the fucking sacrifice.* He cast a look of help at Alex who came pushing through. The witches let the vampire in, and he gripped his hand.

"Don't worry," Alex said. "She made a promise, remember?"

His stomach turned cold. Aurelia and her promises…

She moved to the center of the room and knelt on the rug, thrusting a pillow on the floor and resting the baby on it. "Oberon, sit next to me. Alex, you beside him on the left, and Carn…"

She looked around and the witch ambled through the crowd and sank to the floor. His chin was covered in stubble, his blond hair hanging lank and limp, and the shadows under his eyes threatened trouble. He grunted as he got himself into position.

Zoe knelt on Carn's right, between him and Aurelia.

The coven formed a circle around them. They'd been paying attention. Oberon was still unaware of what was going to happen, but he figured it would involve his blood. That's all he seemed good for these days.

Aurelia drew the athame from her pocket and held the knife in her right hand. "Form the circle."

The witches surrounding them raised their hands, drawing energy up from the floor to the ceiling. The air cooled and electrified. They shifted the position of their hands to face their palms in at chest height to continue the flow. His heart kicked up a notch, responding to the magic, responding to the tension. Whatever they were going to do, it was going to be big. Eight witches, forming a circle, aligned to the cardinal points, and protecting them, filling them with their energy.

Alex swayed in the scent. Oranges strong enough for even him to smell must have swamped Alex's sensitive senses.

Aurelia produced a wooden bowl and placed it on the floor. She held out her wrist, sliced across the skin with the knife, and turned it over to drip blood into the bowl. She squeezed her forearm to pump it faster and when enough had fallen she withdrew, sealed the wound, and passed the knife to Oberon.

"Your turn."

He did it quickly, without thinking, wanting it done. A sharp sting, blood in the bowl. He passed it to Alex.

The vampire didn't bother with the knife, instead biting into his wrist and letting his blood flow. Why Alex's blood?

Carn was next and he sliced his wrist, but before he turned it over to collect it, he put the knife down and waved his hand over the wound. Carn worked his magic and created a small ball of blood above his wrist, shimmering in the light and with magic.

"Thierry, right?" he asked.

Aurelia nodded.

That meant Alex represented Olivier, which made perverse sense.

The blood coming out of Carn tapered and formed a perfect sphere, imbued with magic.

Trickery.

The ball floated to the bowl and dropped into it. Then Carn held the knife out for Zoe whose shaky hand made its own incision across her wrist. She then offered her arm to Carn who repeated the trick for her, forming another sphere, imbuing it with more magic. Zoe didn't look, her face kept still and defiant.

Oberon didn't ask who this blood was meant to represent, but he could guess it was the baby's father, whoever he was. The sphere dropped into the bowl, and Carn healed Zoe's wrist. Alex reached over and closed Carn's wound with his hand.

Aurelia retrieved the bowl and peered into the bloody mix before returning it to the floor in front of the baby. The coven kept up the flow of magic. Viktor stood behind Aurelia and his gray eyes kept watch; his concentration so intense it had weight.

Aurelia rested back on her feet and opened her arms wide, her palms facing up. She gestured for the five of them in the inner circle to join hands.

"You know what you're doing, don't you, Aurelia?" Oberon asked.

She shot him a look that wondered how dare he could question her, but it seemed a valid concern. "Do as I say and remain open."

Aurelia squeezed his knuckles hard enough to make him wince. He tried to fight it, but energy rippled through him from Alex and he tensed before letting it pass onto Aurelia. Strong, thick and insistent it bound their hands together and roped his soul and magic into the working.

He, Carn, and Aurelia balanced the two non-magical people in the circle, but for the power that Aurelia pumped into them, he may as well have been normal too. He tilted his head back as it crashed through him like a cold, crisp waterfall. It pounded him and sank him into the flow as he hurtled through to their common purpose.

"Focus." Aurelia's voice was steady and sure. "Open yourself to the flow but direct it down to where we want it to go. Focus on the charge."

He turned his mind to the working and picked one word to pour his concentration into.

Channel.

He repeated it until the flow shifted. It locked onto the word and rode it along the raging river rushing towards the ocean.

"We call on the powers present to charge the Blood of Five to act as a channel through which the demoness Sinara can enter this world, fully and completely in her true form," Aurelia ordered. "We charge you."

"We charge you," Carn and Zoe responded in unison.

Aurelia squeezed his hand and he did the same to Alex and all five repeated the call. "We charge you."

And again, but this time intoned with the force of the eight witches surrounding them. The sound shuddered through him.

The deluge surged through him once, twice, three times more then, with eyes open, the light poured out of Aurelia, rose up, turned, and crashed down into the wooden bowl of blood, filling it until it glowed red.

Aurelia leaned forward, dipped her fingers into the bowl of blood. When she withdrew it, red light smeared the ends of her fingers. She painted the baby's face, her chest, her arms and legs. Aurelia bit her bottom lip as she did so, and her eyes dimmed. Her fingers shook the longer she went. All the while the babe looked at her. There was awareness in her eyes. Acceptance. Consolation. Aurelia seemed immune to it. Her body lowered to the infant and her breathing shook.

Anointing done, Aurelia shuffled back, wiped the blood off her fingers and grabbed at his and Zoe's hands, resealing the circle.

"All ready?" She took a deep breath. "We're summoning a demon, so I want the circles kept as strong as possible. We can't afford to have any breaks in the flow."

Sweat turned Oberon's palms slick and he wanted to wipe them but couldn't break free. His wriggling turned Alex's attention his way and he gave him a wide-eyed smile, part-good luck, part-what-the-fuck. Oberon chuckled silently.

"Let's start," Aurelia said.

As before the power came through him from the right, drawing the energy around clockwise, pulling it into a vortex that peeled off him and sloped downwards to the center of the circle. A faint glow intensified into bright white light as the energy sailed around and around, gathering strength.

His heart pumped faster, his chest lifted and inflated with energy.

Summon.

The word repeated inside his head, steady, sure, slow, measured. The tempo increased. Slowly. Measured again. But a quickening that matched the beating of his heart. He gripped Aurelia and Alex tighter. Light streamed towards the child and the blood glowed red, brighter, rising off the child's skin to reach towards the sky like fingers reaching for the precipice to pull itself up.

"Join us," Aurelia said.

Energy poured into him. His back arched and his eyes opened. He strained as he took in this added power which poured through him to whirl around the baby and smother it in visible power.

Summon. Summon. Summon. Summon.

Faster and faster the energy spun, wrenching more out of him, more than he had ever felt, more than he ever could have channeled alone. His heart sang with the power of it, with the connection to these people, with the feeling of the divine crashing through him until he lost himself into the torrent and they all became one.

"Sinara!" they shouted.

The world shook like they beat on a giant castle door.

"Sinara!"

The door opened and the power ripped out of them and they were swept into the magnificence that they'd worked. And through the door their power summoned the demoness Sinara.

And she answered.

XIII

Sinara stood where the infant had been: a white demon with feathery wings, gleaming horns and a tail, much like a lion's, covered in velvet down. The coven collapsed after the working to bring her forth. Even Alex was shaken and hunched beside Oberon. He, meanwhile, was still.

This is who I'm going to die for.

Sinara opened her arms and energy streamed through the coven. Refreshed, some warily got to their feet, though most of them chose to remain down, Oberon included. The last time he'd seen Sinara he'd been on the verge of death. He was in no hurry to renew their acquaintance.

Aurelia leapt to her feet and into Sinara's giant arms. The demon towered over the witch. Sinara measured taller than even Carn, who looked a little sick while staring at the demon.

"You did it, Aurelia." Sinara's voice sounded seemingly like two voices at once, a sound and its echo like tinkling glass. "Thank you and thank you everyone for the sacrifices you have made."

"Xadrak is waiting for us," Aurelia said. "He only needs Oberon now."

The demoness looked at him, along with the other eyes in the room. "I'm sorry you have to go through this, Oberon."

He'd stood during their little family reunion. "Well, I suppose I should be grateful that you saved me last time, though it feels a little like it was delaying the inevitable."

She reached forward and her clawed hand hovered over his chest. "We will do our best to make sure you come out of this alive."

He folded his arms. "So, what do we do?"

"We give you to Xadrak."

Black spots flashed in front of his eyes and marked Sinara's white body. He closed his eyes to make them disappear, but his balance wavered, and he was forced to open them again.

No escape.

Aurelia's plans had never inspired much faith, but he'd harbored some hope that the demon would have better options. Instead she was going to wave the white flag, and still he wouldn't survive the war. He was going to die screaming so they'd know what they'd done to him.

"You can't be serious!" Aurelia said.

"We need the portal open, and he needs me to go through it," Sinara replied. "I'm not convinced that he wants merely to get rid of me but also to bring over his loyalists, whoever is left, so they might rule here instead of suffer subjugation on Crion. And to do that he needs to control the portal and neutralize me."

"He'll kill you." Aurelia's face buckled with disbelief.

"Not here he won't. Otherwise I'd return and challenge his rule."

"So, you intend to hand yourself over?"

"And me with you?" Oberon added.

"In a sense."

Coven members grumbled their disagreement. They'd come for a fight. But whatever they expected, it fit in with what Oberon knew to be coming. Either way he would be made to participate in this portal.

"You can't go alone," Aurelia said.

"I won't be alone. I want you there, all of you, but you're not to interfere, you're not to show yourselves until Xadrak opens the portal."

"Why would he do that if we're all there? He'd suspect a trap."

"He'll have to."

"But why?"

Sinara looked at him without a hint of a smile on her muscular face. Her eyes, however, brimmed with pity.

His stomach bottomed out somewhere in the basement.

"She's going to kill me," he said.

"What?" Aurelia's eyes bulged.

"His life must hang in the balance," Sinara said. "Xadrak will have to bring Olivier and Thierry forward. If he doesn't, that'll be the end of it, and he might never get another chance."

Alex held his hand, but Oberon couldn't muster the strength to cling on. Let it be done. Get it over with. Move on, whether through this life or another.

"Do you agree, Oberon?" Sinara asked.

He was surprised when he nodded. He staggered away and left them to argue the logistics. He'd be put where they wanted him, all he had to do was follow orders. At least if Sinara was the one to bring his life on Earth to an end, it might be painless.

Alex followed him into the bedroom. He climbed onto

the bed and sat beside Hame. The oracle's face twitched like his skin buzzed with tiny electric shocks. Was Hame watching this? Had he foreseen it and kept silent? Meanwhile the coven burst into activity. Some went to summon the rest of their tribe, while others remained and subjected themselves to receiving Sinara's additional power. Carn included.

"Do you want to talk about it?" Alex slid onto the bed next to him.

"Not really. I just want it over with."

Would it hurt? Would he still be him? Would he remember this life or simply become one with the brothers? How Thierry must be suffering.

"I'm sorry, Alex. This must be hard on you too."

"It is what it is, and I have to hope that Thierry and you come out of this okay."

"And Olivier."

Alex put his arm around Oberon's shoulder and pulled him close. "And Olivier."

"Do you mind—" He cleared his throat. "Do you mind if we lie down for a bit? I'm exhausted."

Alex laughed and wrapped Oberon into a hug as they lay together. The vampire's strength was more than he expected but he was safe and warm, and with Hame beside them, they were survivors. They just had to do it again.

He dozed—miraculously he dozed—and dreamed of being in Olivier's arms and there being no fear. When he woke, he imagined he was still there. But as he opened his eyes to Aurelia and Sinara peering down at him, his heart jumped into his throat and the happy delusion bolted for cover.

He swallowed the panic. "I guess it's time?"

They nodded and stood back to allow him and Alex room to move. Carn was back by Hame's side and holding his hand. The witch seemed stronger, brighter, though he still needed a shave. He glowed with Sinara's power.

Carn winked at him and smiled. An odd gesture on the blond giant, his features usually so downcast, but maybe it was an act to encourage him along, a celebration and offering to the sacrifice.

Before it got its throat slit.

He followed Aurelia and Sinara. The apartment was even fuller. Witches he'd never seen before had joined with those from earlier in the day. They watched and nodded to him, some smiled, others were grim, battle determined or heady on the power of the demon. Zoe was there and…and she was smiling. Her brother stood beside her, serious and forlorn but upright and determined.

Sinara's magic had worked wonders. But it hadn't returned Zach's eyes.

Aurelia gathered her coven of twenty and rose high enough for all to see her.

"My brothers and sisters, we are going into battle, one that is long overdue. Some of us will not survive, but the sacrifices made will ensure this world is safe from Xadrak and his acolytes. You have served Sinara and me well over the years, when things were hard, when the outcome seemed uncertain, but we will emerge victorious. We will purge Xadrak from this world."

She gazed around her assembled coven, a grateful smile on her lips. Some of them nodded, others beamed up at her with the fervor of devotees.

"I want to thank you." She cleared her throat and her eyes tensed. "You have all meant so much to me. I am indebted to you for your service and for your friendship. After all this time, we are ready for the final push." The softness fled her face, and steel glinted in her eyes. "The battle will not be easy, but we are strong. We are one. And we will prevail!"

A battle cry filled the room and vibrated through Oberon's chest. Alex appeared behind him and he turned to his friend. "Good luck," Oberon said.

Alex smiled before his eyes flickered at something behind his shoulder. "You too." He leaned forward and kissed him gently on the mouth.

A clawed hand pressed his shoulder, a weight so heavy it could have pushed him through the floor. "Are you ready, Oberon?"

He'd never been ready for anything in his life—not the discovery of his power, nor the suffering at the hands of the d'Arjou family—but he was ready for this. His heart and chest swelled with his duty, using it as a drug to numb the terror that would have him flee.

Greater love hath no man than this…

But if Olivier had taught him anything, he was going to tear out a few throats while he laid down his life for his friends.

"Let's do this."

XIV

Olivier and Thierry finished the last of the blood. After the torture Xadrak had brought down on them, they'd needed the nourishment. They lay on the floor and stared through the glass ceiling into the shadows of the warehouse. Day or night, Olivier couldn't tell. The light hadn't changed the whole time they were in there. More tricks.

"Why did you do that?" Thierry asked.

"He would have done it anyway. He wanted me to make a choice."

"I know but you didn't have to."

"I never had to. But I wanted to." If Thierry could remember how they had once been, then he'd see this act wasn't so strange. But too many years lay between that time and this for his brother to realize. Xadrak's approaching stench saved him from having to explain.

"Come back to throw more cheap tricks at us?" Olivier snarled.

The demon's face creased into a smile. "I've heard enough of your shrieking for now, Olivier."

Beside him, his brother was still, and silence stretched across the bond.

"Then what are you doing here? We have better things to do with our time."

"Get up and you'll find out. It's going to be something you've always wanted, Olivier."

"I get to kill you?"

The demon chuckled and the sound was like a scalpel down his spine. "You're going to see Aurelia die."

His mouth dried.

They have Oberon.

He wasn't given the chance to find out more as he and Thierry were bound and gagged with magic and dragged out of the prison and into that in-between place. He didn't know where they traveled to, but when they emerged from that smeared dull world into one of color, it was to stand in a meadow of damp green and yellow grass waking up after winter. Hills cut into the sky, birds wheeled high above, but there was no one around. More importantly, no Oberon.

Where Xadrak walked, the grass shriveled and crumbled to dust. The earth blackened beneath his feet and the further he walked, the starker the ground became until, within seconds, a verdant field became a patch of dirt devoid of life. The acolytes fanned out to form an arch around Xadrak and took up positions ready for an assault.

He and Thierry were marched in front of Franz. Invisible but unbreakable bonds shackled their wrists and ankles. The manacles or the spell or whatever they'd done to Thierry stopped him from turning invisible. Both of them followed behind their…their father.

Henri.

After all these years, the son finally had a chance to confront the bastard father. Despite his size, despite the difference in species, he searched for weak points in which to bury his fangs. He hadn't found any yet. The demon's skin was gnarled and wizened, but even the toughest meat could be chewed with enough patience. Olivier could endure magic. It would hurt and had hurt—hurt without end—but Xadrak—Henri—would weaken. Then he'd strike and pour out all the years of pent-up and not-so-pent-up fury. Oberon would suggest he forgive, but perhaps he'd allow the exception in this case as it would mean saving the world.

"You don't really expect Aurelia to come, do you?" he said to the demon's leathery wings. "What would she gain?"

"Shut up." Franz shoved his shoulder. "Lord Xadrak doesn't have to answer your insolence."

Olivier halted suddenly and Franz's feet scrabbled in the dirt to stop himself from ramming him. Olivier pivoted and let his eyes glow. Franz's wide-eyed insanity slipped a little. He showed his fangs and stretched his mouth in glee.

"I'm going to kill you, Franz. And then I'm going to kill *Lord* Xadrak there—"

Franz thrust his hand onto Olivier's chest, and he braced for an attack, but Thierry slammed into Franz and knocked him aside. The acolyte crashed to the ground, and Thierry fell on him with teeth flashing. Olivier joined the fray, but before they could break skin, Franz repelled them.

Stinging, burning power juddered through their bodies and they levitated off the fallen acolyte and were slammed into the dirt. Franz shot to his feet and pelted them with magic that chipped their bones. But his petty vengeance couldn't quell the ripple of amusement that passed from Thierry into Olivier. He laughed aloud, as hard as it was while his insides melted.

Franz towered over them and the crazy was back in his eyes.

"Enough!" Xadrak shouted.

Franz gave them one last jolt for good measure and the flow stopped. Their muscles relaxed jerkily, and they panted from the ache, but they laughed.

God, it feels good to laugh with you, brother.

"Get up." Franz kicked Olivier in the ribs.

They staggered to their feet and were dragged along behind Xadrak until the demon stopped, turned, and looked down at them.

"The whore will come," Xadrak said.

"And if she doesn't?" He scratched his chin with his thumb, doing his best to appear nonchalant while handcuffed.

"Then I will set fire to the world and everyone in it. I will destroy cities and nations and scorch the earth until Aurelia brings me what I want."

"Aurelia doesn't give a shit about anyone but herself. She'll let others fight her battles, all the while keeping hidden what you seek. And you'll never find it. She's good like that. My sister knows how to keep a secret."

"She'll come. She's her mother's daughter after all."

That brought his head up. "What's Mother got to do with it?"

Xadrak's face folded into the semblance of a smile. "You're not the son of one demon, Olivier, but two, and if I'm not mistaken, and I rarely am, Sinara will come." Xadrak returned to searching the horizon.

Meanwhile, Olivier looked to Thierry for confirmation. His brother gave him an affirmative and apologetic shrug.

"All this time we've been the sons of demons and no one told me?"

Thierry smiled. Was that smile for him? "I guess they thought you couldn't handle any more feelings of superiority."

"It's true. Who'd want to be an ordinary vampire when you can be a vampire borne of demons?" His hands flew to his cheeks. "Wait 'til we tell everyone. They're going to be so jealous."

Xadrak shot forward with a claw and gouged it through the skin of Olivier's chest. He barked out a breath as talons scraped against the tender flesh of his heart. Xadrak breathed sulfur over him. "If I didn't need your mouth for this, I'd rip off your jaw. Until then, keep it shut."

Xadrak withdrew his claws and the skin on the edges of the holes sizzled. Olivier forced himself to stay up as the wound stitched closed.

"Acolytes, prepare for an attack!" Xadrak roared before lowering his voice. "Franz, protect these two from being taken."

"Yes, my lord." Franz replied with a little too much breathy emphasis on the yes.

"Why don't you suck his dick while you're at it?" Olivier sneered.

Franz's eyes bulged like a Chihuahua readying for a good yapping. Olivier chuckled but his laughs stopped when a white demon appeared a few hundred yards away from them.

Enter Demon Number Two.

His mother? *Their* mother? What had he called her? Sinara? Not that it mattered. Met one demon, met them all. But his vision slid off her to the figure next to her.

Everything in him stopped. *No!* She'd brought Oberon. Why couldn't Aurelia have kept him out of this?

"Keep watch!" Xadrak shouted. "She's not alone."

"Search if you must, but we are alone." Her voice carried across the distance as if she stood a foot from them.

She didn't shout or bellow; amusement laced her soft words.

While a score of acolytes hunted, Xadrak turned his fury towards Sinara. "Give him to me. You cannot win this. Prepare for your destruction."

"It has been too long since we have faced each other in earthly battle. I'm almost looking forward to it. At least this time I doubt you will run away."

"You call me coward?" Xadrak's taloned feet scratched the dirt. "After years of sneaking around and getting others to do your work for you? Of sticking to the higher planes and denying a descent into flesh? Even now you play tricks to avoid facing me in true battle." His wings created a small eddy of dust.

"I have seen enough of your face to last millennia. But I will see it returned to Crion where you will suffer the justice you should have received centuries ago."

"You and what army?" He gestured to the empty air. "I will have the key and you will submit."

Sinara positioned Oberon in front of her, claws resting on his shoulder. "We'll have to see about that."

"Seize her and the key!"

The acolytes released their power in streams of colored light.

Olivier hissed at the volleys aimed at Oberon, but they struck a shield. The flow continued but it could not push through. Oberon closed his eyes as a knife appeared in Sinara's claw and she held it to his throat. Olivier's heart ricocheted inside his chest, the beast howling at the gates, demanding to be freed.

No, she couldn't. That's not how this was going to end. Oberon had to survive!

She dragged the knife across his neck, and Olivier roared, the sound galloping out of his mouth and charging towards them as if it were enough to stop this obscenity.

Oberon's blood flowed and he sank to the ground. Sinara vanished.

"Heal him!" Xadrak shouted, but the shield held, and their magic couldn't reach him.

Olivier bashed against his bonds. Oberon couldn't die, not again.

But the witch gurgled from the blood pooling in his throat. His hands scrabbled in the dirt, trying to find something to grab on to and stop himself from holding in his life force. He should be healing himself. He'd done it before.

A chill crept along his shoulders.

They weren't doing this to kill Oberon. They were doing this to force the portal open.

He turned to his brother. "We have to drink from him."

Sad, panicked eyes met his as Thierry realized what this meant.

Save the world, lose Alex.

"Please," Olivier whispered.

A second of pause then Thierry nodded.

"He's going to die," Olivier shouted at Xadrak. "Let us free, or you'll never get what you want."

Xadrak's roars shook the earth, and the bonds shattered. Olivier and Thierry raced across the field and through the shield to collapse next to Oberon. He picked up the witch's dust and dirt-covered hand. Oberon looked at him and knew exactly which brother he saw.

"Hurry." The blood poured out of him and stained his lips. "It's the only way."

He looked at his twin. "Thierry?"

His brother searched around for some sign of his lover, but all they saw was blighted nature, acolytes, and Xadrak.

Olivier's heart fractured into a thousand pieces and their shards scraped his insides raw.

Oh, brother, I am so sorry.

If he could have done this without Thierry, he would have. His brother didn't deserve to lose again. He forced hope into his thoughts and words.

"Aurelia will save you."

Xadrak advanced towards them; he couldn't be allowed to intercede. Olivier squeezed Thierry's shoulder, and his brother took a deep breath. More cuts flayed him from within, but Thierry assented.

Together they propped the witch up between them. With a quick look at Oberon's stricken face, his eyes afraid but insistent, he and Thierry bowed their heads and bit into the tattered skin of Oberon's blood-slick neck, and they drank.

And drank…

And drank…

XV

Aurelia and her coven watched through a scrying glass from a safe place beyond the field. Sinara was still out there, hidden with Carn and bolstering the shield that protected Oberon from having his life saved by Xadrak. Her brothers bit into Oberon's neck and drank his blood. Within seconds, a whirlwind whipped their hair and clothes and gathered dust and light to their bodies.

"Go!" she shouted and her remaining coven of twenty vanished into the ether and traveled to the edges of the battlefield. Cloaked in shields, they landed behind the transfixed acolytes like silent assassins and unleashed their spells.

A bolt of lightning, a flash of fire, a tear of their hearts —unprotected acolytes fell. Aurelia appeared behind a woman and sliced through her flimsy shield. With the fall of their comrades, the rest of the acolytes were on guard. Xadrak released a wave of force that tore the ground beneath their feet.

She and her coven vanished. Fourteen acolytes had

fallen to their surprise attack, but another would not be possible. Still, fourteen was better than none.

They reformed in a V between Xadrak's forces and the portal. Olivier, Thierry, and Oberon disintegrated like houses destroyed in a nuclear blast, and the browns and grays of earth mixed with the portal's blues.

Soon, they'd see Crion. They had to hurry.

Xadrak and his acolytes turned their attack, a massive force stampeding towards them. Aurelia and her coven braced as his assault slammed into them. One of her coven buckled, ripping a hole in their defenses.

"Sinara!" Xadrak roared. "Your weakness is shameful. Come face your demise!"

Sinara did not appear, but an invisible border rose that kept the two armies apart. Aurelia redirected her magic's flow to release a deadly stream which struck the hearts of two acolytes. They fell and she whipped her attack to hit another two. The remaining acolytes redoubled their efforts and struggled against the defenses placed before them.

"Hold!" she roared to bolster her coven. "Hold for yourselves if not for Sinara!"

Xadrak punched the air in front of him and the charge struck and spun her around. Winded, she slammed into the dirt, facing the portal. Her defensive line wavered. She struggled to right herself, corralling her strength as another wave burned her. She screamed from the searing pain and scrabbled to protect herself. They had to defend the portal until—

She opened her eyes and the portal stood strong and proud. Through it the world of Crion shone in its reddish-brown hue. The shield around it held; she just hoped this part of Sinara's plan was going to work out or—

"Sinara!" Xadrak roared.

Aurelia forced herself to stand. Bodies of her witches were strewn about but a force of thirteen still maintained a ragged line. Not enough of the acolytes had been destroyed. She gouged into the depths of her power, but before she released it, a fist smashed into the back of her head. The world shook from the blow, and she collapsed to the ground. She had to stand, but a hand grabbed hold of her plait and yanked her up.

"I've been waiting years to destroy you, Aurelia," Franz hissed in her ear.

She tried to fight back but pain spasmed in her skull. "You…were never…much of a…priority for me."

She struggled against him, but she couldn't free herself from his steel-like hold. Xadrak charged the portal, and her chest seized as he cast aside the lives of her witches.

Franz marched her in Xadrak's wake. The remains of her coven battled, and Viktor made a move to come to her rescue. Only a wide-eyed plea and a frantic flick of her hand kept him back. She couldn't lose him.

He roared, unsettling the brown-haired male acolyte coming towards him. With brutal grace, Viktor wielded a sword in his right hand and an orb of scarlet light in the other and destroyed his attacker in a sickening rend of flesh before rushing to Mira's side and attacking another. Under a berserker's fit he waged battle and disappeared from her sight as she was brought beneath Xadrak's shadow.

The demon stopped in front of the portal. He sensed the shield, a massive confluence of power designed to keep him back—and hide anyone sneaking through the portal. He scraped his black claw down it, hacking into its energy until it shattered. She closed her eyes and hoped Carn had protected himself from the kickback.

There was nothing to stop him entering now, but he

swiveled and scanned the skies. Not finding his old foe he sunk his claws into Aurelia's hair, taking over from Franz as captor. Suspended above the ground, she clung to Xadrak's burning hand, lest her scalp tear from her skull. Her jaw ached from keeping it closed. She would not whimper.

"Sinara! Show yourself. Weak mother that you are, watch as your child dies for your sake!"

Aurelia writhed, unable to grab hold of her power and protect herself.

Mother, hurry.

He raised her aloft, gravity making her twist and ache. "Your daughter will suffer, you accursed whore!"

"She's your daughter too," Sinara snarled from behind him.

And Xadrak was flying, falling, hit from behind with a force that catapulted them across the sky. Power cocooned Aurelia and protected her from the violent jolting until Xadrak's claw unlocked and she was released. She slipped through the ether to disappear farther down the field to land as Sinara advanced, flanked by her army of demons.

Cool relief drowned the sparking panic.

They've come.

They had to be quick before what might remain of Xadrak's followers on Crion could pour through. Xadrak's acolytes quaked at the appearance of the demonic army. She cut through the ether to appear behind one acolyte, placed her hands on her back, and stopped her heart mid-beat. She signaled to Zoe and they split to help the others finish the acolytes, gathering more and more to them to rout the followers. Three broke ranks and vanished but they were pursued. Sinara's demons took to the sky, fanned out, and spread a shield over the field to lock all beneath a dome of white. Xadrak, Franz, and a handful of acolytes remained, but their strength wasn't enough.

The acolytes fell until only Franz and Xadrak remained.

"You have lost, Xadrak." Sinara landed on the earth in front of him.

Franz's face and fingers twisted with rage as he gathered his strength. Aurelia's coven attacked and overwhelmed his power. They dragged him across the field, away from his lord, and dumped him at her feet. She grabbed his hair and forced him to look at Xadrak's defeat: one malignant, hate-filled demon standing under the judgement of angels.

"You picked the wrong side," she hissed into his ear.

"He's not defeated yet."

"No, but you are." She brandished the athame and dragged it across his throat, holding him while his life force drained out of him. His body shook as death spasmed through his arteries and his blood stained the dirt. She prayed he was the last.

"You cannot beat me," Xadrak said. "I will fight you for a thousand eternities, Sinara."

"And I look forward to each and every one." She advanced on him.

He stumbled back, his wings opening and closing, but unable to take flight. The demons, armed with weapons and magic, maintained their line. Xadrak roared again, a wall of sound that shot towards Sinara, forcing her out of the way. It barreled through the portal.

A summons.

A call to arms.

Sinara's eyes widened and she signaled for the army to attack.

The demons released their power and stoppered Xadrak's voice. His arms bound to his side, his wings closed and shredded to ribbons, forcing his mouth to bulge with confined screams. His tail thrashed as he collapsed to the ground. Immune to his cries, the demons dragged him through the portal and were gone. Only Sinara was left.

Aurelia jumped over Franz's dead body and hurried towards her mother.

"You have to close the portal. Who knows how fast Xadrak's loyalists will gather? They mustn't get through." Sinara reached down and caressed Aurelia's face with a palm as soft as feathers.

Aurelia fell into her arms. This was goodbye. This was forever. All the things they could have shared. All the love they could have expressed. All the years they could have been together.

"I love you, my daughter. And I always will."

"I love you too, Mother. I hope…I hope life treats you well always."

"As with you." She squeezed her tighter.

Sinara changed from the white demon into that of her mother when she'd lived on Earth. The smaller stature, her raven hair that she'd passed on to her children, the smell of human skin. She raised Aurelia's head and kissed her on the mouth, and Aurelia's heart broke. Tears burned in her eyes before bursting free and coursing down her cheeks. Her throat hardened and choked with her sobs. And as Elaine separated from her and her form returned to that of Sinara, her heart splintered again.

With a final goodbye caress of Aurelia's head, Sinara stepped through the portal to stand guard on the other side with her army. "Goodbye, my dearest daughter. Save your brothers and save Oberon."

Aurelia nodded and wiped the tears from her eyes. Under Sinara's encouragement, she stepped back and locked away the emotions that wanted to run rampant through her body. She cleared her throat and took a few deep breaths. Viktor came to stand on her right, and Mira and Zoe and the others who remained formed around her. They gave her strength.

Time to finish this.

"Carn!" she shouted.

The blond witch appeared from behind the portal, shattered and shaky, but upright. "Ready?"

As much as she didn't want to lose the portal, her power, and her mother, she'd made a promise and to break it meant losing her life. They had to try. Plus, Olivier and Thierry were the only family she had left on Earth.

"Let's bring them back."

XVI

Thierry and Oberon had disintegrated before Olivier's eyes as they crossed the final threshold and the magic transformed them. He'd sought to grab something, to keep bolted to the Earth, wishing that he was once again manacled, but he had nothing to hold on *with* let alone *to*.

And yet, as he broke apart, he came together, joining with Oberon and Thierry, bound by the blood and forming into a single entity. Part of him gave up the fight to remain by himself, to remain whole, and he welcomed this ethereal blessing, this communion between him and the others. With each passing second it was easier to let go. Until they became one.

They floated, aware that they were not alone, that they were whole but that whole was not one but many. They rested, a weariness they hadn't noticed before stole over them, but as soon as they were aware of it, it passed away. They were peace, in a state they had known but lost. They wanted to cry tears but remembered they had no form and that tears were not needed. They were whole and they were not alone.

But something bothered them. Outside yet within their being there passed a shadow, a shimmer. They heard it weep and beg and then they were crying too. But then it was gone.

After all it was only a shimmer.

Their oneness cracked. They were being pushed away. Stretched. They didn't fight this feeling, it saddened them because they were happy being one, but they didn't want to fight anymore. They knew there was a reason for it and that maybe it was their fault.

I'm sorry, they said without speaking. They had no voice to utter these words, but they trembled through their being. And they took these words because they were meant for them and they accepted the apology. They knew what those words meant and how truthful they were. The pushing stopped, and they were brought back together.

They tried to understand where those words had come from and why they mattered. They came from before. But there was only now.

And they floated. And they grew.

And love swam through them. Warmth and care radiated out from their center and they basked in it. They remembered love. Endless love.

Screams shimmered outside, then passed through them. Something else rippled across and through their surfaces then was gone. They felt them pass but didn't try to stop them. That wasn't what they were there for. They merely watched. And then the sensations were gone, so quickly, and then had never been. Not for them because now was all there was.

And they floated.

And they waited.

And the world passed through them for an eternity.

They were protected in the warmth. They were whole. They were content.

"Olivier."

Where did they know that sound from? It echoed around the whole. The other parts of them flinched and shook.

"Thierry."

This sound meant something too. But as soon as it came, it vanished and couldn't be held, like trying to catch ripples across the surface of the water.

"Oberon."

Another sound they knew without knowing. It snagged on something and attempted to dislodge them out of their infinity.

They remembered hurt.

The words repeated and tugged harder.

Repeated again, and again they were wrenched against themselves and the wholeness strained. Sharp panic streaked in and they were no longer floating but flung back into a maelstrom. Peace wrestled with fury and they broke from the one and he let out a cry that lasted forever.

They splintered into three parts he could see but not see.

And the voice kept repeating those three words.

Names. They were the names of his three parts, of his soul shattering and being stolen from him.

And in burst another sound, a cry, a cry he recognized and loved and had thought lost.

"Olivier."

"Thierry."

"Oberon."

"Olivier."

"Thierry."

"Oberon."

With each repetition, he became himself and the whole separated like dough torn into three equal but different parts. He looked. He saw. He saw his other parts; he saw their forms and he knew them as different from himself. And then he looked at his hands. When had he ever had hands? When had he had a body?

Olivier turned, heaving against the bonds that tied him to his brother. He heard the crying outside them, he heard the weeping, the desperation and he hoped that someone —that he—could rescue Oberon.

"Focus on yourselves," Aurelia cried. "Focus on your names."

Aurelia. His sister. She was with them.

"You are one, individual, the door cannot work if it is broken. Focus, pull against this bond."

Olivier had valued that bond his whole life, connected to his twin the way no other brothers—no other lovers—were connected. But there were others who mattered.

Like Alex—who would miss Thierry and had more of a claim over him because he held his brother's love.

And Oberon—who had never wanted this, who had wanted vengeance and to be whole once more, deserved more than being lost in this endless world, no matter the peace that came with it.

But him?

He did not need to come back. He could leave and they would be happy and perhaps he would be too. Lost, adrift in a world where he had no urge to feed, to destroy, to seek the love of others and claim it through any means necessary.

Thierry and Oberon pulled to return to their forms, and he would aid them. But for him? If he returned, it would be too hard to change. Better not to try than fail.

Especially when failure meant so much death. His time had come.

Six centuries wasn't a bad run.

He braced against them, while they reached towards Aurelia's call. He acted as counterpoint, the stand of a slingshot.

"Use me," he roared. "Push against me."

He'd be lost and become a piece to float away with the other junk of the universe; unable to be joined again with that which would make him whole. But then he'd be dead, be at peace, and he'd know that the others had returned.

Lived.

Loved.

"Push!"

A terrible tearing ruptured their center. The tension gave way, snipping thread by thread, then rapidly unravelling until only a sliver kept them together.

He was going to do it. He was going to be free.

And then he was, and darkness welcomed him, and he stopped fighting. He resisted no more.

The sacrifice fell into the pit.

But a hand reached across an impossible distance, locked onto him, and wrenched him out of the abyss.

Together.

And alive.

XVII

Oberon, Olivier, and Thierry lay in a naked, unconscious heap at Aurelia's feet. The fear locked around her heart unfastened, and she breathed easier with them back to their normal forms. The oath she'd made with Oberon had been served.

They'd done it. Sinara and Xadrak were gone.

And so was their power.

The added source had severed, and she was back to how she'd been not so long ago. It wasn't the loss of power that hurt; it was the loss of the connection with her mother. And while she should find joy in their triumph, it nevertheless felt miserly.

"Aurelia?" Carn said.

She realized she'd been staring at the bodies on the ground. Oberon breathed; her brothers were alive too.

Purple shadows expanded beneath Carn's eyes. "We need to find Hame."

Hearing his name snapped her out of her wistfulness. "Zoe, take the boys back to Viktor's and make sure they don't leave when they wake."

Alex bent down to Thierry and picked him up. His eyes bled tears. Other witches picked up Oberon and Olivier and vanished.

"Viktor, Moroni, take the others to hunt any escaped acolytes." Short nods from the two warriors and, almost without words, they gathered a squad and were walking away to handle their tactics.

Mira, Gabriela, and Carn remained behind. "Let's get Hame."

She'd hoped Hame's freedom would have been granted once Xadrak fell but the oracle hadn't bloomed in her head. He was there—just—a quivering traction that if she'd pushed at would break, but something about the sheer force of it warned her that to do so would destroy him. They had to hurry.

With no time to find somewhere suitable, and Carn looking like he had barely the energy to stand, they lay down in the dirt. The scorched earth dug into her backside and coated her clothes with ash. They lay together, two aligned with two along the arms of a cross, their heads in the center, and sought to calm themselves. Desperation made it harder to let go, the panic keeping her from finding equilibrium.

But the sun aided her, warmed her body, and lying down brought her to the edge of sleep, no matter the worries skittering through her. They had to save Hame. Then she could rest.

She let go and her astral form drifted out of her body and ascended. Sleep wanted to claim her, but she forced herself away from its seductive embrace.

She reached the astral, a slight gray tinge to the blankness, lower than normal and the old alarm that Xadrak might be lurking dragged her down before she rescued herself. He was gone and never coming back. She had nothing to fear from him again. The astral was empty. And full.

And beautiful.

She barked a laugh. He might have gone physically, but the six hundred years of living in dread of Xadrak's ascendance wouldn't be easy to dislodge. Maybe in a few decades.

Carn's form appeared, weary and gossamer. Mira and Gabriela approached. Now the tricky part. Where the hell was Hame?

"Any ideas, Carn?"

"We need to go down. Xadrak created a home base and that's the only place I can think of where he'd keep Hame's astral form."

"Do you know how to get there?"

"Think wicked thoughts." Carn held out his hand and they formed a chain.

Immediately the light dimmed and grew murky. Aurelia's skin prickled at the descent, a subtle change in pressure that shrieked danger. Only Sinara had dared to descend low enough to fight Xadrak and drag him to the gates of death.

He's not here anymore.

She let Carn drag them down until the light turned gunmetal gray and jagged shapes speared the environment. They could have been in a tunnel beneath the Earth as hate and evil took on form, showing its teeth to lost travelers. Her pulse hummed in her veins, but it wasn't the atmosphere; it was the apprehension of what they'd find when they reached Hame.

If they ever reached Hame.

Hold on. We're coming for you.

He didn't respond, but she refused to believe he wasn't

there. Her hope stalled them, and Carn shot her a disapproving look.

"Sorry." Though her heart broke to think it, she let herself believe Hame was dead.

Their descent accelerated down through the winding and hideous tunnels. The back of her neck itched with the attention of unseen things lurking in the lower levels. She held Mira's hand tight and Carn pulled them faster.

Hame's distant roars filtered to their ears.

They hurried and his bellowing grew louder and reverberated in her bones as they burst into an underground chasm. In the center, chained between two stone columns, Hame knelt and strained against a flood of red mist pouring into his head. Carn ran to him but she froze. He was being inundated with images, rapidly shifting between light and shadow as all the prophecies of the world poured into him. Imprisoning Hame hadn't been enough for Xadrak, he had to torture him as well.

"Carn, wait!" she called, wary of any booby traps, but he didn't listen. She gestured for Mira and Gabriela to secure the chamber while she flew forward to protect him. No attack came except for the one that battered her heart at seeing Hame's torture.

He'd chewed through his lip and blood coated his chin. His body strained against the prophecies and protected her and Carn from the onslaught.

"Hame, we're here, we're going to help you," Carn said.

His eyes were screwed shut; he couldn't acknowledge them. She looked into the deluge and couldn't make out one image from the next. He could only endure it, not analyze it, but the constant flow of information would wear him down.

Carn reached forward with both hands.

"What are you doing?" She pulled him away.

"Stopping his ability."

Carn had done this before, gradually blocked Hame from his visions over the course of their two hundred years together, an act to save him from Xadrak's wrath, but it had nearly crushed Hame.

"You think you can withstand the flow?"

"Probably not, but I have to try."

"Wait. Mira, Gabriela."

The witches appeared.

"Carn needs all our strength." She stood behind him and placed her hand on the back of his neck. Gabriela touched his left shoulder and Mira his right. "All of it."

She opened her power into Carn's body. It met the smallest resistance before the flow smoothed. It jerked as Gabriela and Mira merged their energy with Carn's. His back arched and he built up a reservoir before reaching forward with both hands and placing them on top of Hame's head.

He barely made contact before he hissed and snatched back his hands. Aurelia held against the kickback, taking the brunt of it from Gabriela and Mira. They were all weakened and too strong a reaction might throw them out of the astral.

Hame didn't have long. He'd closed his mouth against his screams, his cheeks bulging and jaw tensing so hard he shook. Tears poured down his face, hair matted with sweat plastered to his scalp. They couldn't take him home without first stopping the prophecies.

Carn had to succeed.

She forced her power into him. Her hand splayed and tensed on his neck, holding him in place. She'd drain herself if it meant bringing Hame back.

Carn took a few rapid breaths and plunged his hands

into the flow. He hollered and his hands appeared to burn in flames. But he held on, fighting against a force that repelled him from making contact with Hame's head. He grunted and air charged from between clenched teeth as the distance closed and he pressed against Hame's scalp.

Carn's head flipped back and the light thickened to the color of spilt blood. Xadrak's spell defended itself, jolting through Carn and hammering into Aurelia's sternum. She bore down, taking the blow from Carn, stopping it from passing through. It struck again and she staggered back, her hand clamping onto Carn's neck to maintain the flow.

Blow after blow struck her chest, and though she had no bones to break on the astral, the feeling was the same, that of a battering ram stuck to a massive piston pummeling into her. She buckled.

Someone shouted her name, a plea, but no one else could take this with Sinara's power gone. If there had been more of them, if they weren't already weakened… She couldn't do it to them. They'd already given so much. If saving Hame claimed her life, then that's the price she was willing to pay.

Just hold on a little while longer.

She didn't know what Carn was doing, her eyes closed to concentrate against this attack, but he had to finish this soon or else they'd all perish.

Hurry. Hurry. Hurry.

On and on it battered her and she weakened beneath a force that showed no sign of abating.

Just hold on a little—

Something cracked in her defenses, a weakening that she hurried to shore up. She couldn't syphon any of Gabriela's or Mira's power. She had to remain a conduit to feed theirs through to Carn. The cracks expanded.

Just hold—

A tear eked out from behind her closed eyes. Carn had to save Hame, that's all that mattered. She wished she could have done it and got to say goodbye.

The cracks widened and the blows kept falling. She was buckling. She was going to fail and take them all with her.

Her heart fractured.

I'm sorry—

A hand splayed between her shoulder blades and power flooded into her like a cool river bursting a dam. Shivers raced up her body and her back arched with the influx of energy. This wasn't one witch, this was many, a second line of magic jacked into her passed through a strong and steady hand. Her eyes flew open to see Carn bent but his shoulders broad and his pain lessened. Rejuvenated, she maintained a constant powerful stream that resisted the last vestiges of Xadrak's magic, her heart protected against his weakening strikes.

Above Hame, the crimson grew pink, the images flickered on and off, the gap between one and another growing until finally they stopped, and Hame pitched forward to collapse against Carn's chest.

Relief surged through her as she hugged Carn and Hame. Jagged tears raced down her cheeks as she held the two in her arms. They'd done it. They'd saved Hame. The chains fell and Hame's arms reached around them both and hugged them as tight as he could in his fatigue.

"Thank you," he whispered.

Carn grabbed him, and Aurelia sniffed up her tears.

"Hate to interrupt, but we should get out of here." Viktor's warning and a gentle hand on her arm brought her back. Two of her coven came forward to help Carn and Hame. Two others helped Mira and Gabriela. Viktor was left for her.

She wiped her eyes before facing him.

He stood to attention, shoulders square, arms behind his back, impressive chest puffed up. He looked every part the soldier ready to defy a reprimand.

"Before you berate me, the others were capable of hunting the remaining acolytes, and I wanted to be here for you."

The warrior had fought more battles than she could count yet standing in front of her, he looked like he was about to face a whole legion armed with a spoon.

She fell into his arms and he caught her, lifting her up so she could kiss him. The wounds in her chest healed and together they floated, leaving behind the chasm and the remnants of Xadrak's evil to ascend into the higher realms. Her heart filled with elation, reborn in its happiness. He'd come for her. They'd saved Hame and they'd saved the world.

She gave a thought to Carn and Hame, certain that they'd find their own way home with the others. She wanted to savor this a little longer. Surrounded by a pure world blushed with pink, she broke from Viktor's hungry kisses. He lost his balance as she leaned back, his eyelids drooping and his mouth morphing into a goofy smile before he blinked himself back to full awareness.

"How much energy do you have left?" she asked.

"I think I could sleep for a week." He laughed and nuzzled into her neck and his breath on her skin made her shiver.

Sleep was definitely not on her mind.

"Oh. Well, I was going to say that considering your apartment is command central, would you like to go with me to a little chateau of mine outside Amboise. But if you're too tired, I understand."

His eyes fired up and he bit his bottom lip, the sight of his barely controlled lust sending a thrill through her spine.

She lunged forward, kissing him roughly on the lips, and he devoured her.

All mine.

Screw the chateau. She was going to take him here.

But like a beast soothed by music, he eased back, panting from his own lust, and kissed the back of her hand. He gave her a wink. "See you soon." He vanished.

She almost dropped after him, but the clear landscape stalled her attention. She'd never meet Sinara there again. And with Xadrak gone, her purpose had been served. Six centuries of fighting, of protecting the world from a force it couldn't have handled, and now…

Her life was her own again.

A flash of terror through her veins was soon eased by a calm sense of possibility. There was always something to be done, some purpose she could try, but for now… For now she had a good man waiting for her and she was going to enjoy the fuck out of herself for a change.

XVIII

The scent of cinnamon and caramel had been teasing
at Olivier's senses all fucking day. And it wasn't from the
kitschy patisseries and chocolatiers. A witch was around
somewhere—*the* witch. Oberon's scent got into his sinuses,
into his gums, and wrapped themselves around his fangs.

He refused to think of it as wishful thinking. Not *just*
wishful thinking, anyway.

For two weeks he'd hunted the dull, suburban streets of
an almost unrecognizable Carcassonne, away from the
cobbled roads and towering stone perimeter of the town's
heart. Away from the deluded tourists charmed into a false
sense of security and begging to be taken out. The forest
he'd died in outside the walls was long gone, torn down for
pasture then roads then villages which became housing and
now shiny offices full of ambition and excess. Those streets
were good enough to hunt in.

At least, he'd *tried* to hunt, but that smell wouldn't let
up. Like the buzzing of tinnitus, it subsumed everything.
Even his ability to kill. Three aborted attacks and he'd
eventually given up in disgust and skulked back to the hotel

suite he'd booked for himself with stolen cash. At least no one had died for him to have it. That was…new.

Inside the wood-paneled room was sanitized opulence. In there, he could be anywhere. In there, he could forget the misguided instinct that had brought him back to the place he'd been born. The place he felt sure Aurelia and Thierry would never set foot after they'd watched him leave. If he couldn't rot slowly to death in the ether, then he could almost certainly do it in Carcassonne.

Blue-tinged drapes parted to reveal a terrace where, in the evening, he could stand and look at Porte d'Aude standing sentinel over all who entered or exited the city from the west. Beyond that, the ramparts of the Château Comtal that the do-gooders from World Heritage went so mad for. If they could have seen some of the things that happened behind these walls, they wouldn't be so quick to laud it. And not just the atrocities he'd committed; life was brutal for everyone then. The comforts on tap in this hotel were more than the seneschals of old could ever possibly have dreamed.

The room around him was carpeted where theirs had been cold stone, his bed king-size with not a single parasite, the bathroom marbled and toilets flushing. The room was large enough for a couple of couches, a table and chairs, and a bar. In some ways it was too large. He had nothing to fill it with and sitting watching television had made it feel all the more hollow.

At least in there he had respite from the tease of the witch.

Olivier collapsed onto the hard sofa, his Brioni suit crumpling. Impractical clothes for what he'd gone out to do—the blood stains would have been murder on the wool —but the hunger to feed had taken him by surprise. Something to sate that fucking scent in his nose.

Two weeks—give or take a day—since leaving the witch unconscious in a New York bed, recovering from their ordeal, and he still hadn't been able to ease his craving.

He inhaled deeply, sucking in the recycled hotel air, and the whiff of fake lilacs used to dress the room, but there was no scent of the—

He was out of the sofa and wrenching open the door before Oberon's knuckles hit the wood. The witch startled and laughed.

He, however, wasn't sure a smile was going to send the right message.

"What do you want?"

The witch snorted. "Nice." He didn't wait for an invitation. He slipped around Olivier's body and whistled as he examined the lavishness. "Cool digs. I'm not going to find a body in here, am I?"

Some part of Olivier appreciated the witch's attempts to make light, but that wasn't going to make this any easier.

"You'd know, you've been following me most of the day."

"Guilty," Oberon tossed back over his shoulder as he strolled over to the view. "You can probably close the door. I'm not ready to leave yet."

For half a moment Olivier didn't recognize his own hand still choking the life force out of the door handle. It took everything he had to release it calmly. "It'd be best if you did."

Oberon turned and straightened. "Best for whom?"

That lean, modern body, dressed in a black suit that was even more fitted than his own, couldn't have wrangled one of the pigs in their slaughterhouse, but the strength in those deep earth eyes… The witch would have held his own in this city.

It took him a moment to reconcile Oberon's powerful presence silhouetted against the town he'd grown up in. Old-world and new-world colliding.

He swallowed. The witch couldn't be his any-world. "Best for everyone."

"Well, I think I'll take my chances."

The door clicked shut and Olivier silently fumed. Oberon helped himself to the refrigerator, hooked out three miniature whiskeys in his long fingers, upended them all into a glass and sipped it straight. He looked entirely unaffected by their joint ordeal. Healed. Alex's doing, no doubt. The last time he'd seen Oberon, he'd had the pretty young vampire laying-on hands wherever he pleased. Healing him, sure, but since those were also the hands that got to enjoy Thierry, it had all been a little too…

Shit.

He'd slunk away in the chaos, ignoring his sister's imperious demands for him to stay.

And look where he'd run to.

Oberon drank, the whiskey barely registering in his skin, but watching it work its way down that pale throat got Olivier's fangs all interested. Was it possible he looked even younger than before? Fitter? Is that what near-oblivion had done to the witch? All it had done to *him* was drain him of any will to live.

Oberon leaned against the heavy armchair and watched him. The long silence, the witch's steady appraisal turned him to stone. Heavy enough to crash right through this fancy floor. He forced himself to move, to recover some of his practiced nonchalance. He was normally the one in charge of any situation. This was *his* domain. He shouldn't feel so ill at ease. He stretched out his arms along the back of the sofa and crossed his ankle over his knee.

"You haven't told me what you want."

Oberon took the glass away from his lips, and that made it a little easier to relax. A lot easier not to obsess on them. "I come with news."

"All this way? Just to give me *news*?"

Though, of course, it was a matter of almost no consequence for a witch to cross the planet. He might as well have come from across the hall.

He acknowledged the transparency of his lie with a smile. "And to see how you were doing. After what we both went through."

Both. Like they were some kind of unit.

"As you can see, I'm fine. Perhaps you can give me this so-called news as you leave."

"Carcassonne looks nice at this time of the year. I might stick around a bit."

"It's cold and gray. What's nice about it?" Still, it was warmer than it used to be.

His tone brought a curious intent to the witch's gaze. Made them even less comfortable to be under. "You're not enjoying being home?"

"It isn't home."

"Then what are you doing here?"

Who the fuck knew? "Can we get back to this apparently crucial news?"

Another sip. Another steady stare. "You don't have to worry about being turned into one-third of a portal any longer."

"I hadn't even thought about it." Alright, maybe he had, a little.

"Either way, Carn managed to separate it from our souls and destroy it when we were reformed."

"Thanks for the update. Goodbye."

But Oberon wasn't moving. "Why did you leave?"

Because I'm a coward.

"Our job was done. What else was there for me to do?"

Another small sip of that drink—he smelt it from across the room, ethanol mixing with caramel and roses and cinnamon. He dug his fingers into the cushions against the insistent interest from his cock. The witch had about two minutes left before he broke something, and it was either going to be a canine, a chair, or someone's neck. The one saving grace was that Oberon's heart rate was elevated too.

Fear.

Of me.

Still.

Not unexpected, but not relished either. Not the way he once would have. He'd made the right choice in leaving. His lip curled before he could stop it.

Oberon placed the near-empty glass on the countertop and spun it, a half-turn this way, a half-turn that. Hypnotic and excruciating.

"I'd thought…" A long sigh smothered whatever he'd been about to say. "I don't know what I thought." The smile had vanished by then, banished, and he straightened. "This was a mistake. I'm glad you're alright, Olivier. I'll go."

Oberon walked towards the door without a second glance and the movement was like a blow to the solar plexus. The witch couldn't leave. Not yet. Sure, he hadn't wanted him there in the first place but now he was there…

"Why did you save me?" Olivier blurted.

Oberon stopped. "Would you rather I hadn't?"

"After all I'd done to you, shouldn't you have been thrilled to let me go?"

"I'd made a pact with Aurelia. She made an oath to bring us back alive or else she would have died."

"So, you did it to save her life?"

"I did it to save *yours*, Olivier. Hers was a fortunate by-product."

Somewhere down in the street below, someone's watch ticked.

"Why?" At the last moment, reason chased the vulnerability from his throat. "I didn't ask to come back."

Oberon reached for the door; his voice drenched with disappointment. "Look, if you really want to die, I'm sure someone will gladly give you a hand."

Olivier leapt over the couch and reached him as he touched the handle. It was nothing to him to bar the door more surely than steel. "I'm sorry. I'm not used to…kindness, especially after all that I've done."

Heat blazed in brown eyes that the witch turned on him. "Really? We're going to do this again?" He breathed in and out again slowly. "Yes, I'm well aware of what you've done in your life. Yes, I'm the last person in the world who should want to give you a second chance."

Outright fear chased Olivier back from this vital precipice. Fear that Oberon would leave.

Fear that he'd stay.

"I think we're up to about the fourth, aren't we? You're forgetting I suffocated you back at the cottage."

Oberon gave a short huff and a ball-bearing of tension eased between Olivier's shoulder blades.

"Fine, fourth chance. But I thought if you were rescued, it would be like a fresh start. For you. For me. For everybody. All that blood wiped away. Disinfected slate."

There wasn't enough disinfectant in the world to undo the blood of his past. "I don't think that's possible."

"Why? Because of Thierry and Alex?"

"It's not about them." Wherever his brother and his lover were, he knew Thierry was happy. The ever-present bond hummed along in the background, a radiation he'd learned to ignore. Out there on the ether, he and Thierry had come to a kind of peace—the only kind they ever would—and he found himself being content for them. Even jealous of them. But not because Alex had Thierry. Because of *what* they had. Together.

He fought to keep his own emptiness locked down.

"What is it about?" Oberon pushed.

After all the talking the two of them had done—after everything they'd said and everything they'd seen—words completely failed him.

He grabbed Oberon's hand and pulled him out of the hotel room, holding on fast. At least this way the witch couldn't just walk out on him.

"Where are we going?" Oberon grunted, not quite resisting.

He ignored Oberon's demands for an explanation as he led him out of the hotel and tugged him through the narrow streets of this rebuilt Carcassonne. Past souvenir stores and restaurants, tourist traps and information centers, past all the fake shit that made this place look like a theme park rather than the utter hell it had once been, until he realized that Oberon was walking *with* him rather than *behind* him.

But neither one of them was dropping hands.

On and on they went until finally he reached the spot that was as close as he could figure out. He practically dislocated Oberon's shoulder with the suddenness of his halt.

"Here."

Confused eyes scanned around them. "What am I looking at?"

They stood outside a house, blue painted shutters, white trim. A two-story house that looked pretty much like all the others.

"This is where we lived."

Surprise and curiosity took over. "In there?"

"Near enough. The street's probably a few feet down and the original house long gone, but this nondescript dwelling is where I used to live—" He took the deepest of breaths. "And it's where I was last anything noble, anything good"

The lane they were on was early afternoon quiet; residents were still at lunch or at work or hanging out at other more interesting places. But this is what he'd found, and he'd kept walking past it thinking about all the earth that centuries had dumped on top of the place he'd been born until it was buried. Lost.

Good fucking riddance.

"It was just a house, Olivier."

He dropped the witch's hand. "I knew you couldn't understand." Heat rushed up through him. He should have kicked the witch out and be done with it. What had he expected? What did he *want*?

"That came out wrong." Oberon took his hand back up and threaded his fingers between his own. Then he added the second hand for good measure and stood square on to him. "It's still there. It's part of Carcassonne and always will be. It's foundation, bedrock. It's not going anywhere."

"But what use is it if you can't reach it—?"

"We did reach it. It's right below our feet. And if you're so in love with that shitty hovel, then I'll rip the earth open to get to it, but the house isn't what matters. You forget I've seen your foundations. I've lived and breathed them through your memories. I know what you're built on."

If not for the steel of the witch's grip, he'd have pulled away. And bolted.

"And look at what grew out of the old Carcassonne.

They rebuilt this place from rubble. Centuries of neglect and they managed to restore it."

Someone had done their research. "It's not the same thing."

"Of course it's not, it's just stone. But my point is it's been resurrected. It became better."

He looked around at the tourist tat evident even in this quiet laneway. "You call this better?"

"I call this a city of its time. And maybe you're a man of yours. Maybe you needed to be that man to survive everything you did."

But the *man* was not the issue…

"That's all very well for buildings and cities but let's face it, it won't work for me. I don't know how to be anything other than a monster."

"Who said you have to be? Not all monsters are evil."

Nice try, witch. Not that he didn't appreciate the effort. "Kind of the definition of the word, isn't it?"

"Depends who you ask. For me, a monster shows us the worst of ourselves, so we can do better, it shows us what we're afraid of and how we can best it."

"And when did you rewrite the dictionary?"

"About the same time that I was given an intimate ringside seat into your life. Look, you've done terrible things and—I'm not going to lie—you terrify me at times." He stepped closer. "But all the danger sure gets the blood pumping, and you're definitely not the super-bad boy you once were. Maybe there's a different life for you if you just look for it."

It couldn't be possible. *I'm not worthy of it.* "I can't change. I don't know how."

"Yeah, you do."

Those eyes. Full of compassion. Full of hope. Full of belief in him. When had anyone ever believed in him?

"You think I'm going vegetarian? That I'll start walking old ladies across the street? That's who you think I can be?"

Oberon wasn't having a bar of his doubt. "I know you haven't been killing like you used to."

He opened his mouth and his fangs dropped. "They're still here. Working just fine." He snapped them for good measure.

The lump at the witch's throat jerked up and down at the reminder of what they could do. But it was a good couple of seconds before Olivier realized that it wasn't fear darkening Oberon's gaze. The cinnamon started pumping out full force.

"There's been no torture, no terror. You've killed fast and efficient, and I'd say you've only killed about four since leaving New York."

"Five."

He frowned. "Fine. Five. Some of us have to sleep. But don't think I haven't noticed you're only preying on criminals. That guy you took right after he beat the crap out of his kid. The woman selling meth at the back of that high school."

"So, I'm some kind of avenging angel? Is that your point?"

"My point is, you have changed, whether you're conscious of it or not."

It was conscious. Every neck he bit into he wondered if Oberon would approve. How many deaths would wipe out the gift of forgiveness Oberon had given him? He'd carried it with him, lost as he was, searching as he was, fearful of each new morning in case it would be taken away. He'd resigned himself to believing one day it would so going there had been an attempt to lock it in permanently. But so far, he'd had no luck and each day frightened him.

And the witch had been watching all along.

He took a breath. Then another. Anything to steady the hammering thing in his chest. It wasn't drumming because it couldn't even beat, but something sure as hell was. Just as fast and furious as the terrified pulses he used to get off on.

"I'm not sure I can, Oberon. I'm not sure I even want to. I don't like this nothingness. Fading into the background, invisible and unnoticed. That's my brother's specialty. I don't really do *good*."

Oberon stepped up chest to chest. "You want to be noticed? Become a supermodel. You want redemption? Keep doing what you're doing."

"What the hell is the point? Who'd care either way?"

"You should care. This is your life. Your destiny."

He glared down on the witch. "Who else will care? Seriously, who will give a Carcassonne sewer-rat's shit what I do?"

"You really want me to say it?"

He scoffed. "Don't bother. If you did, it wouldn't be true. I've seen that brand on your shoulder. I saw it when you were healing. *Jamais encore?* You should probably heed your instincts. It's good advice. Never again."

Olivier strode back towards the hotel, a little faster than he'd have liked but then again he was still being driven by something that desperately wanted to be a heartbeat. Oberon let him go, and that was for the best. The witch wasn't up to this; he wouldn't see it through.

All he had were words.

As he entered the Hotel de la Cité's lobby, he knew that wasn't exactly true. Time and again, Oberon had come back to him—at first to torture him, then to help him escape, to keep him from being destroyed, to save him and give him his forgiveness. And even after all that was done, after they'd saved the world and escaped their certain fate, he had come to find him.

That was a whole lot more than words.

That was action.

Not this time though. Looks like he'd finally got the message. Olivier ascended the steps alone and opened the door to his opulent dungeon.

Cinnamon and roses…

The flutter of relief in Olivier's stomach soured. The witch sat in the armchair, his jacket over the back of the sofa, the sleeves of his dark green shirt rolled up to expose the Latin on his arm. He looked royally pissed.

"Do you know why I got that brand?"

"I can guess." Olivier shut the door but walked over to open the window to the terrace to let fresh air in. The cinnamon was going to drive him crazy. It made it impossible to think straight. Not to mention that faint shot of bergamot that had brought him there. "It didn't exactly work out that way though, did it?"

Blood. Endless blood. And the taste. He took a deep breath of outside air, but that only carried more of Oberon's scent into his body. It was all he could do to stifle the groan.

But Oberon clearly wasn't as addled by *his* presence.

"At first it was a pact to never let you or anyone beat me again. But I broke that through my own need for revenge. I thought I could be strong again by beating you, by being *worse* than you."

It'd take a lot more than a few casual torture sessions for him to even come close.

"But after what we shared, after the memories, after the blood, and after our joining, it came to mean something different, something better than I'd meant when I scribbled it on a piece of paper in the tattoo parlor."

Olivier turned in the doorway, his arms folded across his chest. "Came to mean what?"

Oberon stood and walked towards him, the anger having faded and kindness softening his lips. "*Never again* will I let vengeance make me its prisoner. *Never again* will I use my own selfishness to harm others. *Never again* will I berate myself for taking a chance, for giving aid or offering love."

The thundering moved up into his brain until he just about passed out. "Well, good luck with that."

He made to move, but Oberon grabbed him and held him still. "Listen, Olivier, there's more between us than what we once were to each other. You need someone to give your life meaning, to make the passage of the years easier, to keep you from falling into darkness again."

He hated the words even as the idea seduced him with its potential. "You think you know me so well, witch?"

"Know you?" He laughed, but nothing in his body said it was funny. "I was a few brutalities shy of *being* you. You've had so much longer to perfect the art. You've been through so much more."

"I'm not your project."

"I don't want a project. I want you."

The thundering stopped long enough to make him wonder if a man could die twice.

"You don't know what you're asking." It was perilously fucking close to a whisper.

"I'm asking a strong, fearless, slightly damaged vampire to take what is perhaps his most daunting risk ever and find out if all that love he once had and all that love he still has could find a home, could find someone who wanted it, who felt the same in return. I'm asking you to make yourself vulnerable and to let someone love you for a change. Olivier d'Arjou, will you let me?"

Something vital and alive rushed through him, swilled in his veins and soaked out into the singular elements of his flesh. The last time he'd felt anything near this heady was the day Rellius had turned him. The day the color and vibrancy and richness of the world had first been revealed to him.

How the hell had he forgotten it existed? And when had he stopped noticing it?

"*Slightly* damaged, you say?"

Oberon hissed. "Fine. A fucking write-off."

"You know I don't like witches," he said with the slightest flick of his mouth.

"And I'm not all that keen on vampires but perhaps we could both make an exception? At least for a little while."

It was only the fracture in Oberon's voice that told Olivier how tight the witch was holding himself inside. How much he'd put on the line.

And how much braver one little light-thrower was than the most feared of vampires.

"How long are you thinking?"

Every sentence he uttered that didn't start with 'get out of my sight' visibly ratcheted Oberon's anxiety down a notch.

"A century, give or take?"

Chuckling sounded almost ridiculous on his tongue. But it felt kind of right. "You think you're going to live that long?"

The witch flicked his chin, and his game was an unexpected turn on. "You're not the only one who's immortal."

"Aurelia gave you that too? Wow. You've definitely got the touch. No one else can work her like that."

"Well, it took her a while. She delivered in the end though. I think motherhood softened her. Or maybe the Russian."

The idea of anyone penetrating that ice-cold heart was almost inconceivable.

As inconceivable as some witch penetrating his.

He stepped in closer and peered into Oberon's fearless gaze. "I'm glad to see you finally got what you wanted."

"Well, I haven't got everything…"

"What else is there?"

A century seemed to pass as Oberon visibly gathered the fortitude to close what little distance remained between them. A warm kind of pleasure raced ahead of his lips and Olivier finally recognized it for what it was.

Pride. He was proud of his witch, sucking up the fear and reaching out with both hands for what he wanted. That took guts. After everything they'd been to each other. And done to each other.

None of which was a patch on what he was aching to do to him. Starting with that mouth…

Oberon leaned forward and closed the last of the distance between them. His lips pressed his, brushed his, and those skilled hands traced up to do magic on the back of his neck. Everything in him wanted to take, take, take; hard and fast and nasty. But that was a different Olivier d'Arjou and he was done hurting this witch. His fingers slid up under Oberon's shirt and traced the welt letters on his shoulders.

And touch became vow.

He lifted Oberon off the ground, taking his weight easily, their mouths pressed hard together. Tongues met, gently, slowly, and the contact sent warmth coursing through his body before swirling to a point behind his sternum. Right where his heart used to beat. Oberon clung to him harder and demanded more, and he was only too happy to give it. Where once he would have conquered, now all he wanted to do was please. Where once he would have thrilled at generating fear, now he moved slowly, to nurture. To cherish.

Who knew he even had cherishing in him?

There was something strangely appealing about seducing this man who could throw him across the room with blue light if he wanted to. Even a fully fed vampire. God, how would it feel to be dominated like that for a change? Once. Right before he took control back. Passion cut a streak through him and he slammed the witch up against the wall to get a better purchase on that mouth. Yet, it wasn't rough, and Oberon wasn't afraid.

And neither was he yielding.

His kisses begged forgiveness for that, they begged union, and he knew that Oberon wanted to be equal in this carnal dance. Needed it.

And suddenly he was all about what this man needed.

He held him aloft, gentle but supportive, giving rather than taking. Kissing as though his life depended on it. The longer they mouthed each other, the tighter his skin grew and the harder it was to keep his fangs sheathed. His flesh vibrated with tension. Or maybe it was the moans reverberating through his body. This was a force building to a storm, a monsoon that would wash away everything.

And then it stopped.

Dead.

Oberon twisted out from his hold and stepped clear of the broiling tsunami.

He turned his head, needing the strength of the wall to stay upright, but long enough to see what it was that had changed the temperature all of a sudden.

Oberon's gaze fixed squarely on his fangs. He hadn't even realized they were out.

"It's okay—" Olivier began, one shaky hand raised.

"Shut up."

"Wh—?"

"Shut. Up."

The witch paced back and forth like an agitated tiger, his focus never leaving the fangs Olivier knew glinted with saliva. Working himself up to something.

Olivier pushed himself away from the wall and turned, his hands out to his sides, as non-threatening as a man with death in his mouth could be.

Oberon frowned at the gesture, then stilled his pacing. His heart hammered even faster than when he'd had him pinned to the wall. He was visibly talking himself into something.

Olivier wondered who he had to pray to in order to make sure that '*something*' wasn't a walk-out.

Oberon puffed out a quick breath, a runner on the starting block, then marched purposefully, inexorably, towards him. As soon as he was close again, he raised his fingertips gently to Olivier's mouth and feathered them across one of his fangs, learning its shape, its texture. Studying the place it ruptured from his gums.

Silently introducing himself and getting their measure.

Olivier stood frozen—not capable of movement to save either of their lives—not willing to break whatever spell the witch was under.

When the introductions were over, Oberon leaned in against his chest, hard body against hard body, and slowly raised his mouth once again. His breath was a sauna against the ultra-sensitive dentine of his fangs.

Something in his leg muscles started to fail.

But before they did, Oberon raised his eyes to his and held them. Forever. Then he whispered against the wetness of his half-open mouth. "Hey."

Impossible to look away, Olivier was in thrall as sure as he had been once to the vampire who'd made him. Except this was an entirely different kind of fascination. Something thudded in his throat.

"Hey," he breathed back.

Witch brushed vampire. Once. Twice. Slower and softer than before and focusing on the fullness of his bottom lip. Then, with no warning and even less sense, Oberon dashed that delectable tongue across his right fang, before returning to the kiss.

Again, his knees wavered. But they held.

He wanted to gather Oberon up again in his arms and march him straight over to the sofa—or even bend him over the back of the sofa—but something in him accepted that this was Oberon's seduction.

The witch needed to drive.

Again with the tongue-swipe, but this time it was his left side. A deep shudder ran through him. Before Olivier could do much more than moan, Oberon twisted his tongue around to press gently against the glinting tip of his fang.

Olivier's gasp was as much for that as it was for the repeated threat from his legs.

Oberon pressed again.

It took a vampire's super-sensitive hearing to hear the tiny pop of fang rupturing tongue, but a moment later it was completely lost in the blinding flash of white that detonated in his vision. His spine curved backwards, and he inhaled sharply, freezing as the pleasure surged through his body, holding onto this exquisite magic, lest it slip away. His knees finally did buckle then and the two of them slid, entwined, down the wall, as Olivier closed his mouth over Oberon's and made the kind of seal needed for the kind of feeding the witch was offering him.

Freely.

Not forced by a monster. Not coerced by a witch. Not obliged by all of destiny.

Gifted. With love.

Caramel filled his mouth and senses and sent his eyes rolling back beneath his fluttering lids. Cinnamon swilled around them both and Olivier swallowed deeply as he supported Oberon against his body. The witch seemed to stiffen with every new swallow, but it was a good kind of stiffness, the kind he liked best; a full-body, ready-to-break kind of stiffness that told him Oberon was as deeply into this as he was.

And just as liable to fracture.

But fracturing was not an option; at least not yet. When the witch went—and he would go, several times— Olivier wanted him exhausted and trembling from need, stretched tighter than the leather on his fancy sofa.

He wanted this to last. In case it was the only chance he got.

Suck became kiss and kiss became worship as Oberon's tongue eventually fell away from his fangs long enough for them both to draw breath. Long enough that Olivier was able to mumble against his jaw. "What *was* that?"

"Magic." Oberon chuckled weakly.

He managed to lift his head. "Actual magic, or…?"

"*Us* magic." He settled more comfortably against him. "You like it?"

"Do you have more surprises like that planned?"

"I didn't plan that one. I just felt like I needed to establish…terms…with those big boys."

Both big boys twitched to rupture again. And soon.

Oberon slumped his head forward to rest against Olivier's neck. "You know…rules of engagement. Going forward."

It can't have been easy, facing them so directly after

everything his fangs had been party to. But the idea that there was a 'forward' to be had gave him another little thrill.

"Consider them tamed."

If that was their reward, he'd happily shackle them for life. Even if life was a millennium long.

He felt the witch's smile against the skin of his throat and the teasing hotness of a chuckle chaser.

"Oberon North—vampire slayer. Who'd have thunk?"

And who'd have thought a vampire would ever long to be slayed. But he had just now. And he still did; every part of him was hungry for a repeat.

He rested his chin on Oberon's shaggy hair. "It's right up there with Olivier d'Arjou—witch lover."

Oberon lifted his head and tackled that word head on. "You talk a good talk, d'Arjou. But can you deliver?"

Faster than he could narrow his beautiful, earthy eyes, the witch bounced back against the over-stuffed leather of the sofa. Olivier half kneeled on it and reached for his belt.

"When have I ever not delivered?"

ABOUT THE AUTHOR

Daniel de Lorne writes about men, monsters and magic (often with a bit of mayhem thrown in). In love with writing since he wrote a story about a talking tree at age six, his first novel, the romantic horror *Beckoning Blood*, was published in 2014.

In his other life, Daniel is a professional writer and researcher in Perth, Australia, with a love of history and nature. All of which makes for great story fodder.

And when he's not working, he and his husband explore as much of this amazing world as they can, from the ruins of Welsh abbeys to trekking famous routes and swimming with whales.

You can contact Daniel through his website or sign up to his newsletter to receive all the latest news on releases, giveaways, cover reveals and more.

Connect with Daniel
www.danieldelorne.com

ACKNOWLEDGMENTS

It's been a long road to get to this final book in the *Bonds of Blood* series, going on nearly ten years from the first blush of an idea to finally getting my act together and wrapping it all up. There are a few people who have made this possible.

First is my good friend Nikki Logan, who encouraged me at the beginning to get it down and to make it better, who loves these characters almost as much as I do and helped me right through to the end.

An enormous thanks to Kate Cuthbert and Escape Publishing for giving *Bonds of Blood* its first home. It was wonderful working with you.

To my husband, Glen, for being my biggest—and most insistent—fan, who gives me the freedom and encouragement to keep going, who tries his best not to break a writer's fragile ego, and always shares in the joys and comforts me through the lows.

And finally, thank you to you, the reader. I hope you enjoy this book and more to follow.